THE REALMGATE WARS
HAMMERS OF SIGMAR

The Gates of Azyr
Chris Wraight

Legends of the Age of Sigmar

Fyreslayers
*David Annandale, David Guymer
and Guy Haley*

Skaven Pestilens
Josh Reynolds

Black Rift
Josh Reynolds

Sylvaneth
*Robbie MacNiven, Josh Reynolds,
Rob Sanders and Gav Thorpe*

The Realmgate Wars

War Storm
Nick Kyme, Guy Haley and Josh Reynolds

Ghal Maraz
Guy Haley and Josh Reynolds

Hammers of Sigmar
Darius Hinks and C L Werner

Call of Archaon
*David Annandale, David Guymer,
Guy Haley and Rob Sanders*

Wardens of the Everqueen
C L Werner

Warbeast
Gav Thorpe

Fury of Gork
Josh Reynolds

Bladestorm
Matt Westbrook

Mortarch of Night
Josh Reynolds and David Guymer

The Prisoner of the Black Sun
An audio drama by Josh Reynolds

Sands of Blood
An audio drama by Josh Reynolds

The Lords of Helstone
An audio drama by Josh Reynolds

The Bridge of Seven Sorrows
An audio drama by Josh Reynolds

The Beasts of Cartha
An audio drama by David Guymer

Fist of Mork, Fist of Gork
An audio drama by David Guymer

Great Red
An audio drama by David Guymer

Only the Faithful
An audio drama by David Guymer

THE REALMGATE WARS

HAMMERS OF SIGMAR

DARIUS HINKS
C L WERNER

A BLACK LIBRARY PUBLICATION

Hammers of Sigmar first published in 2015.
This edition published in Great Britain in 2016 by
Black Library,
Games Workshop Ltd.,
Willow Road,
Nottingham,
NG7 2WS, UK.

10 9 8 7 6 5 4 3 2 1

Produced by Games Workshop in Nottingham.
Cover illustrations by Paul Dainton and Dave Greco.

The Realmgate Wars: Hammers of Sigmar © Copyright Games Workshop Limited 2016. The Realmgate Wars: Hammers of Sigmar, GW, Games Workshop, Black Library, Warhammer, Warhammer, Age of Sigmar, Stormcast Eternals, and all associated logos, illustrations, images, names, creatures, races, vehicles, locations, weapons, characters, and the distinctive likenesses thereof, are either ® or TM, and/or © Games Workshop Limited, variably registered around the world.
All Rights Reserved.

A CIP record for this book is available from the British Library.

ISBN 13: 978 1 78496 284 5

No part of this publication may be reproduced, stored in a retrieval system, or transmitted in any form or by any means, electronic, mechanical, photocopying, recording or otherwise, without the prior permission of the publishers.

This is a work of fiction. All the characters and events portrayed in this book are fictional, and any resemblance to real people or incidents is purely coincidental.

See Black Library on the internet at

blacklibrary.com

Find out more about Games Workshop
and the world of Warhammer 40,000 at

games-workshop.com

Printed and bound by CPI Group (UK) Ltd, Croydon, CR0 4YY

From the maelstrom of a sundered world, the
Eight Realms were born. The formless and the divine
exploded into life.

Strange, new worlds appeared in the firmament, each one
gilded with spirits, gods and men. Noblest of the gods was
Sigmar. For years beyond reckoning he illuminated the realms,
wreathed in light and majesty as he carved out his reign. His
strength was the power of thunder. His wisdom was infinite.
Mortal and immortal alike kneeled before his lofty throne.
Great empires rose and, for a while, treachery was banished.
Sigmar claimed the land and sky as his own and ruled over a
glorious age of myth.

But cruelty is tenacious. As had been foreseen, the great
alliance of gods and men tore itself apart. Myth and legend
crumbled into Chaos. Darkness flooded the realms. Torture,
slavery and fear replaced the glory that came before. Sigmar
turned his back on the mortal kingdoms, disgusted by their
fate. He fixed his gaze instead on the remains of the world he
had lost long ago, brooding over its charred core, searching
endlessly for a sign of hope. And then, in the dark heat of
his rage, he caught a glimpse of something magnificent. He
pictured a weapon born of the heavens. A beacon powerful
enough to pierce the endless night. An army hewn from
everything he had lost.

Sigmar set his artisans to work and for long ages they toiled,
striving to harness the power of the stars. As Sigmar's great
work neared completion, he turned back to the realms and saw
that the dominion of Chaos was almost complete. The hour
for vengeance had come. Finally, with lightning blazing across
his brow, he stepped forth to unleash his creations.

The Age of Sigmar had begun.

TABLE OF CONTENTS

Stormcast – Darius Hinks   9

Scion of the Storm – C L Werner   201

STORMCAST

Darius Hinks

CHAPTER ONE

Lord-Celestant Tylos Stormbound

The hammer falls.

Vengeance tears from my throat, ringing through the bloodless metal of my mask. 'God-King!' I cry in a voice that is no longer my own.

'God-King!' howl my lightning-born brothers as the tempest hurls us from the sky.

The ground gives as we land but Zarax rides on, ignoring the odd, yielding terrain. I cling to her scales, as blind as a newborn. The others are close behind and I hear their metal boots pounding across this broken, benighted land. Weapons are drawn, oaths are howled and I take my first breath of mortal air. Sulphur pours through my mouthpiece and I gulp it down, relishing the bitterness.

The storm thins, revealing plumes of smoke and embers. I whisper to Zarax and as she slows I sense the others gathering around me. I almost pity those we have come to destroy. Who could dream of such an enemy?

The smoke drifts, revealing glimpses of a tortured landscape. We're heading down a glistening, crimson road that seems to have been carved from a flayed corpse. Sigmar's tempest has landed us on a butcher's block of body parts and thrashing, broken wings.

It's a shameful sight but I don't avert my gaze. I must be vigilant, aware. I must understand this place quickly.

I look harder and realise that it's not a road, but a bridge of meat and chains, hazy with flies. Its span is vast beyond measure, stretching miles ahead before disappearing into a crimson wall of smoke. Over the side I glimpse wisps of cloud and realise we're far above the ground. Shrieks fill the air and I see that the bridge is alive. The whole structure is made of living birds – thousands of them, broken and burned together by hot irons and fixed to a mesh of thick, oily chains. It's the stink of their ruined flesh that fills my lungs. It's their thrashing bodies I'm riding across and their pain I can hear.

I want to roar in outrage, but I bite down my fury and keep my voice level.

'Advance,' I say, rising up in my saddle and turning to face my army.

My heart races as I see what I command. The storm has spawned a golden host. Even in this stinking, bloody wound, they are a vision. Every one of them is clad entirely in gleaming armour, still crackling with the fury of the storm. Pennants trail above glinting, haloed helmets, bearing the divine sigils of Sigmar and the Celestial City. No army ever looked so glorious, so *dignified*. And Sigmar has entrusted it to me.

The vanguard is a seamless wall of shield-bearing Liberators; numberless ranks of heroes, marching towards me in perfect unison. Then come the retinues of paladins – striding goliaths that dwarf even the Liberators, clad in blessed, god-wrought suits of armour. Some carry great, two-handed hammers that look like they could topple city walls, while others wield pole arms – long, gleaming glaives with lightning in their blades. In the rearguard are my divine archers – hundreds of Judicators, moving with the same precision as the rest of the army, readying their shimmering bows. High above, riding the thunderheads, are our winged guardians, the Prosecutors: radiant, inviolable and more dangerous than the lightning.

I almost laugh. *Stormcast Eternals* – the God-King's unbreakable fist. Removed from the golden halls of Azyr, we shine all the brighter.

I turn back to the bridge and see the sky for the first time. It's almost entirely obscured by rock. A vast sphere of smouldering ore, hundreds of miles in diameter, hangs directly over our heads. Such a star-burnt hulk can only be a moon, dragged from the heavens by divine will. It's moving towards us, shedding sparks and boulders as it glides majestically through the clouds. The sky ripples in its wake like water in the lee of a ship.

'Lord-Celestant.'

I look down from Zarax's back at Lord-Relictor Boreas. I can barely recognise my brother's dry tones. His arcane duties have left their mark on his speech, just like every other part of him. As I was being drilled and remade in the Celestial City, Sigmar sent my brother through death and beyond. Eternity echoes in his every word.

Unlike the rest of us, my brother's mask resembles a bleached skull, and I find myself wondering what lies behind. Would I recognise his face? Unlike me, he has endured Sigmar's fire a second time. He knows what it really means to be immortal.

The rest of my captains stand back in respectful silence as he approaches.

'What are your orders, Lord-Celestant?' he asks, speaking

formally, giving no hint of our shared past. He glances at the heavens. 'This was not prophesied. None of my auguries indicated that we would land here, on this bridge of birds.'

I look back down the road, blanking out the thrashing wings and the insanity hanging overhead.

'The tempest can't have strayed too far off course, Boreas.' I nod back down the bridge. 'We've clearly found our foe.'

There are figures emerging from the fumes – a barbaric, crimson-clad rabble scrambling along the bridge, pouring from the smoke like blood from a wound. The moonlight shows them in sickening clarity. They wear jagged, red and brass helmets and their bare chests are lashed with scarred muscle. They carry repulsive, brazen idols and axes as tall as men, scored with foul sigils, and every one of them is draped in skulls and glistening with blood.

'Bloodreavers,' says a voice edged with hate. 'Finally these snorting dogs will receive some justice.'

I turn to face the speaker. 'Liberator-Prime. There can be no victory without discipline.' I nod at the lines of Liberators marching towards us. 'They will follow our lead, Castamon. Show them what Sigmar expects.'

He nods, humbled. 'Lord-Celestant.'

I turn back to the bloodreavers. As they run they fill the air with a dreadful din. They are trailing something that clangs and clicks along the chains of the bridge but at this distance I can't make out what it is.

The rest of the Liberators clatter to a halt around us, moving with such well-drilled precision that they could be on a parade ground.

I point my hammer at the bloated moon and raise my voice.

'Remember this, Stormcasts: nothing is forsaken. Look deep enough into the darkness and you will always find Sigmar looking back.'

They remain motionless and silent, but I feel their battle-hunger; it radiates from their gleaming armour.

'Lock shields,' I say, and there's a deafening clang as the vanguard snaps into place. The entire army moves as one, bodies, shields and armour, fitting together to make an impenetrable bastion of sigmarite.

Struggling to suppress my pride, I raise my warhammer, Grius, to the crimson heavens. It flashes in the moonlight, and Zarax lets out a roar. As the dracoth rises beneath me she opens her reptilian jaws and unleashes pure white fury at the clouds. The air crackles and spider legs of electricity dance across my armour.

I give the signal to advance and as we meet the enemy lines I become one with my expressionless mask – an emotionless implement of Sigmar's will. Anger is forgotten. Grief is suppressed. Everything falls away: the sound of shields rattling on greaves, the torment of the bridge, the lunacy of the moon – all I know is this moment. I feel the long, slow arc of my life reaching its culmination. Finally, I face the monsters I was born to slay.

Gold and crimson collide. There is an explosion of grinding metal as the vanguards meet. Sparks glitter in the darkness, axes clang against shields and bucklers smash against armour.

The lines of Liberators hold steady and I order them onwards. Their shields lock tighter with every step and they drive the enemy back across the bridge of birds. Even from a few rows back I can barely breathe for the stink of the bloodreavers, a ripe stench even more powerful than the sulphurous moon. They fight like wounded animals, snorting, spitting and howling as they throw themselves against the Liberators' shields, trying and failing to break our line. I glimpse deranged faces, eyes rolled back in sockets, delirious with rage. They're more stampede than army.

'Drive them back!' I shout as the bloodreavers' frenzy grinds us to a slow plod. 'Drive them back to whatever dark vaults spawned them!'

They begin to drop, felled by lightning hammer-strikes, golden flashes that lash out from behind shields, crushing armour and bone. It seems that victory will come before I even have chance to gauge the strength of my army.

I hear a cry of pain from the shield wall.

I peer through the serried, golden lines and glimpse one of my Liberators clutching at his throat. His armour has been rent and there's blood, lots of blood, rushing between his fingers. He vanishes from view as the phalanx closes around him.

His choked screams scrape around my skull and I drive Zarax forwards, keen to be done with these animals. Even the dracoth cannot easily wade through such a crush, so she unleashes a gout of lightning, tearing a channel through the enemy ranks. The smell of cooking meat intensifies the stench.

A bloodreaver bounds over the shield wall. He vaults several rows, screaming hysterically, and lashes out with a pair of jagged axes. Another Stormcast staggers as the bloodreaver crashes into him.

Before the Liberators can respond, a paladin strides casually forwards and brings down his huge, two-handed hammer. He moves with a languid, easy grace but his blow lands like a thunderclap. The bridge rocks and blinding light envelops us all. Even Zarax stumbles.

When the glare fades, the bloodreaver is gone and the paladin has calmly resumed his place. If it weren't for the gore sliding down his breastplate there would be no sign that the Chaos creature had ever existed. I take note of the Stormcast's markings.

'Retributor Celadon,' I shout, disguising my pride beneath a stern snarl. 'Wait for my command.'

More of the howling curs manage to scale the shield wall, disrupting our faultless lines. It's becoming harder to match the dispassion of my mask. Anger boils through my limbs. I clutch one of my honour scrolls and recite the Oath of Becoming.

Dozens of the bloodreavers are falling to the Liberators' hammers and swords but I hear Stormcasts crying out too. Such noble beings were not made to succumb to such soul-sick dogs and my patience starts to fray. The crush of bodies becomes oppressive. My eyes blur with sweat and my muscles burn with the effort of holding myself back.

Another Liberator falls and a whole section of the shield wall gives.

The bloodreavers seize their chance and wrench the gap wider with a flurry of axe blows.

I signal to the paladins, finally giving them permission to advance, and they surge forwards, led by Celadon's brutal blows.

'Close ranks!' I roar, rising up in my saddle and ordering the Liberators back into position as the paladins storm ahead. They try to obey but the bloodreavers are becoming even more feral. They fight with no structure or reason. Something is driving them into a boiling frenzy. It's bewildering.

Another Stormcast cries out in pain and I will take no more.

'For the God-King!' I roar, launching myself from Zarax's back and into the enemy, joining the wave of paladins.

Ranks of warhammers rise behind me, along with a chorus of battle cries.

The fight begins in earnest.

I pick out the largest bloodreaver and bear down on him. His face has been warped beyond recognition by deep jagged scars and there are thick hoops of brass hammered through his biceps. Every inch of him has been transformed by a lifetime of war. The din of battle is everywhere, but I'm deaf to everything beyond the deep, phlegmy rattle of his breath. He snorts like a boar, drooling and bestial as he smashes his axe into my hammer.

The blow jolts through me and I rock back on my heel, gauging the weight of him against my own strength. He is as heavy as iron, but I'm easily sufficient for the task, and after the crush of the shield wall I relish the chance to lash out. The stink of his breath is worse than the rotting bridge – he growls something in his disgusting, dark tongue and I recognise the smell of human flesh.

I smash Grius into his axe and savour the sensation of my armour-clad limbs. My body feels like a new weapon, forged in the stars. There's a strength in me that I can barely fathom.

The bloodreaver recovers and swings but I'm faster. *So* fast. Grius crunches through the mouthpiece of his helmet, tearing it away in a shower of sparks and blood. His head snaps sideways and he reels away from me, jaw hanging loose from his head.

I stride after him, barging deeper into the crush, and draw back my warhammer for another blow.

Laughter explodes from his throat. He tears away what remains of his jaw, hurling it to the ground like the remnant of a meal.

There's something so obscene about this that I pause – only for a second, but long enough for him to slam his fist into my golden mask. My head rocks back as a long, iron spike grinds through the eye socket of my helm. Pain explodes across my face and my helmet fills with blood. I stagger backwards, reeling across the thrashing birds, blinded in one eye, and almost drop my hammer.

He gurgles grotesquely as he lunges after me, blood rushing from where his mouth used to be.

Pain only makes me faster. My hammer connects with the top of his helmet and brass crumples beneath god-forged sigmarite. His skull collapses.

He gives a last, porcine, grunt and topples back into the throng.

I down another opponent with a backhanded blow, then step back to survey the scene. I've unleashed a storm. Freed from the crush, the paladins are striding through the bloodreavers like a tempest, their voices raised to Sigmar, lightning flashing across their hammers. The bloodreavers topple before the combined onslaught of Liberators and Retributors. It's a massacre. My army flows like gold from a brazier. In minutes we have shattered their ranks, scattering heads and axes as we go. The battle is almost won.

Boreas fights beside me, smashing his way through the enemy with slow, precise determination, splitting shields and heads.

I wipe the blood from my golden mask and realise that we're mirroring each other as we strike.

'Victory and honour!' I cry, and he raises his hammer in reply.

I take a fume-filled breath and look around. There's a vast shape looming up from the smoke further down the bridge, punctuated by ominous crimson lights.

'That's not the Crucible of Blood,' I call out to Boreas. 'We must finish this quickly and find out where the storm has landed us.'

He peers at the distant tower. 'You have eyes in the heavens, Lord-Celestant.'

I nod and look up into the darkness. 'Drusus!' I cry, fending off a blow and peering back down the bridge. At first there's no reply so I battle on, scouring the heavens for my cloud-borne Prosecutors.

The moon has fallen even closer. The sight of it is dizzying, vast beyond understanding. Such a colossal, dazzling sphere has no place looming so low. As it gets closer it starts to affect the bridge. The structure sways so violently that birds are being torn free and hurled up towards the sky, and the chains reach up to the clouds, dancing like serpents.

'Lord-Celestant!' cries a voice.

I make out the golden form of Drusus, flying overhead.

Divine light gilds his wings as he dives through the fumes, trailing Sigmar's heralds of death behind him. He banks and rolls, clutching twin hammers. Even the blank expression of his mask can't hide his excitement.

'See what this bridge has in store for us,' I shout, levelling my hammer at the shadows up ahead.

Drusus nods but remains overhead, struggling to hold his place, buffeted by a new storm that has sprung up.

'Lord-Celestant,' he cries, pointing one of his hammers back to where debris is flying up from the bridge. 'The moon is falling.'

Before I can reply, a circle of bloodreavers surrounds me, each clutching an axe as tall as I am. If they've noticed their losses, they don't show it. They lope towards me like drunken brawlers.

As I ready myself, I feel a charge in the air – traces of Sigmar's wrath circling once more, crackling in my joints, responding to my faith. I raise my warhammer to the clouds and cry an oath.

The bloodreavers charge and my armour blazes white, ignited by the remnants of Sigmar's tempest. Grius erupts as I bring it down between my feet.

There's a thunderclap and a ring of light slams into my attackers.

Blood flies from their mouths and they arch in pain as their backs break.

'Make for the towers!' I cry, vaulting their twitching corpses and hurling myself back into the throng. Whatever Drusus has seen, the battle is nearly over and we need to advance.

My leap takes me unexpectedly high and I have an odd sensation of weightlessness. It takes me several seconds to land back on the bridge. The battle rages on, but most of the bloodreavers are dead and the rest are in disarray, so I call my retinues back into formation for the final push. We will finish this with the same dignity with which we began it.

I'm still a few paces away from the phalanx when my feet lift off the ground again and my face turns to the sky.

Deranged laughter fills the air as I try unsuccessfully to grasp on to something. Dozens of birds are being torn free and hurled into the ink-dark sky. The whole bridge is bucking and heaving.

I spin in the air, thrashing my limbs. As I turn I see that some of my Liberators have been thrown to their knees while others, like me, are rising into the air.

'Lord-Celestant!' cries Drusus from somewhere nearby. 'The moon is too close!'

An iron-hard hand locks around my throat and I turn to see one of the berserk warriors laughing wildly as he drifts up beside me, several feet above the bridge. His axe swings towards my face.

The sickening sensation of weightlessness slows my reactions. I bring Grius up but only quick enough to deflect his blow, and the axe slams into my gorget. The blessed sigmarite holds, but we continue to spin away from the ground.

The bloodreaver still has hold of my throat and we pirouette through whirling embers. His breath reeks of death. His scarred, leathery muscles are slick with blood and his battered helmet is daubed in tribute to the Blood God. His face is near enough for me to see cracked, corpse-dry lips and thin, blackened teeth. He's too close for me to swing my hammer so I pound the handle into his face, breaking his nose. He just laughs harder as we float higher.

Then he twists his voice around words I can understand.

'Fly home,' he says, his voice an obscene gurgle. Then, with a snort of derision, he tries to shove me away, but my speed has not entirely left me; before I'm lost to the storm I manage to grab hold of his axe.

The fool is so rabid that he won't let go of his precious weapon, so I haul myself down its length, grabbing onto his arm with one hand and swinging Grius with the other. It connects squarely with his head and I hear the *crack* of his breaking neck. He slumps in my grip.

I roll again, hanging onto his corpse and get a sickening bird's-eye view of the battle below. Dozens of my Stormcasts are being lifted up from the jolting bridge. Only the paladins are too heavy to be moved. Most of the bloodreavers are dead, but the survivors howl ecstatically as the moon wrenches us from victory. Finally, I realise the significance of something that has been bothering me since I first saw it. Every one of the bloodreavers is shackled to the bridge.

'Their chains!' I cry, grabbing hold of the one attached to the corpse and lashing it around my leg. 'Drusus!' I can see him and the other winged Prosecutors still hurling hammers of lightning at the foe. 'Their chains! Lash us to the bridge!'

He stares at me, confused, then nods and waves his retinues into action. They dive into the crowds of drifting Stormcast Eternals, grappling as many as they can back down to the bridge. Our orderly attack has become an airborne riot. As Drusus' Prosecutors attempt to lock chains around their brothers' legs, the remaining bloodreavers lash out with their axes, hacking them down as they struggle to secure the chains.

My head pounds as Liberators rush up through the clouds, snatched by the lunar storm and thrown to the heavens. The moon is so close the air is groaning beneath its incredible mass.

Drusus and the other winged Prosecutors lash countless dozens to the bridge, but others are disappearing from view, flashing like reclaimed comets as they rush towards the firmament. My Stormcasts rage as they are dragged from this world. Anger boils in my knotted gut as the storm spins me faster.

The grinding of the moon becomes deafening, throbbing in my still bleeding head until I think it might split.

CHAPTER TWO

Vourla – High Priestess of the Steppe

My sorcery is almost spent; my books have been burned. What does that leave? Just a weak old woman, waiting to feel a blade at her throat. The gods played a cruel joke when they chose me as the steppe's last chance for vengeance.

I shift in my chair, throwing shadows across the octagonal chamber. The floor gleams in the torchlight like a piece of perfect marble, but I've walked across it many times and know the truth. Hakh's throne room is carpeted with human teeth, hammered and smoothed to a sheen. They spiral across the room in their thousands, circling a thick, pitted grindstone. The teeth are only a small reminder of the lives Hakh has taken. I doubt he considers them more than decoration, but I feel the pain of every sundered soul. Sometimes I run my hands over them, tracing the contours and cracks, recalling names and whispering a promise: I will avenge you. For a long time I did not know how I would achieve such a feat, but now, finally, it is in reach.

The throne beside me is the carcass of a great beast – a

beautiful, feline thing from the time before Chaos. After killing it, Hakh hollowed out the corpse with his bare hands and had it cast in brass. Now it hunches over him, frozen in an eternal roar. The warlord sits silently and hasn't moved for an hour, but I know he's awake. He's long beyond such mortal frailties as sleep. There are weapons everywhere, but if I took a single step towards him my game would end. I must bide my time. Vengeance is so close I can feel it in my tingling palms.

Hakh's generals have yet to arrive and my only entertainment comes from his hounds. Most of them are as motionless as their master, slumped at his feet, but a few circle me, their claws scraping and clattering across the gleaming floor. Even after all these years they've not given up hope that Hakh might rethink my importance and present them with a meal. They're not real dogs, of course, but hulking, reptilian things, the colour of flayed muscle and as tall as a man. Their enormous, canine heads are crowned with horns and their bodies have been bloated into a grotesque parody of nature, torn out of shape by heaving muscle. Smoke leaks from their jaws as they pad back and forth, their eyes always locked on me.

The spiked collars at their throats crush the magic out of me and they stink of the hell-pits that spawned them, but I've become fascinated by them. There's a mystery to them that I can't fathom: Hakh loves them. When slaves become too weak to work, he feeds them, still living, to the hounds. I've been forced to endure the screams more times than I wish to recall and, as the slaves die, I always keep my eyes locked on Hakh's. They burn with pride as his hounds do their work – the pride of a devoted father. The thought fascinates me. I can't stop thinking about it. There seems to be something profound just beyond my comprehension. This murdering, poisonous monster *cares* for something. What does that mean? What does it mean for his wretched subjects? These gore-hungry executioners own everything now. They own those pitiful few of us who still live on the Kharvall Steppe. Slaughter, hunger and fear are the only things we will ever know now. Few of us can recall the days when animals like Hakh's great cat still breathed and hunted, moving through a realm unshackled by Khorne's brass towers. The monster sitting in the throne is all we have, and he loves something. What does that mean?

The door swings open and Hakh's eight generals march into the chamber, paying me no attention as they approach the throne. A more wretched group of stooges and villains never drew breath, but, as always, they adopt the mannerisms of proud, disciplined knights. Their twisted red and brass armour flashes in the torchlight as they drop to their knees and rest their foreheads against their axes. How furious they would be if they knew that a frail, human woman like me had written their death warrants. Not only have I convinced Hakh to call them home, but I have also convinced him that they are worthless. I have driven a blade so neatly between their shoulder blades that they did not even feel it.

Hakh remains motionless for a few more seconds, then his ember-red eyes flicker into life. The lord of the Blood Creed is still a man of sorts, I suppose, but he has more than a foot in the realm of daemons. The thick serrated plates of his armour cover most of his body, but his head is horribly exposed. Years of dark worship have earned him a pair of bestial, ridged horns that swoop up from his brutal, heavy brow. His face has the grey, greasy pallor of a month-old corpse.

For a while he ignores the newcomers and stares at me. My fear was long ago matched by hate and I hold his gaze, but I can't read the thought in those inhuman eyes. Has he seen through my ruse? Will he turn his generals on me?

He waves a hand, allowing them to rise and bark out their tallies of atrocities, presenting them as proud victories. They list every head they've taken for their lord, but I've already told him a convenient truth: that they have nothing to boast of. They no longer have an enemy to fight. This kingdom is no longer on its knees – it is supine.

'I have tightened the yoke on the cities of Iphilaus and Chius,' cries one of them in strident tones. His massive frame is encased in jagged brass armour and he has the pure white pelt of a wild cat slung across his shoulders. 'Their princes will not ask you for leniency again.' He hurls a sack to the foot of the throne and bloodless heads spill out, tumbling across the floor with a sickening series of thuds.

Another of the warriors strides forwards. He wears a heavy, blood-drenched cloak that leaves a crimson smear behind him as he walks. His gauntleted hands are locked around a daemon-forged glaive that shimmers with inner fire, revealing a cruel leer deep inside his hood.

'The Volpone River now runs red, Lord Hakh. The Volpone Knights seemed unsure whether they should kneel to you, so I helped them decide. I removed their knees. Three thousand of them are now feeding the fish at the bottom of their sacred river.'

As he listens to their boasts, Hakh leans forwards in his throne and starts to tap the blade of his sword against the floor.

I notice that Hakh has started to tremble and I edge back into my stone chair. His growing anger would be obvious to anyone with sense, but the generals carry on oblivious, crowing over their petty victories.

Hakh is a goliath – there is something almost bovine about his armour-clad bulk. But when he finally explodes, it's with surprising speed.

The general nearest to the throne topples back into the others as his head flies off, removed by one clean swipe of Hakh's sword.

The warlord roars as he storms across the room to grab the severed head and smash it against the wall. The others try to raise their weapons, but Hakh attacks them with the head, slamming it into their faces until it becomes a bloody lump of bone and metal. He roars as he kills, and then, when every one of them is dead, he hurls his dripping weapon at his throne, where it bursts like a flagon of wine.

I feel a mixture of nausea and pride at what I've done.

He's not finished. Still roaring, Hakh strides across the chamber and gouges the wall with his horns, sending wood and masonry clattering across the floor.

Then he turns, panting like an animal, and locks his gaze on me.

I scramble backwards but there's no escape. The doors are unlocked, but even if I could get through them, where would I go?

He crosses the chamber and stares at me, blood dripping from his horns.

'You were right again,' he says finally. 'They found nothing. They failed.'

His voice is a low growl that makes my language as vile as his own.

'What else do you know?' he asks.

I'm terrified but, even now, he won't hurt me, I'm sure of it. As the hounds throw themselves around the chamber, snapping and snarling, he bats them away, sending them sprawling across the floor.

'What do you *want* to know?' I ask.

He snarls and jabs one of his bloody, brass-plated fingers at my forehead.

'No games.'

'Why would I tell you anything more?' I ask, playing a fool; playing along with his lie.

He relaxes visibly, thinking he still has me in his power. He points his sword at a space in the floor of teeth. 'It's not finished. You know who's next.' He leans close, dripping blood onto my face. 'I'll make an exception and kill them slowly.'

For a moment, I allow myself to imagine that his words are true – that I have a family to save, that they're still alive somewhere, waiting for my powers as a sorcerer to buy their freedom. I picture their trusting, beautiful faces and it almost breaks me. My eyes fill with tears and the idiot thinks it's because I'm afraid for them. He thinks I don't know they are long dead.

His breathing quickens as I nod.

I sneer at his butchered generals. 'They were wasting your time. They lacked the wit to find the real threat.' I look beyond him, out through one of the narrow windows. 'But there is still an enemy. There *is* a way you could shine.'

His eyes blaze and he moves to grab me, stopping himself at the last minute as though he's afraid of shattering a precious jewel.

'And if I slay this enemy?'

'If you could slay the man I've seen, your future will be secure.' I glance at the sign of the Blood God, Khorne, carved into the back of his throne. 'You will have served your god well. He'll be in no doubt as to which of his lords should rule this land. You'll become lord of the Kharvall Steppe.'

He growls again and I wonder if he might finally kill me. But no, he's just overcome with excitement. He's picturing his peers – all the other lords vying for control of the steppe – and thinking of how he will feel when they kneel before him.

'Show me.' He sounds awed.

I shoo him away like a dog and, incredibly, he backs away, taking his hounds with him and sitting back on his throne. I take a cloak from one of the corpses and fling it around myself with a flamboyant gesture, as though it's a beautiful robe. My sense of the theatrical has not entirely left me. Then I walk to the centre of the chamber and climb up onto the grindstone. It's a huge ring of pitted granite, five feet high and almost as thick. I wince as I haul myself up onto it, but the thought of what comes next gives me strength.

For one ridiculous moment I wait for the musicians to start, but then I remember that they're all dead. I look at Hakh, unsure what to do. He's hunched forward in his throne, holding back his hounds and staring at me with such devotion that I almost laugh.

With the hounds restrained, a ghost of my power returns. I start to hum the Song of Summoning and beg my body for forgiveness as I subject it to another ordeal. My muscles remember what I do not and, as I start to dance, I hear the dead musicians in my head, willing me to succeed.

The whole performance is quite ironic. These meat-headed morons despise magic but they can't remove it fully from their towers any more than they can bar the passage of the air. As my stiff, bruised limbs twist themselves into the old shapes, a breeze springs up around the grindstone, snapping through my borrowed cloak and whipping up the fragments of broken wall. It's no natural breeze and as I look over at Hakh I feel the urge to laugh. To leave such sorcery unpunished is clearly a torment for him.

It only takes a few moments for the images to appear. My mumbled verses become an impassioned hymn and the breeze turns into a whirl of places and scenes. I spin faster and Hakh rises from his throne, staring in wonder at the figure forming in the tempest – a great lord, clad from head to toe in gleaming armour. His face is hidden behind a smooth, expressionless mask and he carries a great rune-inscribed warhammer. He's leading a vast host of golden knights into battle, some borne on wings of lightning and all of them wielding hammers that flash with the light of the storm.

I've known of his coming for weeks, but now I see him I'm as enraptured as Hakh. The lord's armour sparks and flickers as he moves, charged with some kind of divine energy, but it's his demeanour that shocks me. I've never seen anyone move through a battle with such solemnity. He strides calmly through the fighting, untouched by the violence and corruption that surround him. Great chunks of the ground are being torn free and hurled up towards the sky, but he maintains a cool, regal majesty. As I study him, a painful thought creeps into my mind. It's that most treacherous of worms: hope.

'Is this him? Is this the warlord I must face?' Hakh staggers towards the apparition, reaching through the flashing lights. 'Who is he?'

My plans are forgotten. I stare in wonder.

'He is called Tylos.'

CHAPTER THREE

Lord-Celestant Tylos Stormbound

Duty keeps me sane. I will not let my brothers die.

I haul myself down the chain and step onto the bridge, ignoring the pain, the screams and the madness of the storm. I drive down my anger and level my thoughts. I study the fastening around my leg and see that the bloodreavers have designed them for a specific purpose – so that they might travel through the lunar storm. This must be something they endure regularly, and it must therefore be something that passes. I look up at the moon and see that it's already swinging back up towards the stars. We will ride this out. We will sanctify the Crucible of Blood.

I fasten the chain tighter and stagger across the lurching bridge, barging between crowds of tumbling bodies. I grab those I can, fixing them to the structure, while crushing those in red with Grius until they are as broken as the birds. It's hard to fight cleanly in this madness, but I refuse to slip into brutality. I'm no longer the animal Sigmar lifted from the slave pits. I'm a good man; a devout man. Every kill I make is in Sigmar's name.

My men follow my lead and soon we're on the attack again, bloody and shackled but twice as determined. The laughter of our foes ceases as they find themselves once more facing a wall of hammer-emblazoned shields. I doubt we look as glorious as when we arrived, but I'm sure we are more terrifying.

Drusus and his men loop through the night sky, supporting our advance, hurling Sigmar's twin-tailed judgement.

The bloodreavers fight on. They can't hope to win, but the pitiful few that remain throw themselves at us, fuelled by a senseless kill-fever, thrashing and hacking as we trample them.

The final push is over in minutes. The storm is definitely fading now and the bridge becomes calm. Eventually, the moon is high enough that we can smash our chains and charge, finishing the bloodreavers in a silent, efficient slaughter.

I grab the last of them by the throat and drag him to the edge of the bridge. He kicks as I hold him out into the night, studying him with silent dispassion. He stops struggling and spits on my mask, his phlegm sizzling angrily on the metal, and stares at the blood flowing from the eyehole of my mask.

'Blood for the Blood God.' He starts laughing.

I remain silent.

The bloodreaver's eyes become lucid and I am pleased to see that I have confused him. He continues to laugh but it sounds forced. He strains to free himself whilst staring at my mask, trying to see what lies behind.

There was a time when I would have crushed him just see his pain, to see him beg for mercy, but I stay my hand. I am no longer that man. I brought the bloodreaver out here to denounce him, to list his crimes and vent my rage, but now I realise that would be as clumsy as revealing my face.

I drop him from the bridge.

As the bloodreaver falls from view, the insanity of this place hits me. I know the name of this kingdom – the Kharvall Steppe – but little else. I had assumed that the bridge spanned a great river, but the thundering noise I can hear is coming from something far stranger. Below us is an ocean of black fire, boiling with tormented creatures. I have no doubt that this place was once magnificent, but now it's a monstrous sight. I look down on a frenzied tsunami of reptiles, mammals and crustaceans, bound together by flames and ash, tumbling and rolling over each other in a furious rush to escape the heat. Some of the scorched creatures resemble things I can recognise, but others have been warped into lunatic creations of horn and scale. The moon paints them red; a torrent of claws and blood.

Boreas' cool tones interrupt my thoughts. He has left the other commanders behind and followed me to the edge of the bridge. Now that we are alone, he finally drops my title.

'Your first taste of victory, brother.'

'Victory isn't enough,' I reply. 'You know that. If we're to win the wider war, we must be a beacon. We must ignite these realms, not with flames but with hope. Vandus' victory at the Igneous Gate has bought us passage this far, but we have to be worthy of him. We must show the people of this land what they can be.' I draw back my shoulders and take a deep breath. 'We must show them how to be stronger, better.'

Boreas glances back across the bridge. 'Sixty Liberators are gone,' he says, with no trace of emotion.

I look past him and see the truth of it. Of those that remain, many have dark stains on their golden armour.

'The pull of the moon,' he explains. 'I can do nothing for them. They will endure hours of agony before their souls can return to the Celestial Realm.'

I look up at the sky. Which of those lights are not stars but men, screaming as they drift into the lonely void?

I turn to Boreas, wondering what kind of man he is now. We have shared so much and yet I feel like he is a stranger. Where has he travelled in Sigmar's name? Every inch of his golden armour is draped in talismans: skulls, bones and scrolls, all inscribed with tales of the underworlds. There is a grandeur to him that I don't recognise, and a coldness.

'The scholars of the Celestial City did not foresee this,' he says. '*I* did not foresee it. The storm should have landed us inside Hakh's kingdom, at the foot of the Crucible of Blood. Instead it brought us here, to the Red Road.' His words trail off and he shakes his head. When he speaks again, his voice is so soft that I can barely hear him. 'Dawn will soon be here and there are now many challenges between us and victory. Hakh's realm is encircled by a great fortress known as the Anvil. My visions have–'

'Brother,' I interrupt. 'There are no walls tall enough to stop this army. You know that. It doesn't matter where we've landed, Sigmar will not abandon us. We will reach the Crucible of Blood.'

He nods. 'I just want you to know what lies ahead. After the Anvil, we will reach Lake Malice, a mile-wide stretch of lava. Our souls may be immortal, but our flesh is not. You will need to find a way across that liquid inferno.'

'Then we have little time. How fast can we reach the Crucible of Blood?'

'If we follow the road for another mile or so past the bridge's end we'll reach the Anvil. Lake Malice is not much further from there. If we can find a way across, the Crucible of Blood will be in sight.'

'How long before the sun rises?'

'Maybe as little as three hours.' He looks up and I find myself trying to discern the eyes behind his skull mask. There's something strange about the colour, or maybe it's the absence of colour? I step closer, intrigued.

'If the sun rises before we capture the crucible, even Sigmar can't help us,' he says, turning to the horizon.

'Then three hours will have to suffice,' I say. 'Do you still have our key?' I glance at the collection of relics that adorn his armour. 'Is it intact?'

He takes a heavily bolted box from his belt and opens it with a muttered prayer. Then he lifts out a fume-filled bell jar. The opaque, green glass is thicker than my shield and locked to a silver base by a row of filigreed clasps. The jar is beautiful, in stark contrast to the contents. As Boreas lifts the glass from its base, a cloud of mist drifts away to reveal a shrivelled, black heart. The Kuriat, ancient beyond imagining, a living fossil from another age, still beating with a steady, unceasing thud. Tiny lights flutter around it, golden motes that dance and sparkle as Boreas holds the relic up in front of his mask to study its rhythm.

'The Kuriat has already slowed,' he mutters. 'The radiant storms have been cast astray. Something has perverted the will of the Celestial City. Or some*one* perhaps.' He glances at me, then looks down again. The golden lights billow and roll, forming symbols under his fathomless gaze. He reads something in the tiny constellations and nods, before closing the jar and locking it carefully away again.

'The Kuriat is still true. Its potential is undimmed. If we bring it to the Crucible of Blood, Khorne's legions will find that a new power has dominion over their prized realmgate.' He notices the crimson smear across my metal mask. 'You're wounded. Let me see.'

I remove my helmet and allow him to examine my eye.

Pain explodes across my face as he touches me but I consider it just penance for being so careless. How absurd to have been injured in my first battle.

'The eye is punctured,' he says, a hint of humanity in his voice, a hint of my brother. 'And the cut is messy. I'll need to mend the wound as best as I can to avoid infection.'

I try to shrug him off, impatient to move on, but he points at the madness below. 'Lord-Celestant, this is not a place to be careless, and your life is too precious to be taken lightly. Your soul may survive a corrupted wound, but your flesh will not, and I do not intend to lead this army in your stead.'

I loosen my grip on his arm. 'Then work quickly, brother.'

He takes an object from his armour and presses it to my face. Something plunges deep into my eye socket. The pain doubles and fresh blood pours down my face, then the world turns crimson. I struggle to see what my brother does next. He chants in a language I've never heard before and the words sound furious and alien, then he reaches up, as though trying to grasp something from the air.

'How long will–' I start to say, when a blazing column of light slams into us. It hits me with such force that I almost topple to the ground. Only my brother's firm grip holds me upright. The air crackles with arcane power and a sickening heat washes over me.

I try to cry out but my body is shaking so violently that I can't speak. My weapons drop to the ground and I slump in my brother's grip. Light pours through me, cramming my consciousness with dazzling energy as the celestial majesty burns through my skull. For an agonising, rapturous moment I feel not Boreas' hand but Sigmar's on my flesh. The light deepens and grows before revealing a hellish vision: thousands of grinning cadavers, rising up from a shattered wasteland. They crawl from their graves and swarm towards me, carrying ancient, rusting spears. One of them is a great, winged horror and, as it dives towards me I see its bleached skull in gruesome detail. I'm about to cry out in defiance, to denounce it, when the vision vanishes, replaced by the polished skull mask of my brother's helm.

The light fades and night returns. Strength floods back to my limbs and as I look around, I see that I'm still on the bridge of birds.

'You saw something,' says Boreas, keeping hold of my arm. 'What?'

I shake my head, confused.

He stares at me in silence for a moment, then gives a disapproving sigh that takes me right back to our childhood.

'You are doubly blessed, brother. The God-King has worked a miracle through my humble flesh. I only meant to safeguard you from infection, but it looks as though Sigmar does not wish to be served by one-eyed lords.'

I blink and realise that he's right: the vision has returned to my eye. As I study the storm clouds overhead, though, I feel as though I am seeing more than I should. The heavens are strangely vivid and mobile. I shake my head. 'We need to go.'

I click my mask back into place and clasp my brother's shoulder in thanks, then we stride back across the bridge to the others.

Some of them are wounded but there's no doubt in their eyes as they see me approaching. Zarax is there, waiting patiently for my return. She looks unharmed and is scratching and pawing at the bridge, eager to carry on.

Drusus lands a few feet away and as he removes his helmet I feel again that I'm seeing more than I did before. Now I can clearly see how the Reforging has changed him. When I first met Drusus, barging his way to the front of a crowd of aspirants, he was a broken man, tormented by an illness of the mind. Now a steady, missionary zeal burns in his heart. He folds his lightning-bright wings behind his back and drops to one knee. The trust in his face feels like another inch of armour across my chest.

'Forgive me, Lord-Celestant,' he says. As he speaks, his head twitches to one side, a ghost of his former madness, but he refuses to let his voice waver. 'I will not fail you again.'

'True,' I reply. 'You will not.'

Ranks of Liberators, Retributors and Judicators climb slowly to their feet. They raise their weapons in silent tribute, ready to begin again. I'm so proud I could roar.

I climb onto Zarax's back and survey my incorruptible host.

'Your baptism is complete,' I cry. 'Prepare for war!'

After half an hour's march we leave the bridge of birds and I lead the army through avenues of cloud-scraping, shattered towers. Drusus and his Prosecutors glide overhead, slicing through storm-wracked clouds, clutching their hammers and javelins as they search for signs of danger. From Zarax's back I survey the lines of Liberators marching ahead of me. Even their presence in this wretched place is an act of defiance. They move in flawless, perfectly symmetrical phalanxes, illustrating everything that an army should be. They're riven with faith and pride. Behind me stride the paladins, Celadon at their head and further back march the ranks of Judicators. Chaos-spawned horrors scuttle for safety as our boots crunch towards them.

'Soon,' says Boreas, looking up at me. There's a trace of humour in his voice.

'Soon?'

He waves his hammer at the army that surrounds us. 'Soon you'll have your chance to truly test them and see what Sigmar has entrusted you with. It won't be long until you can show your mettle.'

I smile behind my helmet. How easily he still guesses my thoughts. I glance at the heavens, trying to discern our home in the stars. 'They say that when Vandus opened the Igneous Gate, the heavens cried out in gratitude. They say a chorus of lost souls sang his name.'

Boreas nods. 'You have a lot to live up to.'

We reach the plateau and leave the shadow of the towers, heading for a glittering, moonlit expanse of scorched earth that leads to endless fields of rippling grass. There's a tinkling sound on the breeze, like hundreds of tiny bells. I look back and notice that the lunacy of this place is so profound that the moon has already resumed its natural place in the night sky. Sigmar's tempest still flickers overhead and clouds race through the darkness. Our target is clear though. I don't need Boreas' relic to point the way. Across the fields stands a vast wall of shadow. It stretches over the horizon and flickers with crimson pinpricks of light.

'The Anvil,' says Boreas. 'The border of Hakh's kingdom. Manned by an army to make those bloodreavers look like a gathering of fishwives.'

'Instruct my captains,' I say. 'Order them to spread the army out.'

Boreas snaps out commands to my captains and Zarax carries me to the edge of the fields. The tinkling sound grows louder and I realise my mistake: what I took for blades of grass are in fact real blades. We're standing before an expanse of rusting metal – millions of swaying, broken swords, each one held erect by a rotting skeletal hand that juts out of the dusty soil. They chime gently against each other in the breeze.

'What's this?' I say looking down at Boreas.

'The Field of Blades. The last army of the Kharvall Steppe.' He steps closer to Zarax and looks up at me. 'Khorne found their attempts to defend themselves amusing. He buried them here in mockery.'

I glance back at the paladins. 'Do we need to clear a path?'

'No, Lord-Celestant, there's no threat left in this army. They are simply a warning. Not even a warning – an illustration of what happens to those who brave the Anvil.' He prods a sword with his hammer. 'We'll pass through them easily enough.'

'There are so many,' says Drusus, landing a few feet away.

He's right. I look out at the Field of Blades and attempt to estimate the size of the army that Khorne found so unworthy. There must be millions of weapons quivering in the breeze while the Anvil overlooks them all, like a sated lion.

'This must have been the greatest army that ever bore arms,' says Drusus.

I laugh and signal the advance. 'The *second* greatest.'

CHAPTER FOUR

Vourla – High Priestess of the Steppe

Hakh parades me along the battlements like I'm a prized pet rather than a woman. There's no chain, no leash; the fool is so sure of his hold on me he never dreams I could be a threat. Others are less sure. As we pass ranks of crimson-armoured soldiers, they stare at me, outraged by the sight of a sorceress in their brainless ranks. None of them would dare to question Hakh's will, though, not if they treasure their heads. Even the hounds don't bite, although their presence is enough to cause me pain. As they pad at my side, the power of their collars crushes the magic out of me, draining me of power. They are as tall as I am and so close I can smell the brimstone in their veins.

I stagger on, playing the part of a tyrant's consort, pausing occasionally to glare at one of Hakh's soldiers, as though singling them out for punishment. They're more afraid of the figure walking behind me. Vhaal is captain of Hakh's honour guard and almost as massive as his lord. He's clad in the same thick plate armour, painted blood red and edged in brass, and he carries a double-headed axe that I doubt I could move, let alone lift. From the neck up, though, he's dramatically different to Hakh: the skin of his face has been flayed, leaving a mask of glistening muscle. His flesh is so corrupted that it never scabs. Blood weeps constantly from his eyes, flowing down into a long, knotted beard that hangs like a piece of intestine from his dripping chin. Hideous as his face is, it is his expression that unnerves me most. His peeled, lipless mouth seems to wear a constant smirk, as though he knows something that nobody else does.

I turn away from Vhaal and shiver. The Anvil is as high as a mountain and my tattered cloak does little to keep out the chill, but it's a relief to be outside again. The Dark Gods long ago robbed us of clean air, but even this fume-filled miasma is better than the stench of Hakh's throne room. Furnaces and forges work constantly in the Anvil's bowels, rumbling and hissing behind the wall, and we are surrounded by lurid sparks that spiral up into the darkness. But high in the heavens I glimpse true stars and they hurt me more than the hounds' collars. Their untouchable beauty is an unwelcome reminder of what has gone. As Hakh snaps orders at his men I recall folktales I learned as a child – tales of gods drenched in light, rather than blood. My father used to sing of immortals that walked the heavens, riding great star drakes into battle, driving back the daemons of the void. I try to shake my head free of such nonsense, annoyed at myself. Khorne's butchers killed my father long ago and such thoughts can only bring me pain. My only hope now is revenge and I won't risk it by dreaming of things that can never be.

The golden knight has done this to me. Something about him has turned me into a little girl again. I look down at the floor to give myself a reminder of the truth. The Anvil is hundreds of miles long and every inch is carpeted with shattered human teeth. This, I remind myself, is the true story of the Kharvall Steppe.

Hakh spends ten minutes or so inspecting his defences and berating Vhaal, but I can see his mind is elsewhere. His violence is cursory and half-hearted. Barely a dozen sentries have felt the sharp end of his sword tonight and, as soon as he reaches a watchtower, he heads back inside, taking me with him.

He leads the way through a series of skull-choked passageways and corpse-strewn antechambers until we come to a large, barred door. Guards step from the torchlight to challenge us, then quickly salute as they see Hakh's bulk.

Vhaal steps forward and shoves one of them towards the lock, and we are shown into a long, rectangular chamber. The guards rush to light the torches, disturbing clouds of dust as they clatter back and forth. It's clear nobody has been in here for a long time. As the flames sputter into life I see why – this is a repository of knowledge and learning, which are not Hakh's favoured subjects. Maps and charts cover the walls and there are tables piled with obscure astrological devices and books.

Hakh catches my surprised expression and looks even more furious than usual. It almost seems that he is embarrassed.

'Where is he?' he grunts, waving his sword at the maps.

I realise that I've not been clear. Whoever this Tylos is, he is about to present himself at the foot of the Anvil. Hakh has no need to go trekking across the steppe to find him. I'm about to explain this when I realise how stupid that would be.

'I don't know, exactly,' I lie. 'But I know where he's headed.'

Hakh nods, tapping his sword impatiently against the floor.

I stroll across the chamber to the window and beckon him to follow. There I point at the butchered landscape that lies beyond the Anvil.

On this side of the wall, the steppe leads to a blinding expanse of lava. It stretches three miles to the east, where it spits angrily onto a distant, fume-shrouded shore – a black horseshoe of basalt that rises even higher than the Anvil. Even from here I can glimpse our destination – the prize that the lake protects. Even through the smoke I see a flash of bronze; a brazen warning beneath the gathering clouds.

Hakh nods slowly. 'Of course. The Crucible of Blood. The golden warlord seeks a route to Khorne. He seeks daemonhood.'

Even after all I've witnessed, I'm momentarily stunned by how moronic he is.

'He isn't going to find Khorne,' I explain. 'He doesn't worship your god. Think of how he looked in all that golden finery. He's dressed in tribute to the other gods – beings who ruled before you came. He imagines himself as a hero from some older, nobler age. He hasn't come to pass through the gate – he means to conquer it.'

I see rage growing in Hakh's eyes as I dare to lecture him, so I change tack quickly. 'Just think of what it would mean if you could stop him. The Blood God would see without a doubt who should be lord of the Kharvall Steppe.'

Vhaal nods with his usual ironic smile. 'Amakhus and the other warlords would have no choice but to kneel to you.'

Hakh grips the lintel so tightly that his gauntleted hands start to crumble the masonry. He glares at the captain. 'They would never kneel. Nor would I give them chance. Once my lord has made me a prince, I'll use their skin for banners.'

I nod. 'Heroes forgot this kingdom a long time ago. I don't know what brought Tylos here now, but you could wait an age and not see his like again. If you seek a chance to prove your worth, this is it.'

Hakh takes a ragged breath and backs away from the window. 'When? How long will I have to gather my armies? They're scattered along every mile of this wall. When will he reach the crucible?'

I frown, genuinely unsure. I barely touched Tylos' mind, but I sense that he understands the Crucible of Blood. I think he knows what will happen when the sun rises. 'He means to reach it before dawn.'

Hakh spits. 'Dawn? That leaves me no time at all. Dawn is a few hours away.'

'What time do you need?' I ask, surprised by my growing confidence. 'What do you need to stop one knight and a few of his men?'

Hakh stares at me, and I curse myself for overplaying my hand. Vhaal steps closer, lifting his axe.

Hakh throws back his head and laughs. 'You have more guts than any of these worms, Vourla.' He waves at Vhaal. 'If you were a man and less of a runt, I'd give you his axe.'

I shrug, hoping he can't see how close I was to running.

'The golden warlord can dress up as any god he likes,' continues Hakh. 'It won't fix his head any tighter to his neck.'

He turns to Vhaal. 'Gather the Blood Creed.'

'All of them?' Vhaal's cheeks glisten as his smile widens.

There's a clicking sound as Hakh rolls his head back around his shoulders. I presume he's about to take the captain's head, but he just laughs. 'No. I'll take half of them. That will be enough. You wait here with the rest of them. Someone needs to guard this place against old women and peasants. And you can prepare my victory feast.' He waves at the window. 'There must be a few hovels left. Find me some new meat.'

Vhaal's grin freezes on his face. After a pause, he gives a stiff bow and departs. I hear him barking out the call to muster as he strides down the passageway and before long I hear the braying of tuneless horns echoing along the battlements.

'Will you leave straight away?' I ask.

In reply, Hakh drags me out into the courtyard and within half an hour we're mounted up and riding east across the steppe, with the spires of the Anvil disappearing into the haze behind us. We ride on huge, iron-clad monsters and I can feel evil simmering through the metal saddle beneath me. Death is rushing towards me now, but so is my chance; my one chance to strike a blow.

CHAPTER FIVE

Prosecutor-Prime Drusus Unbound

The voice is still there, whispering urgently at the back of my thoughts, but its power is gone. I'm no longer Drus Unaki, the man who let Ghuldiz burn; I am Drusus Unbound. I have been given a second chance. Sigmar's heralds follow *my* command and I am trusted. Tylos has given me duty and hope and, by all the fire that burns in my wings, I *will* give him victory.

We're flying so high that the Anvil looks like a nest of knotted serpents – a poisonous tanlge of guardians encircling the entire steppe with their crest of spine-like towers and countless crimson eyes. I lead my men into a dive and as the ground rushes towards us it's hard to remain calm. These are the towers that encircled Ghuldiz and Tersoos. These are the fires that burned down those ageless, jasper halls. These are the serpents that took my life.

The voices in my head grow louder, but I refuse to listen.

As the final wisps of cloud part, I see the Anvil appear in lurid detail. It's actually two walls – we are flying towards an outer curtain wall protecting a space like the outer ward of a castle. A hundred feet beyond that, a taller, inner wall rises up into the clouds. Two parallel lines of impenetrable rock. The whole structure is mind-numbingly huge and the towers that punctuate it are built around slender white spires, like huge, petrified talons. I remember my purpose and look back at the outer wall.

This will be easier than Tylos imagined.

The guardians of the Anvil are spilling out of their fortress. There are hundreds of the bare-chested berserkers we fought on the bridge – bloodreavers, Tylos called them – but they are striding out into the darkness as though preparing for a hunt. From my vantage point I can see my brother Stormcasts advancing through the Field of Blades towards them, but the bloodreavers are oblivious. I have to stifle my laughter.

White metal flashes in my peripheral vision as Prosecutor Sardicus approaches. His golden mask reveals nothing but I can hear his eagerness for battle.

'Prosecutor-Prime,' he calls out over the noise of the storm. 'The Lord-Celestant said we would find the right moment to attack. Do we wait or do we strike?'

I look down at the bloodreavers, still oblivious to the danger. 'I say we warm things up a little in readiness for our commander.' Divine light tears through my body and forms hammers in my palms. The sensation is terrifying and wonderful. I'm a conduit for pure, unshackled vengeance. 'I say we bring them Sigmar's fire!'

I hurl the bolts down into the crowd at the gate and throw myself after them, summoning celestial fire from my fingers as I go. A chorus of war cries greets my words as my men dive too. A storm of light flies past me, slamming into the bloodreavers.

As I near the ground, it erupts with dozens of detonations. The bloodreavers are so close I can see the shock on their brutal, scarred faces, followed by outright fear.

I hurl another pair of hammers, filling the gateway with a plume of crimson dust, then seconds before crashing into the ground I swoop back up towards the clouds, screaming Sigmar's wrath as the wind howls through my helmet.

The others do the same. When we reach a safe distance, we pause to look down at our work. The ground before the gate is a mess of charred craters, filled with wounded and dead. Twenty or so of the bloodreavers fail to rise, and many of those that do are carrying terrible injuries.

They slam the gates behind them but remain outside to roar and howl at us. Our attack has distracted them from the golden phalanx that is emerging from the Field of Blades. Before the bloodreavers have the chance to ready a defence, Tylos and the others crash into them, driving them back across the craters and bodies.

I lead my men over the outer wall to see how many bloodreavers are inside the gate. As we near the battlements I see movement and pause. At first I think it must be more bloodreavers, but the battlements themselves are moving, coming to life; shapes I mistook for gargoyles and grotesques rear their heads and twisted creatures of Chaos rise from the stone, bellowing and snarling as they fix their gaze on Tylos and the others. As they draw back their heads, like snakes preparing to strike, I sense a new kind of energy pooling around me.

I realise what's going to happen, but too late. As I lead my men in another dive, aiming for the monsters on the wall, they unleash a torrent of blood from their crumbling jaws. Some of the crimson liquid hits us but most pours down on Tylos and the others.

They raise their shields seconds before they vanish inside a mushroom of red flame.

'For Sigmar!' I cry, launching a furious volley of thunder

strikes at the wall. My retinues follow suit and several of the stone creatures explode. There are still dozens left intact though and, ignoring us, they vomit another tide of crimson at Tylos. The dome of red fire burns so brightly that I have to look away. One of my Prosecutors tumbles through the clouds, his armour trailing smoke and sparks as he tries to right himself.

I order Sardicus to his aid and lead the rest in another dive, blasting the stone monsters with so many hammer blows that the air starts to warp under the strain. Another of the daemonic shapes topples and I look back to the figures below.

The red cloud dissipates and there, scorched but unbowed, stands Tylos. At first I think no one has been harmed but, as Tylos leads his warriors forward to clash again into the bloodreavers, I see that several of the Stormcasts are left sprawled on the ground, their armour warped into odd, liquid shapes. I hear terrible cries of pain as the metal eats into their ruptured bodies, then lightning spears past me, enveloping them in white heat. When the light dims, the bodies have vanished.

We dive to join the battle but Tylos needs little help. The columns of light have ignited something in him. He crashes through the bloodreavers on Zarax, his armour blazing like a fallen star. For a moment I falter, awed by the sight of him. This is no longer a man. This is the God-King made manifest.

This is Sigmar bringing bloody redemption through Tylos' willing flesh.

CHAPTER SIX

Vhaal the Skinless, Captain of the Blood Creed, Executioner of Kyphanto

I taste your blood on my lips and your strength in my arms. I know that nothing else is real, Lord of Skulls. I see what gift you have offered and I will not refuse it. My spirit is ready. The hour of Vhaal approaches. Soon these pale shadows will fall away and I will join you in the Great Slaughter.

I hear the sound of battle through the gates and my blood surges in answer. Death is out there in the fields, screaming my name, but I hold my fury in check as the ranks of the Blood Creed line up behind me in the courtyard. Hakh has only left me with half an army but as they jostle into position, readying their axes and fixing their helmets into place, I know that all along the Anvil the other towers are emptying. Soon there will be thousands of puppets dancing to my tune. Nothing here is real, of course; not the Blood Creed nor those outside the gates. These talking sacks of blood are baubles, nothing more – tempting distractions that you have draped before me as a test. Even as a child, I knew that you and I alone were real. Before I could walk, I saw through the facade that surrounds me. Soon I will ascend and stand by your side.

Lord of Skulls, I know I am your son. Why else would you let Hakh be tricked away by that devious woman? Why else would you leave me this choice offering?

The outer wall is lit up with flames and embers and as I look up into the fumes I catch glimpses of gold and white, blazing wings.

'Tell me again,' I say, turning to the nearest warrior.

'A golden knight,' he replies, breathless after his run from the tower. He's still fastening his helmet into place and I see the bloodlust in his eyes, but I know it's only a pale mirror of my own true hunger. I watch him closely, hoping to catch the trickery in his words.

'Maybe a king,' he continues. 'They're all dressed in pretty gold suits, even the winged lightning wielders, but their leader looks like...' He pauses, almost looking surprised or confused. 'Like the paintings in the temple of Kaslov.'

That temple was a ruin long before we got to it, but his words only fuel my sense of destiny. This is the great lord that the witch was discussing with Hakh.

My scarlet lord, you have given me a chance to prove my worth. I understand everything. The great game nears its end. I thank you for this blessing and I give you my solemn oath: in this very hour that golden king shall give you his blood and I shall give you my soul.

The sound of battle moves closer to the gates and my men look expectantly to me for the order to advance. I won't be fooled by such tricks. I know they would lead me astray if I let them. We must wait patiently and let you do your work. I can see you from here, pouring your fury down through the spirits on the walls. In their powerful shapes I see your form.

I look at the design that decorates the centre of the courtyard – hundreds of skulls hammered into the ground to create a stylised image of one enormous skull. Once I've torn apart this golden champion I will plant his fake heart in tribute. I will show you that I am ready to return to your citadel.

'Wait,' I snap, ordering my men to take up positions on either side of the gate. When the golden knights break through, the final act shall begin.

CHAPTER SEVEN

Lord-Celestant Tylos Stormbound

Blood-acid slams against my borrowed shield, hissing across the charmed metal. The blast hits me so hard that I'm almost forced from Zarax's back, holding the shield over my head as the liquid forms a crimson dome around us. Most of my men do the same, but some are too slow. Just a few feet away, I see Liberator Arion tumble backwards, his shield torn away as the blast envelops him. His head warps like metal in a furnace and blood sprays from his gorget. The pain must be horrific but he does not cry out; he thrashes and rolls across the ground, unable to breathe, and clutches at the molten metal. The men nearest to him look on in horror, powerless to act as they crouch beneath their shields.

A figure races towards him through the madness – Boreas. He is holding his bone standard aloft as he runs, and power is radiating from it, blasting the acid away.

My brother plants the staff of his grim reliquary in the ground, lifts up one of his artefacts, a bone-handled knife, and starts writing invisible symbols in the air over Arion's head as the Liberator paws at the congealed mess that used to be his face. A moment later, he ceases his thrashing and slumps back onto the broken ground, seeming to be at peace. He grips Boreas' arm in gratitude.

The clouds part and light engulfs the pair of them as a column of lightning slams down into the ground. The Liberators standing nearby are thrown clear by the blast and the world is plunged into shadow by the brightness of Arion's pyre. After a few seconds the light fades and when Boreas heads my way, there's no sign of the fallen warrior.

'What becomes of us when we fall?' I ask Boreas as he comes to stand beside Zarax. 'What have you done to him?'

He is too exhausted to speak for a moment and the storm is still crackling across his armour. Whatever happened between him and Arion has left him trembling and dazed. He watches the sparks dancing across his gauntlets.

'I have…' He pauses and closes his fist, extinguishing the light. 'I only ended his pain, brother. Sigmar did the rest.'

He says nothing more on the subject and looks back at the Anvil.

'We're almost through,' I say, jabbing Grius at the bloodreavers. 'They're trapped at the foot of the gates. Drusus and the rest of his Harbinger retinues are swinging back through the clouds, preparing for another attack on the gargoyles. When they strike, we'll charge. We'll slaughter the remaining bloodreavers and enter the Anvil. After that I will mount the walls and bring Sigmar's judgement down on those stone horrors.'

The sky burns white as Drusus leads another attack. His Prosecutors form a dazzling 'V' as they dive from the heavens, hurling hammers at the walls. The torrent of blood ceases as the gargoyles are thrown back, enveloped in jagged arcs of light.

'Advance!' I cry.

Zarax hurls me forwards, bounding over charred, buckled limbs and leaping at the line of bloodreavers. As she locks her jaws around her prey, I bring Grius down into the first face I see.

Each hammer blow takes me further from my undisciplined past. Bones and teeth splinter around me as I advance with cold, inhuman precision. Zarax, meanwhile, is a vision of taloned, snarling fury. Her blue-scaled hide burns in the gloom and lightning pours from her jaws as she careers through the enemy lines.

The bloodreavers collapse before her in a shower of blood and broken weapons and I bring Grius down against the gates with a prayer. The runic hammer blazes like a star, a blinding fragment of Sigmar's soul.

A splinter races up the centre of the door, glinting like quicksilver. Zarax roars and my men pause mid-strike, joining their voices to hers. The sound floods my mind and my second blow is twice as hard. As Grius hits the door again, it shudders beneath the blow and the crack widens to reveal rows of moonlit buildings.

Blood-acid rains down again as the gargoyles recover from Drusus' attack, but Zarax and I are sheltered in the threshold and I swing my hammer for a third time. Grius burns with a flame so bright it lights up the whole doorway as it gives way.

My men roar as Zarax carries me through the splintering wood.

Their cheers falter as the dust clears and we see what lies beyond.

Gathered in the courtyard beyond, at the foot of the Anvil's second wall, are ranks of red-armoured knights. As my vision clears I see that the guardians are heavily clad in suits of thick, brass-rimmed plate and their faces are hidden behind brutal, jagged helmets, all crowned with the icon of the Blood God. They wait in disciplined, orderly lines, and they're huge – maybe as big as my own men. Standing ahead of them is what I take to be their captain. He's as heavily armoured as the other knights but his head is uncovered and the reason is clear – his face is an angry mess of exposed muscle that he clearly wishes to display. As he strides confidently towards me he gives me the strangest look – a wry smile that implies we're sharing some kind of joke. The idea that I could share anything with him turns my stomach but, before I can call the charge, Boreas steps through the broken gate and speaks.

'There are too many,' he says, looking up at me.

My men are clambering through the broken gate behind him, smashing the hole wider as they rush to escape the red death outside, but the crimson ranks make no move to advance. The one with a wound for a face is holding them back, studying us.

Boreas is shoved against Zarax as others crowd into the passageway. 'Look at them,' he says.

There are countless hundreds of these goliaths and they display a carefully drilled discipline quite unlike the lunatic barbarians on the bridge.

I look down at Boreas, unable to hide my anger. 'Remember what we are, Lord-Relictor.'

I catch another glimpse of Boreas' strange eyes and I see that he's taken aback. For the first time since we landed in this hellish realm I've surprised my brother.

'If you think we can't break through by strength of arms,' I continue, 'use whatever secrets Sigmar has entrusted you with. This first strike against Chaos cannot falter, Boreas. Sigmar's Stormhosts must be free to advance without fear of constant attack from behind. We will reach the Crucible of Blood and we will sanctify it.' I reach down from Zarax's back and grip his shoulder, hauling him towards me. 'Forward is the only way.'

A clanging sound echoes across the vast courtyard as the red-armoured knights prepare to advance.

'What would you have me do?' he asks, an edge of pride in his voice.

I keep my tones level, not wishing to sound like the common street fighter I once was. 'You carry death in you, Boreas, I can smell it. Bring it to our aid.'

'I'm a storm-priest, Tylos, not a necromancer. Whatever you might remember from my past, I'm–'

'Boreas!' I wave at the mass of towers looming on the far side of the courtyard. 'You've been to places I could barely dream of. Do what you were created to do.' There's no plea in my voice, only command.

He looks up at the Anvil and then back at me. 'You'll be stalled here for too long. When dawn comes you'll still be battling through these dogs.'

As always, Boreas is infuriatingly insightful. I tighten my grip on his arm. 'Then find us a way through.'

Horns blare out as the knights begin their charge.

I give an order and my men close ranks. A shield wall forms around Zarax and I turn to my rows of archers.

'Seriphus,' I cry, calling over the leader of my Judicators. I point at the steps inside the gate. 'Take up positions inside the outer wall. Wait for my call.'

The Judicator leaps to obey, scaling the battlements and ordering his retinues to ready their bows.

'Sigmar is with us,' I say, looking back at Boreas as the archers take up their positions. 'And I will win this battle'. I soften my voice. 'But you must do whatever the God-King demands of you.'

He looks back through the broken gate at the Field of Blades and nods. 'Hold them here. I will return.'

Then the battle engulfs me and Boreas is gone.

CHAPTER EIGHT

Lord-Celestant Tylos Stormbound

The guardians of the Anvil are no more human than we are. The air simmers and recoils from them as they approach, as if they are chiselled from hot coal. Their huge frames are bolstered by layers of red and brass plate and they smash into us like automata, animated by a rage so potent it pours off them like smoke. Blood warriors. Since Sigmar drove them back from the Gates of Azyr, their name has become infamous as Khorne's most fearless attack dogs.

Zarax rears up and brings her claws down onto the first crimson-clad brute to reach us. I draw my runeblade, Evora. My heart swells at the sight of her intricate inscriptions. Like me, she is a holy weapon, forged in the heat of the stars. She sings in gratitude as I bring her round in a wide arc, slicing easily through shields, greaves and necks, toppling whole rows of Chaos warriors. Her voice is the sound of the heavens, a soaring, celestial chorus that rings out over the din of battle, elevating the bloodshed to the noble endeavour it should be. I join my voice to hers as we kill.

My Liberators hold steady under the weight of the attack, proud and determined behind their shields, an impassable wall of blue and gold. Their hammers meet with jagged, brutal axes and the air rings with the sound of breaking metal.

I see a flash of crimson. Something bolts through the crowd and slams into Zarax's flank. She staggers to one side but I manage to stay on her back. I swing Evora down in another singing arc. She cuts through arms and faces and I follow her with Grius, swinging the warhammer with my other hand and crushing crimson helmets to a mangled pulp.

I fight with all the power and grace I learned in Sigmar's golden halls, thrusting, lunging and pounding without ever fully losing myself to the violence. Faith is my lodestone, directing my every step. As Evora sings, I let her voice calm me. I feel like I'm taking part in a grand ceremony, rather than riding through a crush of armoured knights.

I order Liberator-Prime Castamon to advance and he leads his retinue with composed blows. The emotion I saw in him before is gone and he pounds through the blood warriors with cool, lethal efficiency. Every few paces, his shield wall drops and he strides forth, lashing out with his warhammer. A crimson-clad colossus attacks, swinging an axe at his throat. Castamon raises his golden shield, deflects the blade and drops the blood warrior with an armour-splitting blow.

Lines of blood warriors charge towards him but Castamon is already gone, swallowed by a wall of shields as his Liberators reform their phalanx. The enemy crashes uselessly against an impenetrable wall of sigmarite and the Liberators march on, implacable and unstoppable.

I ride towards Castamon, noticing something odd. However many times Castamon's Liberators strike, the enemy aren't falling back. My armour has turned as red as the enemy and my muscles are screaming with exhaustion, but I haven't moved. I'm still just a few feet into the courtyard.

I take a moment to look around.

Castamon and the Liberators are still locked in their gleaming phalanxes – gilded fortresses, battered by tides of red and brass – but they haven't gained an inch. However terrible the wounds we inflict, the enemy never falter. If I couldn't see scarred, sunburned chins jutting out from their helmets, I would think they really were automata. They have no concept of pain and more of them are flooding into the courtyard all the time.

Zarax rears beneath me again as an enormous creature locks its jaws around her throat. She staggers under its weight and I see that it is a flesh hound of Khorne – an enormous reptilian thing, coated in red scales and armed with talons as cruel as Zarax's own. As it attacks, it lets out a dread howl – a sound so full of animal bloodlust that it could only have come from the bloody plains of Khorne.

Sigmar's wrath floods my limbs and I hurl the flesh hound back into the ranks of blood warriors. It crouches and roars, iron-hard spines bristling along its grotesquely muscled back, but before it can pounce, Zarax charges forwards and I slam Grius into its drooling jaws. White fire blossoms beneath its scales and it tumbles back into the enemy ranks.

As the flesh hound collapses into ash, the blood warriors crush around Zarax, grinding me to a halt with their armour-clad bulk. Grius and Evora do their work, surrounding me in a storm of sigmarite, and dozens of blood warriors fall away, but more pile in, careless of the wounds I am inflicting.

Then I see the lord with the skinless face wading through the battle towards me. He still wears that same, knowing smirk, but his arms are a frenzied blur as he hacks through his own men to reach me.

My heart quickens. This is my chance to behead this army and end the fighting so we can keep moving. Sigmar did not send me to fight for the Anvil. We should be far from here by now. As the lord approaches, I seize my chance.

'Seriphus!' I cry, standing in the saddle and raising my voice over the din so that the archers on the wall can hear me. 'Now!'

A roof of white flame spreads overhead as the Judicators launch their lightning-charged bolts. The front row of blood warriors evaporates, replaced by an explosion of blood and dazzling arcs of power. Bodies are hurled into the air and a huge swathe of the army collapses.

Zarax is thrown backwards by the blast and, when she turns back to face the enemy, there's no sign of the flesh-faced lord. The Judicators' volley has had little effect other than that, though. Blood warriors are still pouring from the wall and the whole courtyard is now full of them.

'Retributors!' I cry, seeking another way to end to this deadlock. I smile as hundreds of the hammer-wielding paladins break ranks and line up before the phalanxes of Liberators. They step slowly, encumbered by armour that would crush a mortal man. Until now I've kept them behind the other Stormcasts. They carry no shields on account of their colossal two-handed weapons, but they still resemble a wall of metal.

The blood warriors finally pause, not afraid, but intrigued. As the paladins march to my side, the ground cracks beneath their weight and storm-charged air flickers over their amour.

While the enemy are momentarily thrown, I give a signal to the Judicators on the walls. Another storm of blazing arrows whirrs overhead and slams into the enemy. The blood warriors' vanguard erupts in white flame and I order my paladins to attack. They pound across the courtyard – metal-clad titans with blazing hammers. Their blows land with supernatural force and another series of detonations rocks the enemy frontline. More arrows slam home. I order the phalanxes of Liberators to follow them.

The enemy are still reeling when the Liberators' shields crash into them and finally we start to make some headway.

Zarax rears beneath me. Blood is streaming from her flank and several of her iron-hard scales have been torn away, but she roars lightning as she carries me back into the fray.

CHAPTER NINE

Lord-Relictor Boreas Undying

More than any of us, Tylos has been reborn. I've travelled so deep into the darkness that his soul is clearer to me than his flesh. Sigmar's forges have made him anew; my brother is a celestial lord now, not the faithless sell-sword that tormented my youth. As I leave the Anvil and turn to the Field of Blades, I hear him leading the charge. I know he will fight with honour, but I wonder if he sees how close we are to disaster. His eagerness to match Vandus' heroics could be a dangerous distraction. The Anvil stretches for miles across the steppe, and every minute Tylos spends fighting in that hell pit will see hundreds more blood warriors pouring from the battlements. This is not the battle we were sent to win – I must find a quicker way to end it.

As the clamour of battle fades behind me, I reach the solemn quiet of the Field of Blades, where skeletal hands clutch useless weapons in an eternal vigil. Tylos and the others recoiled at the sight of this place but as the cemetery chill reaches up through my boots, I feel a blessed peace. I almost relish this chance to turn away, to sink back into shadow.

I drop to one knee and take out the Thin Man. The jumble of claws and bone lies innocently in my palm. Such an ugly little thing and yet it contains incredible power – the power to bridge worlds.

I've toiled so long in the shadows that my memories play tricks on me, but some things remain painfully clear. I feel a rush of anger as I think of the man who gave me this gift, so many years ago. 'One day you *will* wish to return,' he had said. 'Keep this as a parting gift.' I had sworn I never would, but other, more powerful oaths have left their mark on me since then and I must crush my pride. Tylos is no longer my hot-headed young brother; he is my Lord-Celestant, an avatar of the God-King, and I must do whatever he needs of me – even if it means facing my oldest ghosts.

I grab one of the skeletal hands and prize the sword from its grip. The weapon crumbles at my touch and I push the Thin Man into the open hand, clenching the fingers around it in a fist. Some snap, but the relic stays in place. Then I hold my own hand a few inches from the bones and begin to pray.

The swords around me rattle as Sigmar's tempest flickers in the dust. The sound of fighting coming from the Anvil grows fiercer, but I pray harder, summoning the God-King's fire from the heavens. The dust becomes a whirlwind, spinning around me and cutting through the gaps in my armour. Finally, as my words become a howled song, the skeletal hand grips mine and the Thin Man turns to ash, his promise finally fulfilled.

Reality slips away.

Damp, bone-aching cold seeps through my armour as I enter the Realm of Death. Serpentine mist coils around me and I see bestial faces in the ether – spirit hosts, pawing at my armour, trying to wrap their deathless claws around my heart. An unholy chill seeps through my breastplate but such insipid souls are no threat to an emissary of the God-King. I grab one of my honour scrolls and mutter a prayer, driving them back with a powerful stream of litanies and oaths. They whir and spiral away from me, letting out thin, moaning wails as they tumble back into the shadows. As they fade from sight, I see how the heavy boot of Chaos has transformed the Tolgaddon Marshes.

Wherever I look there are cloud-scraping talons – Chaos citadels with brutal, triangular towers. They punctuate the horizon like a stone forest, spilling shards of crimson through the tumbling clouds of spirit hosts. I feel as though I am in the jaws of a beast. Hordes of bloodreavers are marching through the gloom, mustering for battle beneath crude, brazen standards bearing the sigil of the Blood God. They are accompanied by columns of smoke-belching monstrosities that could either be war machines, metal-clad beasts, or an unholy hybrid of both.

I tremble with rage as they barge past, screaming their obscene battle cries, but I have the sense to keep silent and stay in cover. The Thin Man has led me to a ditch full of brackish water, piled with mounds of armour and old clothes. It's an undignified way to arrive but it gives me a moment to study my surroundings. I peer over the edge and see nothing familiar. The great charnel palaces that once filled the marshes have been destroyed. There are a few crumbling remnants of one of Nagash's corpse cities, but they're so defaced and ruined that I can't work out where I am. It looks as though the Supreme Lord of the Undead has been usurped and driven from the marshes by a more potent power. If Nagash's citadels have been overrun, what does that mean for the one I seek?

'Where are you?' I mutter, scouring the banks of wailing mist.

Whatever has happened to the underworlds, my former master still lives, I'm sure of it. I can almost hear him, scratching away at his rolls of vellum – endlessly recording and reviewing, oblivious to the sound of his world falling down around his ears. I have no other option but to follow my instincts, so I wade off through the knee-deep mire in the direction that feels right.

I grimace as I barge through the floating mounds that surround me. They're not clothes as I first thought, but corpses, bloated and deformed by the water. White, lifeless faces roll to stare at me as I shove the bodies aside, following the course of the ditch. Every few minutes I risk a glance over the top. As I near the fortress, I grow more alarmed. The Chaos bastion is built on a scale that defies nature. It's so vast that clouds drift around its towers and the huge armies pouring through its gates resemble billows of glittering dust.

I'm starting to think I should head back to Tylos when a sound makes me pause. There's something approaching from behind me. I can't see through the gloom but I can hear the slurping, slapping sound of feet tramping through the mud and gore. I hurry around the next bend and freeze. Up ahead of me, there's a figure hunched over the bodies, feasting on their ruptured flesh as if it were a glorious banquet. The creature is a stooped, grey-skinned horror, covered with open sores and threaded with writhing worms.

At the sound of my approach, the ghoul whirls around and stares at me with wild, rolling eyes. It's carrying a half-gnawed femur, and at the sight of me it scampers through the filth, swinging the bone at my face.

My warhammer lands with such force that the ghoul's skull collapses. It cartwheels back through the ditch, losing its makeshift weapon and collapsing into the bodies it had been feeding on. The blessed sigmarite of my weapon is engraved with holy tracts and as the monster tries to rise, its body collapses and burns under the weight of my faith, shrivelling and boiling into a pale soup that seeps away into the mud.

I'm now left in no doubt as to what is approaching from the opposite direction so I stride on through the bodies, keen to avoid making any more noise, but before I've taken more than a few steps, the bodies start to rise. Dozens of the corpses are revealed as wild-eyed ghouls, identical the one I just destroyed. They moan and gurgle as they lurch towards me.

My hammer flashes in the dark as I charge through them. There's no time to stand and fight and no way to return. All I can do is race on and pray I reach my destination before I draw Khorne's bloody gaze.

The ghouls swarm around me, rising from the mud and viscera like a pallid fungus. They've clearly been waiting for something to fall within their cadaverous reach, too afraid to venture out into the open.

Finally, a whole wall of grasping, broken-clawed hands slams into me, barring my way. I strike them down with furious blows but, eventually, they clamber towards me in such numbers that I'm driven up the wall of the ditch and out of cover.

The nearest of the warbands is less than a hundred yards away and, as I stumble into view, still pummelling the mob of leering ghouls, my golden armour flashes in the moonlight. I am seen.

Horns blare with renewed violence and there's a great clattering of armour as a host of warriors turn to face me. At the head of the column there is a knight in thick, spiked armour. He bellows a command and his men break ranks, racing towards me with a deafening roar.

'Where are you?' I gasp, racing through the darkness. There's nothing waiting for me but another mound of bodies. 'You promised me a way back!'

The ghouls are butchered and trampled into the ground as the Chaos warriors bear down on me. I find myself surrounded by rows of heavily armoured killers. They slow as they approach, readying their brutal axes, intrigued by my strange armour.

I back onto a mound of bodies, my hammer raised before me, then laugh as I see what I'm standing on. Piled beneath me are the slaughtered remains of a library – charred remnants of books, trampled into the ash and mud. They are as familiar to me as the faces of my own family. I spent my youth cataloguing these ancient texts and I understand immediately what they mean. He *has* left me a way back – a way through the glamour that has shielded him from the Blood God. I grab a book and start to chant the old litanies, waiting for the necromancer to hear me.

The Chaos warriors howl in rage as I start to fade from sight.

It's autumn, as the necromancer likes it, and as my boots sink deep into a mulch of muddy brown leaves I can't help feeling a little impressed by what he has achieved. The Dark Gods have left their mark everywhere but here. Not a single brass tower mars the sombre beauty of his estates. The valley is lined only with leafless, rain-lashed trees and long, grasping shadows. The necromancer is ancient beyond even my understanding, more of a relic than the trinkets he collects, but despite everything that passed between us, I can't deny that his learning has served him well. He claimed once that he was born in another age, long before the coming of Chaos. Such talk no longer seems quite so fanciful. Few have the power to mask themselves so completely that even a god cannot discover their presence. I never learned to pronounce my master's true name, but the appellation I always gave him still seems apt: Mopus.

The fane itself was one of Mopus' earliest finds. It's the grandest of his homes and it squats at the end of the valley, as though ready to scuttle away; a crumbling mountain of faceted turquoise, forty feet tall, twice as wide and carved in the likeness of a colossal deathwatch beetle. Its compound eyes watch my approach with hunger and I pick up my pace, jogging through the whirling rain.

I hurry through the gloom and realise that not all of the shapes lining the valley are trees. I stop, peer through the drizzle and realise that there are hundreds of pale figures standing in rows around me, clutching ancient spears and staring away from the fane. They're as motionless as the trees, but a cold light flickers in their shattered skulls. I step towards the edge of the path and see that the ranks of undead continue out of sight. There must be thousands of them, an army waiting patiently for a command. They pay no attention to me, but their presence gives me pause. Mopus was never one for wars. That was our great bone of contention – the wedge that drove us apart. It seems that many things have changed in the realm of the dead. I continue on my way with even more wariness. If Mopus is still the master of this place, then he is not the man I remember.

The entrance to the fane lies between the beetle's broken antennae at the base of its head, and as I hurry towards the door a pair of milk-eyed cadavers step from the shadows to greet me. I would expect to be remembered at this place, but I lift my hammer just in case.

Mopus' attendants twitch, as though tugged by invisible strings, then back away into the shadows, leaving the way clear.

I climb the steps to the towering slab of turquoise that passes for a door. It's buried beneath a robe of dead ivy and clearly hasn't been opened for months, so I am forced to tear and pull at the knotted mass until, finally, I uncover an iron handle. The door is locked, but the handle is so rusted that one good shove breaks it free and the door screeches open. A gentle sound seeps out through the gap: a whispered tapping, the sound of tiny pebbles pouring into a tin bowl.

I glance back and see the sentries staring blankly at me. They make no move to attack so I shove the door wider and stumble inside.

I'm met by a wall of clocks and mildewed books, stacked in mounds and filling the entrance hall. The smell of damp is overwhelming and there is something tragic about the scene. The books are rotting into an inseparable mass of gilt-edged pages and sagging, broken spines. It's like the site of a mass burial. The clocks are in just as poor condition but, by some charm of Mopus, they are all still ticking. This is the tapping I heard – so many mechanisms working at once sounds like a distant hailstorm.

Cold blue light pours through the walls and washes over the dying books, revealing how tightly packed they are. For a moment I think there is no way to proceed, but then I spot a gap near the ceiling, to the right of the passageway. Time spent in the fane will bear no relation to the battle at the Anvil, but I cannot allow myself to dawdle. Already I can feel the lure of Mopus' quiet cold, and I doubt the God-King would offer me a *second* chance at salvation.

I clamber up the wall of books and clocks, wincing at every torn cover, and reach the ceiling. The gap is too small but the air is so damp that I can shove my hammer through the barrier as though it were a bank of mud. After a few moments I manage to haul myself through the hole.

On the other side there are more piles of sodden books and broken timepieces, but I am able to crawl across them, just inches below the ceiling, until I reach the lintel of a wide doorway. I squeeze myself through the gap and into another room.

I slide down the slope of books but there's still no sign of a floor. In this chamber, as well as more books, there are mounds of idols and fetishes. I see bronze, dog-headed statues and carved, wooden birds piled together with no obvious sense of order, but I notice that all of them carry Mopus' tiny, handwritten labels.

It's only as I approach another door that I notice I'm not alone. There are figures slumped amongst the relics. Some look up as I pass, but most remain intent on their work, poring over drooping pages or scratching at mouldering paintings. They're as pale and lifeless as the monsters guarding the door, and the eyes that turn towards me are clouded and blue. Mopus has long made a habit of employing the studious dead and I start to feel more confident that my journey will not be wasted.

No one speaks so I hurry on. It's a long time since I visited the fane, but I easily remember the way to Mopus' chambers. If he lives, there is no question of his being absent. That much, at least, I can be sure of.

Another pair of hooded figures is watching over the entrance to his chambers, but, again, they back away at my approach, and I step through the door.

Everything is as I recall, a fact I can't help but find comforting. Tapestries still cover every inch of the antechamber, so threadbare and thick with dust that the heroic scenes have faded into abstraction. The blurry, indistinguishable shapes, combined with the hazy, filthy air, make me feel almost drunk. That, along with the gloom, spare me from seeing most of the other things in the room. Crooked bookcases lean against much of the wall space, crammed with crumbling tomes and rows of jars. There's enough light for me to see that the pale, half-formed shapes suspended in the jars are twitching and moving, excited by my arrival. There are countless other mysteries vying for my attention: abandoned sketches, broken pieces of scientific equipment and piles of bleached human bones, all covered with Mopus' little labels.

I walk through into Mopus' study and, to my surprise, the ancient scholar almost rises from his desk. He can't quite force himself to leave his mouldering texts, but he sits in a more upright position than I have seen before, and actually turns to look at me. His face is as pallid and skull-like as ever, but his eyes flash victoriously as I approach his desk. His skin is so tightly stretched around his skull that it seems to shine in the candlelight. Every inch of him is tattooed with intricate, cabalistic designs – spidery blue wards of protection that enable to him to converse with even the most dangerous spirits. His gaunt face conjures up memories of our final fierce argument, but I can't help feeling a little pleased to see that, amongst all this death, Mopus is still clinging to life.

I notice other figures loitering in the darkest corners of the room – ephemeral wraiths, draped in robes of pale mist, and newcomers to the fane. They drift a few feet above the dusty floorboards and I can see at a glance that Mopus has dragged them from the grave. The candlelight refuses to illuminate them fully, but I sense them staring at me with interest.

Mopus shows no anger as I reach his side, only pride that I could not stay away. Whatever passed between us, I sense I am forgiven. He waves me to a chair and grasps my hand as I sit. His long, filthy digits lock around my gauntlet and he gives me a smile of genuine friendship.

'The Crucible of Blood,' he says finally. His age-ravaged voice is hard to understand. 'You kept me waiting for all these years, Boreas. You left me here alone, with no word of your whereabouts, take up a new religion, and then you embark on adventures without ever asking me for help. Why didn't you come to me, Boreas? Can it really be that you no longer value my advice?'

I have few cards to play. The old scholar clearly knows why I'm here, and my new name. He probably knew my purpose before I did. I nod and then glance again at his spectral attendants. His tone is pleasant enough, but I'm in no doubt as to how much danger I'm in. His guards carry weapons of some kind, knives perhaps, but they're too hidden in mist for me to make them out.

'Look,' says Mopus, shifting rotten books from the pile on his desk until he finds the volume he's after. It's a slim portfolio of prints and sketches and as he flicks through them he laughs. 'Have you seen the thing?' He jabs one of his crooked fingers at a particularly disturbing painting. It shows thousands of daemonic beings boiling in a vast pool of blood, surrounded by a rim of brass. Even so crudely rendered the daemons make a shocking sight.

I look away from the painting and he smiles at me again, making his face even more skull-like. 'I imagine your new friends did not explain the whole story, did they?' He traces his finger over the text beneath the image and reads aloud. '*Beneath the ruins of the Nomad City stands the Crucible of Blood. It is an enormous brass skull. It is a gruesome relic of an ancient war, filled with the blood of a thousand mortals. It is charged with the power of the Lord of Rage.*'

Mopus gives the robed figures a wild-eyed glance, as though expecting a reply. They give none, so he continues.

'*The skies above the Crucible of Blood are filled with the drifting fragments of the Nomad City. The ruins may once have been a great civilisation or perhaps, a single, fortified structure, crafted by forgotten beings in the time before Chaos.*'

Mopus shakes his head in wonder as he stares at the painting. Then he turns to me, his eyes narrowing. 'What have you got yourself embroiled in, young Boreas?'

So he doesn't know everything; his omniscience clearly doesn't stretch as far as the Celestial City. He doesn't seem to know the significance of the crucible. So much has changed since we last met. Mopus, the great scholar of our age, is ignorant of our prize. His books have finally failed him.

He leans across his desk and, as he moves, his thin, parchment skin slides over his ribs. He peers through the eyeholes of my mask and runs one of his bony digits across the golden sigmarite of my armour, tracing the contours and sacred runes. 'A uniform.' The idea seems to amuse him and he glances mischievously at the figures in the shadows. 'Boreas has joined a regiment.'

I say nothing.

'But he has become no less taciturn,' he laughs, flopping back into his chair and spreading his arms. 'What do you want, boy?'

'I do value your advice, Mopus, and I need your help.'

He keeps smiling but I sense that he also wears a mask. Behind that smile he's worried. Another sign of how much things have changed. I can't remember ever seeing fear in him before. He looks from me to the painting of the Crucible of Blood and then back at me again.

'We all need help, Boreas,' he says. 'There's still magic in the fane that those Chaos wretches could never hope to comprehend, but it's failing.' He grimaces and looks at his empty palms. 'You know I have no appetite for war, but I have been forced to prepare for it just the same. I fear my solitude may soon be taken from me.'

I nod, thinking of the pale legions I saw in the valley.

'And, after all these centuries, my second sight is failing.' He waves his hand. The gesture draws a column of letters from the pages on his desk and they begin to whirl and spin. Mopus licks his ink-stained fingertips and jabs them at the luminous characters. After a while, images appear in the storm of words. I see Tylos and the others, battling furiously, trapped in the heart of the Anvil. I lean closer, trying to discern details.

'They won't break through.' Mopus stares at the images, fascinated. 'I can still see that much. Not without my help. Which, of course, is why you came.' He peers at the tiny gold figures. 'But what are they? I have scoured my libraries for a clue but found nothing.' He turns to me, looking at my armour again. It must be galling for the great collector to see such an unfamiliar design. 'What's happening, Boreas? What have you become?'

'The Age of Chaos is over.' I try to keep my voice flat and impassive, but the words ring out through the darkness. 'The Celestial Gates have opened, Mopus. The Lord of Storms has returned.'

Mopus licks his thin, cracked lips and glances at his shadowy entourage. 'Sigmar?' He frowns. 'If that were true – if you are really his vengeful host – this is not the most impressive crusade, is it? You're trapped in the Anvil, miles from the Crucible of Blood.'

'We were thrown off course. We should have landed in the ruins of the Nomad City, right at the foot of the Crucible, but the storm was sent astray and we landed in the borderlands. We should already have completed our mission.' I glance at him. 'We were betrayed.'

'So, Sigmar's great homecoming ends with a whimper, just because you got lost?' He softens his voice. 'Come home, Boreas. Take off that ridiculous suit. Study with me, as you did before. Since you left, I've collected treasures you can't imagine. Why get yourself embroiled in the wars of gods? They've always fought and they always will, but only we get killed. They're not like us, Boreas. They don't care about us. And there's still so much to do here – so much to learn. There is knowledge here that you couldn't dream of. If you joined me we could survive a hundred wars.'

'Survival isn't enough,' I say calmly. 'Murder and cruelty can't just be ignored. Things have to change, and we have to change them. I won't hide any more.' I nod at the image of Tylos and the other Stormcast Eternals. 'This is just a fragment. You're seeing the tiniest glimpse of what will follow. We're a raindrop at the cusp of a great storm.'

He keeps staring at me and I sense that I've touched something in him – some vestigial spark of honour. Then he slumps back into his chair.

'I've lived too long to follow heroes, Boreas. I tried that once before. Their failure caused me more pain than all the gods combined. Change is not so easily brought about. I could get you past the Anvil, but I can't see why I should. You've made it clear I no longer have your allegiance.'

For years I've suppressed my disappointment in him, the fury I felt at our final parting, but now it boils out of me. 'You're not the things you own, Mopus. You are not dead. You have knowledge and possessions here that could make a difference. You could end the suffering of thousands if you dared to apply the things you have learned. But you hide yourself away here, studying life so that you don't have to live it.'

His expression hardens as I dig at the old wound. An awkward silence fills the room and I see something dangerous in his eyes. I curse my lack of tact – my anger may have cost me everything.

'You're not so changed, Boreas,' he says after a while, staring at my armour. 'For all your grand words, you still have an eye for interesting trinkets.' He points at the box hanging from my waist. 'You've not taken your hand away from that toy since you arrived.' He studies the runes around its base. A few lonely threads of colour start pulsing in his cheeks. 'It looks almost as old as I am. How important you must be that your new masters decorate you with such baubles.'

I back away, keeping a protective hand over the relic, and curse myself for revealing its importance.

I sink into one of the spectral figures. While we've been talking, they've formed a circle around the desk. They're as cold and cruel as the spirit hosts outside. I struggle but I can't force my way through and I'm reluctant to fight in front of Mopus. I turn to face the spirit. Its hood is deep but I see a gleam of skinless bone and grinning, bleached teeth.

It shoves me back towards Mopus with surprising strength.

'Are we enemies, then?' I growl, looking back to Mopus and glaring from behind my mask.

He still has a troubling brightness in his eyes. 'Far from it. In fact, I'm beginning to think I might be able to help you. There's more to life than friendship, after all.' He stares at the bell jar. 'If that's as important as you obviously think it is, perhaps you have more bargaining power than you realise.'

'Mopus,' I growl, unable to hide my anger. 'This means nothing to you!'

He laughs without smiling and I see that I've lost all hope of reasoning with him.

'By the gods,' he says. 'You *are* eager to keep it. It must be very special. Why were you never this interesting when you were hanging off my coat tails?'

I can see his pulse racing angrily beneath his translucent skin. 'If you give me that trinket,' he continues, 'the Anvil will be nothing more than a bad memory. You and your shiny soldiers can march on to fight whatever hopeless battles you choose. In fact, I'll ensure your safe passage to the very mouth of the Crucible of Blood. Nothing shall bar your way. I'll see to it. My reach is long. I'm sure you remember that much about me.'

'Anything else,' I say.

The fury in my voice just makes his eyes gleam all the more.

I feel like smashing the room apart. Without the Kuriat, capturing the Crucible of Blood will be impossible. Sigmar's artisans spent years forging an icon that could reclaim the realmgate, and I know Mopus is only demanding it through spite. He has no idea of its true worth.

I'm about to storm out when I see the swirling image of battle still raging over Mopus' desk. Tylos and the others are fighting with all the nobility and heroism I would expect, but the wall of blood warriors before them is impenetrable and growing larger all the time. Khorne's legions are flooding from the surrounding towers, cramming the courtyard with a forest of axes. My head pounds. To give away the Kuriat means defeat, but Mopus is my only chance at breaking that bloody deadlock. For all his faults, Mopus is not a liar. If he says he will ensure our passage, then he will. If I refuse, Tylos will still be mired in battle when the sun comes up. And then all will be lost anyway.

When Mopus speaks again, his voice is cold and flat. 'If the God-King is all you believe him to be, Boreas, what does it matter? Is there any deal you can make here that will hold him back?'

He's mocking me, but he's right. We must survive the Anvil and there *is* another way. 'Forgive me, Tylos,' I mutter as I unclasp the bell jar from my belt. I stare at it for a moment then reluctantly drop it into the necromancer's grasping hands, whispering a prayer as I do so.

He tears off the lid and stares at the still-beating lump of black meat.

'What will you do to the Anvil?' I demand, all thoughts of friendship forgotten. 'When will we be free to advance?'

He gives me a brief, unreadable look, before turning back to his desk and his endless reading. 'It's done. You should hurry. You're missing all the fun.'

CHAPTER TEN

Lord-Celestant
Tylos Stormbound

Sigmar's light envelops me, blazing white, blue and finally crimson as it cooks our enemy alive. As the paladins advance in their hulking, star-forged armour they dwarf the surrounding Liberators, and each blow from their massive lightning hammers rocks the courtyard, scattering blood warriors and smashing craters in the ground. They look like gods torn from the heavens and as I lead them into the enemy, the ground shatters beneath their wrath. Hundreds of my Liberators are wounded, limping and staggering as they lash out with their hammers, but they hold their formations and advance close behind us.

Zarax tenses beneath me and unleashes another bolt of celestial fire. Finally we're making some headway. The lines of Chaos knights are thinning and drawing back. The paladins are clearly too much for them. I wave the army on as Zarax tears into the reeling enemy warriors.

Only at the last minute do I realise that this is too easy; too quick. My instinct screams out at me that we're being tricked and I shout an order, halting the advance.

As the Liberators lock their shield walls back into place, I see that I was right. The space that opened up before us is not the sign of a retreat. The smirking Chaos champion is ordering the bulk of his army to back away from us, making way for some new strategy. He barks out a command and his army parts, creating an avenue of armour and axes.

The ground judders as though a stampede is approaching. From my vantage point on Zarax's back, I am the first to see the cause of the thundering sound.

Hundreds of skinless horrors charge from the opening in the enemy ranks, pounding across the courtyard towards us. They're all eight or nine feet tall and lashed in glistening, blood-slick muscle. Tentacles burst from their raw, wound-like flesh as they hurtle towards our lines. We now have blood warriors on either flank and these newcomers charging us head on.

I act fast, ordering the Prosecutors into the fray. Drusus leads them over the battlements, dodging blasts of crimson from the walls as he hurls his lightning-charged hammers at the monsters.

More detonations rock the Anvil and the world turns white, but when the blaze dims, the monsters are still there. I manage to cry 'Charge!' seconds before they wade into us.

Revolting tentacles lash out from their armoured shoulders, hammering down against our rows of shields. Dozens of Liberators are forced to their knees but others rush to take their place.

Zarax does not wait for me to spur her on; she bounds forwards, crashing through the golden ranks of Stormcast Eternals and fastening her jaws around the head of the nearest monster. I bring Grius down into the head of another and, as it reels away from me, trailing blood from its obscene maw, a paladin pounds through the crush and lands his blazing, two-handed hammer between its cloven feet.

The creature is eviscerated, but the explosion also jolts Zarax to one side; she staggers, almost throwing me from her back.

Bodies crash into my steed and the echo of the blast grows louder. The ground shakes harder as the noise becomes a deafening rumble and I ride on through the scrum of bodies.

The monsters have forced us back through the archway. Hundreds of my men are now outside the Anvil, being driven slowly back towards the Field of Blades.

I yell a command but my words are drowned out by the rumbling noise. It sounds like the world is being torn in half. The tremor is now so violent that the walls around the gatehouse are crumbling and splitting. I look up, expecting to see the crimson moon overhead again, but the sky is empty.

Then I see Drusus. His incandescent wings hurl him through the darkness, lighting up the expressionless masks of the other Prosecutors.

'Pull back!' he cries, catching sight of me.

I shake my head, outraged by the suggestion of retreat, but then look up in shock. Weapons and shields are lowered as everyone in the passageway takes in the bizarre sight unfolding within the Anvil.

The cloud-high spikes that jut out of the watchtowers have started to move and the battle is forgotten as we all turn to stare. The rumbling is now so loud the cause is unmistakable: the Kharvall Steppe is in the grip of an earthquake. The huge talons around which the Anvil has been built are juddering like wind-lashed trees. We're forced back, reeling out of the passageway as it collapses around us, filling the air with dust and spinning fragments of rock. A few hundred of the Chaos knights stagger into the Field of Blades with us and we quickly despatch them, but most remain trapped in the huge crush of bodies that fills the courtyard.

'Lord-Celestant,' says a voice from behind me.

I look down from Zarax to see Boreas striding through the Field of Blades. He looks no different, but as he reaches my side the scent of death pours from him. He reeks of the grave.

'What have you wrought?' I ask, looking from my brother to the tumult that surrounds us.

'Lord-Celestant,' he says, 'we must back away from the Anvil.'

'This is our only path.'

'Trust me,' he says and there is an uncharacteristic note of urgency in his voice that makes me listen.

'Fall back!' I cry, pointing Grius at the Field of Blades.

We barely make it clear in time. As my army floods into the rows of broken swords, the rumbling sound behind us becomes deafening: an oceanic roar followed by masonry whistling past my ears. As huge chunks of stone slam into the ground all around me I glance back and see what Boreas has done.

The talons at the centre of the watchtowers have risen into the sky, like the shoots of a strange plant. As they rise they're tearing the Anvil apart, creating a new wall of dust and crimson light. As the spikes rise higher I see that they form the spine of an enormous fossilised serpentine skeleton – a snaking mass of ancient bones big enough to dwarf a mountain.

'They never knew,' cries Boreas, over the din. 'They built the Anvil on the back of a fossil.'

I try to speak, but my words are lost beneath a new sound. As the mountainous, twisting skeleton rears up into the clouds, shrugging off the Anvil like a coat, it opens its jaws and bellows. The sound is unbearable, a cry of torment so loud that my ears ring when it ceases.

The ground rolls like a storm-lashed sea and whole towers fall from the sky. I'm blinded by dust and deafened by falling rocks, but my mind is racing. The blood warriors were still inside the courtyard. Nothing could survive this. I see Boreas up ahead and stare at him. Who could summon such a thing from the grave? What has my brother become?

CHAPTER ELEVEN

Vourla – High Priestess of the Steppe

We emerge near the shore, slipping from the fumes like a troupe of ghosts. Smoke whips up over rippling basalt, coating our metal steeds in ash and making us all gleam in the moonlight. It's less than an hour since we rode out from the Anvil and we're dead already; Hakh just doesn't know it yet. I find it hard to suppress a victorious smile. The warlord rides on, blinded by his lust for power, carrying me behind him through the blazing heat. Tylos must be attacking the Anvil by now and I thank the fumes for the eerie, muffled quiet. If Hakh realised my trick, he might still have time to return and fight a battle he could win. I'm not going to give him that chance.

The Blood Creed ride behind us, the hooves of their hideous mounts crunching across the black rock. They make a monstrous sight, but it won't make any difference. Nothing will survive what lies ahead. Not even Tylos and his gleaming host. As I recall his noble figure striding through the battle I feel a trace of guilt, but quickly suppress it. I didn't choose Tylos' path – I'm just turning it to my advantage.

Shapes loom out of the smoke and I gasp. The lakeshore is crowded with hulking beasts. They're crouched menacingly on the rock, as though about to charge.

Hakh grunts with what might be laughter and rides on.

As we near the shapes I see that they're not creatures but buildings – hovels, built in the shape of enormous horned heads. They're all painted blood red and, as we walk past the mouth-like doorways, terrified faces peer out at us. There are few survivors of the old kingdoms left but some still eke out a pitiful existence as slaves and lackeys for Hakh and his ilk.

'My kinsmen,' I mutter.

As they realise that the Blood Creed hasn't come for them, a few dare to wander out into the moonlight and I see their strange outfits. They've made costumes from scraps of wood in an attempt to impersonate the monsters they've based their homes on. They wear horned, wooden helmets, painted to resemble brutal, bestial faces. They look so absurd that I would laugh, if not for the pitifully deranged expressions on their faces. My beloved people have descended into superstition and barbarity. Khorne has broken their minds as completely as he has broken their land.

Our destination looms into view – a blackened fort, a hulking slab of scorched metal layered with dozens of smoke-belching chimneys and oil-spewing pipes. The artifice of the Blood God may be graceless, but it is powerful. I feel a growing nausea as we near its grumbling walls. Unlike the towers of the Anvil, the fort leans back at a drunken angle, as though straining against the huge chains that link it to the bubbling lava. The chains are each thicker than Hakh's chest and there are so many of them that they form a kind of rattling skirt, spreading out from one side of the tower.

There is only one door and Hakh strides towards it, climbing a row of steps that circle the tower's base. He leaves his army behind and drags me along with him. There's nowhere I could run even if I wished to, but Hakh won't let me out of his sight. As we wind around the scarred rock, I get a better look at the strange machinery that adorns the metal bastion. Illuminated by the hellish light of the lake is a vast collection of gears and spindles, scorched and blackened but still intact and coated in thick black tar. The chains are threaded through various wheels and jammed in place by hunks of rusted iron. I've seen such infernal engines in use before and I prayed never to do so again.

After several minutes, Hakh reaches the door – a brutal riveted slab of brass tall enough to admit a giant but with no obvious handle. Next to the crudely wrought door is a stone plinth, topped with a long, curved horn.

Hakh glances at me, then pounds the door.

The clanging echoes through the tower and soon I hear the slamming of doors and the clattering of armoured feet on metal walkways. After a few moments, the door swings inwards with a grudging moan. We're greeted by the smell of old machines and rotting meat.

There are figures in the gloomy entrance hall – more of the brutish, armour-clad Blood Creed – and one of them steps out into the moonlight. I've met Khorlagh the Keeper once before but familiarity doesn't lessen the shock. He's almost as massive as Hakh but, rather than weapons, he carries the brutal tools of his trade. His bloodstained armour is adorned with billhooks, iron staves and thick, studded manacles. In his hand he clutches a jagged trident, warped and glowing with heat, as though recently drawn from a furnace. Tucked into his belt is a cruel, barbed whip. It's not the brutal implements that make me shrink away from him though; it's his skin. It is corpse-white, marbled with indigo streaks, and sags away from his body like an ill-fitting suit, revealing glimpses of the glistening flesh beneath. The effect is made all the more disturbing by his oddly gracious manner. He performs a ridiculous, formal bow and then gestures towards the open doorway.

'My Lord Hakh,' he says, his words turned into a moist rasp by his flapping, bloodless lips. 'What an honour. What an honour indeed.' He glances back at the figures loitering inside the tower. 'I received no word from Vhaal that you would be inspecting the fort. We have made no preparations.' He tries to tidy his face, tucking his skin back into place and smoothing it down like a courtier adjusting his wig.

'Get us across,' says Hakh, nodding at the ranks of knights gathered below.

Khorlagh frowns and then laughs. 'For a moment there I thought you meant you were going to the crucible right now.' His laughter causes his skin mask to sag again. 'But of course you don't mean that.' He waves us inside again. 'You'll have to excuse our lack of preparation. You can use my chambers to rest until it's safe to make the crossing.'

Hakh grabs Khorlagh by the arm and hurls him towards the brass horn. 'Now.'

Khorlagh looks shocked. 'My Lord, we can't cross now. It's nearly dawn.'

Hakh lets go of me and clutches his sword in both hands. 'Are you the only one here who can take me across?'

Khorlagh briefly shakes his head, but then he sees sense and nods. 'Yes, My Lord!' He waves his trident at the lake of lava 'No-one else can control them. Without me, passage is impossible, I assure you. I've spent long decades mastering the techniques and understanding the–'

Hakh silences Khorlagh by raising his sword a little higher.

'Of course.' Khorlagh turns to the horn.

He swings the mouthpiece to his lips and a harsh braying sound fills the air. Khorlagh's lungs seem bottomless and the noise grows to an unbearable volume. I clamp my hands over my ears and almost topple down the steps, but Hakh drags me to his side.

Finally, Khorlagh lets go of the horn and staggers back from its stand.

For a while, there's nothing but the echoes of the horn blast, but by the time Hakh has led us both back down the steps, a great din is booming out from the walls of the tower. I hear the rattle of machinery lurching into life and the roar of huge furnaces. The narrow windows spill crimson light out into the darkness – daemonic eyes, opening one by one.

Whatever engines are contained in the tower are so powerful that the ground beneath us starts to judder and shift. Geysers of oil and smoke burst from the ground and the pipes that go down start crackling as energy blasts through them.

'How long?' asks Hakh, ignoring the tower and staring out at the lake.

'Not long,' mutters Khorlagh. 'The beasts do not dare keep me waiting.' A little pride creeps into his voice. 'Such monsters are difficult to control. Many died before I managed to perfect the machines. Too much power and they'll die. Too little and *we'll* die.'

I wish that I could take his trident and plunge it into his chest. Whatever creatures are out there, they deserve a better fate than to be tormented by Khorlagh's sweaty hands.

Khorlagh catches my furious expression and stares, as though seeing me for the first time. Hakh doesn't notice; he's too busy watching the cluster of chains that have begun winding back in from the lava. The lake hisses and booms as the metal lurches from the depths, glowing and sparking as it rises.

Khorlagh smiles proudly as his machines do their work. A few hundred feet away an island of coiled, scratched brass rises, an entire headland wrought of spiralling, pockmarked metal. As the chains drag it towards us I see Khorlagh's monstrous slaves: towering, ox-headed beastmen, with brutal, swooping horns and four arms, all lashed to the sides of the metal island. There are hundreds of them heaving the great disc of brass from the boiling lake. Their bodies are crackling and smoking like roasting meat.

'Ghorgons,' says Hakh, with a hint of respect in his voice.

Khorlagh nods proudly.

'How do they survive?' I ask. 'Why doesn't the lava burn them up?'

Khorlagh nods at the pipes and chains joining the tower to the lake. 'These engines have girded them with the wrath of the Blood God. It doesn't protect them from the pain, but it certainly keeps them moving.' He laughs and pats his whip. 'They're more daemon than beast now, but they wouldn't dare defy me.'

'How will we ride it?' asks Hakh, staring at the quickly approaching island.

Khorlagh laughs. 'With care. And getting on isn't the only challenge.' He points his trident at the clouds of ash overhead. 'When my servants rise, they always bring a crowd with them.'

I look where he's pointing and see nothing but embers, falling from the night sky.

Hakh clearly sees something more. 'Ready your axes,' he bellows, looking back at the Blood Creed. 'We're going to have some sport.'

'I must prepare for the landing,' says Khorlagh, heading back into the tower, yelling orders as he goes.

The ghorgons make a horrific sight as they haul the metal to shore, straining and thrashing at their bonds as gangways hurtle down from the tower, locking the island into place. Khorlagh's men dash back and forth through the lava spray, acting out a lethal dance as they fasten more hooks and chains onto the limbs of the giant beastmen.

Then, suddenly, with a grinding screech, one of the ghorgons breaks free. It charges through the lava, bellowing and making straight for us. Dozens of Khorlagh's men are smashed from the walkways as they try to halt it, thrown to their deaths in the lava below.

The ghorgon reaches the shore and does not pause, still running straight at where Hakh and I are waiting. I back away but Hakh just glares at the monster. It towers over him but he looks at it as though it's no more dangerous than a stray dog.

Khorlagh cries a command and grappling hooks blast out from the walls of the brass tower. They slam into the ghorgon with such force that they punch through its chest and send it hurling back the way it came. It crashes to the ground, lifeless.

I glance at Hakh, wondering if the attack has deterred him in any way, but he barely seems to have noticed. His gaze is still locked on the far shore and the tantalising glint of brass that lies beyond the walls of the crater. I've completely ensnared him. My heart races but I try to calm myself. It's not done yet. My visions have misled me in the past.

After what seems to me a painfully long time, Khorlagh's slaves succeed in pinning the island down under a forest of staves, chains and walkways. The ghorgons heave and roar, unable to break their bonds, and Khorlagh appears from the tower, his skin-mask in complete disarray.

'Be quick, my lord,' he cries, waving us towards the walkways and rushing to meet us there. He points at the clouds. The embers now look more like shooting stars, rushing towards the lake. 'We must board before they attack.'

As we climb across ramparts and onto the trembling jetties I see crowds of Khorlagh's slaves hanging from chains as they try to hold the ghorgons in place. As they crank their gears and shove their levers, the bonds tighten, finally silencing the monsters' feral cries.

We're only halfway across the gangway when there's a scream of grinding metal and we are all thrown off our feet. Several of Hakh's knights are hurled into the lava and, for a moment, I think I might follow them, but Hakh still has hold of me.

Another one of the ghorgons has broken free and is thrashing from side to side.

More slaves are thrown to their deaths before Khorlagh can reach the scene. He and several of his lackeys arrive carrying a long pipe that ends in what looks like a diamond harpoon. They fire the point deep into the ghorgon's thick neck and it drops from view.

As they run back down the gangway, Khorlagh waves at figures lining the battlements of the brass tower. There is a flash of sparks and flame as they activate another machine and send a bolt of energy down the pipes. The metal crackles with power and the ghorgons twitch. The air crackles as they start to heave the island back into the lake.

Khorlagh grins as he runs back up the walkway, waving us on, towards the centre of the island.

The heat makes me feel sick and embers settle on my face as I run, scorching my skin, but the Blood Creed do not falter. Khorlagh leads us up an incline until I see where he's taking us. There's a scorched, blackened hole blasted right in the centre of the metal island. It has created a kind of walled enclosure lined with jagged terraces and trailing masses of chains. Khorlagh and his men wave us down into the scorched pit but the Blood Creed need no instruction; they flood down into the hole and begin fastening the chains to their armour. Hakh drags me down with him and binds me to his jagged plate armour with a thick chain.

We're barely settled when Khorlagh gives another signal, eliciting more blasts of energy. There's a clanging din as the Blood Creed are thrown to their knees, and I'm forced to cling onto Hakh's armour. For a terrifying moment, I think we're going to plunge beneath the lava, but the furious ghorgons keep the metal above the surface as it powers back out into the lake. Heat pours over me and I can't seem to catch my breath. I try to rise and cry out, but then the world turns black.

When I come to, I'm on my back, looking at a mixture of stars and spinning embers. Hakh has gone, but I'm chained securely to a shard of heat-warped brass. At first, I think I must be delirious, the scene is so nightmarish. I'm surrounded by the howling, grunting ranks of Hakh's knights, and they're fighting for their lives. The air is teeming with huge, ferocious animals – snarling, feline monsters with great leathery wings and broad, slashing claws. Before my books were burned I spent long hours studying the creatures of myth and legend, and a name tumbles from my lips: manticores. They're roaring furiously as they dive, tearing Hakh's warriors from the metal, and feeding on them like gulls fighting for scraps.

The more the manticores kill, the more enraged their shrieks become. They hurl corpses into the lava and roar with bloodlust.

The manticores are almost as massive as the ghorgons but the Blood Creed are inhuman and utterly fearless. After the initial shock, they soon start to revel in the slaughter. They laugh at the terrifying creatures as they cut them down. Hakh has unshackled himself and climbed to the lip of the silver crater, surrounded by fumes and sparks. He's like a captain at the prow of an infernal ship, howling as he cuts the manticores from the sky.

The beasts fight on, berserk, but the end comes quickly. As the last of them plunges to a fiery death, I lie there on the scorched metal, shaken by the horror my world has become. Chaos has tainted every part of the Khavall Steppe. Everyone I ever loved died at the hands of Hakh's armies. Is revenge really enough?

As Hakh's knights celebrate their victory I can think of nothing but Tylos, striding towards me through the flames, blazing with valour.

CHAPTER TWELVE

Lord-Celestant Tylos Stormbound

As the Anvil entombs our foes, the fossil that destroyed it whirls away, leaving a tornado of dust and rubble as it hurtles across the steppe.

'Follow it!' cries Boreas, struggling to be heard over the din, battling through the falling debris to reach me.

The rest of my army emerges from the swirling clouds of dust, bloody but unbowed – looking for my command. As they stagger from the wreckage towards me, I'm distracted by the skeletal colossus filling the sky, blocking out the moonlight and shedding towers the size of mountains. Truly, this realm is full of wonders.

'Hammers of Sigmar!' I roar, rising up in my saddle and pointing Grius at the disappearing fossil. 'Witness a miracle! Witness the power of the God-King.'

Boreas staggers to a halt nearby and the rows of expressionless masks turn to face me.

I keep Grius pointed at the enormous skeleton crashing across the steppe.

'The realms will kneel no more!'

I bring Grius and Evora together over my head and they erupt in a ball of holy fire. Faith and fury pour through my skin and armour, surrounding me in a blinding nimbus of light. 'For the God-King!' I cry, as Zarax rears beneath me, spewing lightning from between her gaping jaws.

The Stormcasts reel away from me, shaking their heads in wonder, even Boreas. Then, as Zarax tears off in pursuit of the skeleton, I hear them echo my war cry and join the chase.

At first the going is slow, as we struggle over the ruins of the Anvil. Most of its defenders are buried beneath a landslide of broken masonry, but every few feet I see a grim reminder of the warriors who seemed so unstoppable a few minutes earlier: twisted, bleeding hands jutting up from the rocks and lifeless faces, staring up at the sky, their skulls sheared apart. I allow Zarax to hurtle past most of them but there is one corpse, skewered on a fallen spire, that catches my attention. I rein Zarax in and look down at the still muttering warrior. It's the champion with the skinless face. His body has been torn almost entirely in two by the piece of masonry but he's still clinging to life.

At the sight of me he laughs and tries to rise, but he only succeeds in pouring his viscera across his broken legs.

'You do not exist,' he gurgles through a mouth full of blood. 'The Blood God and I–'

Before he can say more, Zarax roasts him alive with a blinding flash of lightning. I make the sign of the hammer as he crumbles into ash, then urge the dracoth on.

As I leave the ruins behind I see that Boreas' warnings were not exaggerated. The fossilised serpent is heading directly east, towards a shimmering line of fire that stretches across the entire horizon.

'Lake Malice,' I say out loud, recalling my brother's description of the impassable lake. I would never let Boreas know, of course, but I have no idea how we will cross this final hurdle. Even god-forged Stormcast Eternals cannot simply wade through lava.

As it nears the lake, the skeleton is lit up in red and gold and I have the strange sense that we're chasing a lost soul, plunging into the depths of the underworld.

I rein Zarax in and allow the others to catch up. Boreas is at the fore and I'm about to praise him for destroying the Anvil when he speaks.

'Lord-Celestant,' he says. His voice sounds angry rather than pleased. 'Our passage through the Anvil was not bought cheaply.'

'I understand, Boreas.' I glance at the quickly disappearing monster. 'Sigmar sees all. Whatever pain you've endured–'

'Tylos, you don't understand.' He glances down at the relics hanging from his armour. 'The price was the Kuriat.'

I can't hide my shock. 'The heart? Boreas, what do you mean?'

'I bought our passage with it.' He steps closer. 'It was the only way. We're almost out of time. The tempest was sent astray. If we'd spent any longer trapped in the Anvil–'

'Yes,' I interrupt. 'I understand.' Anger pounds in my chest and it takes all my strength to keep my voice calm. The Kuriat was the key to the Crucible of Blood. Without it, there's no way we can seize control of the realmgate. For the first time since we landed, I feel the ghost of my past rising to challenge me. I grasp the hilt of my sword in an attempt to steady myself. I hear a harsh voice at the back of my thoughts: the brutal, honourless killer I was before the Lord of Storms tempered me. I grip the hilt tighter until my heart steadies.

Boreas watches my hand on the runeblade.

'I had no choice,' he says.

The rage passes. I am as true as Evora's blade. I dismount.

'Boreas, do you trust in Sigmar?' I place my hand on his shoulder.

He nods.

'Then trust in me. We both know what we must do.'

He grips my arm. 'Brother,' he begins, 'I swear that there was nothing else–'

'I know,' I reply, returning his grip. 'And we both knew it might come to this.' I manage to keep my voice level as I consider the path left open to us. 'There can be no return.'

Before either of us can say more, an explosion tears the night open. Golden light flashes in the polished metal of my men's masks. Boreas and I both turn to study this latest miracle.

The serpent has thrown its entire length across Lake Malice. The liquid sprays and hisses over bones as big as mountains and it is enveloped by a liquid heat haze.

'You bought us a bridge,' I say, turning back to Boreas with a laugh of disbelief.

He nods and, despite everything we face, I hear laughter in his voice too. But then he becomes serious again. 'Not for long, brother.'

I follow his gaze and see what he means. Even through the haze I can see the skeleton smouldering and warping where it lies in the lava. As we stare, it raises its fanged skull and lets out a ghostly roar.

'Move!' I cry, leaping back into the saddle and waving Grius at the lake. 'The Lord-Relictor has bought us a passage to victory. Our journey ends on the far shore.'

Zarax leads the charge, speeding me across the black rocks. Boreas and the others rush to follow as Drusus leads the Prosecutors overhead, scouting the night sky for signs of attack.

By the time we reach the shore, the skeletal serpent has left a trail of carnage. The area is littered with strange architecture – weird, domed houses built in the shape of bull-headed monsters, destroyed by the giant fossil. Zarax vaults over broken horns and shattered snouts. As we career through the strange scene, I get my first glimpse of those we've come to save: emaciated, wide-eyed mortals, cowering in outfits as ridiculous as their homes. They make a tragic sight and I raise my head, determined to show them what humanity can be.

As we near the lava, I see the remains of a bastion that must have been crafted by the same brutal hand as the Anvil. The smashed remnants show signs of jagged, taloned battlements and thick, brass walls. On the side facing the lake there is a pile of broken machinery – wheels and pulleys that were previously linked to great chains, now all gone, torn free by the impact of the bone serpent.

Zarax pounds on. As we near the bubbling lava, an intense wave of heat penetrates my armour. The skeleton is sinking fast, the fossilised remains slumping and snapping as the lava devours them, and I'm about to cry out a warning when Zarax makes the leap. The fossil's tail holds as her great, scaled bulk crashes down on it, and the Liberators follow close behind, clambering onto the splintering ivory arch as though they were simply crossing a brackish stream. Again, I'm hit by the incredible charge I've been entrusted with – what kind of warriors would follow me across this searing heat, with death only a single misstep away? Only those born of the God-King's immutable will.

Unlike the others, I have only to hold my nerve as Zarax carries me towards the far side. As the bones jolt and crack under her weight, gouts of smoking lava lash out, but Zarax has the heat of stars running through her veins and she charges on, dodging every blast the furnace can throw at us.

Boreas' fossil has lowered its head and I can clearly see our goal ahead – a flash of moonlit brass, glimpsed over a ridge of basalt. The Crucible of Blood is painfully close, but so is the dawn. The dazzling lava beneath me makes it impossible to be sure, but I can't help thinking that the sky is getting lighter.

'Faster!' I cry, turning back to my men. They're already showing god-like heroism by hurling themselves over these bones, but I will not face Sigmar as a failure. 'We have to reach the Crucible before the sun rises!'

They pick up their pace, but fossilised bones do not make for easy footing. The paladins in particular struggle to heft their massive suits of armour over the crumbling vertebrae and the heat is now so intense that the fossil is starting to spark and flame. Soon the whole thing will be ablaze, but I'm forced to rein Zarax in halfway across and wait for the others to reach me.

I can feel the seconds ebbing away and it is a torment to sit powerlessly, so close to my goal. I cast my gaze out across the lake and see a shape rushing in our direction. There's something moving through the lava, making for the burning skeleton.

'Faster!' I roar, looking back along the fossil. The vanguard of Liberators has almost reached me and the Judicators are with them, but the retinues of paladins are trailing way behind, with Boreas at their head. Drusus has led his Prosecutors down from the clouds to help. They are hovering over the struggling paladins, pounding their celestial wings as they attempt to lift their brothers over the crumbling, sparking bridge.

Boreas sees more shapes rushing towards us, raises his hammer into the rolling fumes and cries out a litany. Whatever the things are, they must be as tall as oaks. I can't hear my brother's words over the hissing and burning of the lake, but I can sense a growing charge in the air as he prepares for an attack.

'Lord-Celestant,' shouts Liberator-Prime Castamon as he reaches my side. He waves his hammer at Boreas and the paladins. 'We need to head back!'

I shake my head. 'There is no going back.'

Boreas is standing proudly at the head of the paladins with his banner of bones and his hammer raised in defiance. The paladins form ranks behind him, readying their weapons for whatever is about to emerge. They're perched on flaming, shattered bones a few feet above a lake that would burn them alive. They're about to be attacked from all sides, yet even now they show no trace of fear.

The lava erupts as a goliath bursts into view. It has the head and legs of an ox and four, powerful arms, two of which end in jagged iron hooks. Strange, crackling energy shimmers over its scarred hide and the lava leaves no mark on it. The monster bellows as it crashes into the bones, surrounded by a rolling cloud of flames and sparks.

Boreas vanishes from sight and Castamon cries out. 'Ghorgons!' he yells, preparing to charge back down the bones.

I slam him back into place.

'Hold your nerve,' I growl and he nods, stepping back into line.

The place where the paladins were standing is now a wall of flaming spray and pounding, sparking limbs. I see golden figures dashing through the flames, bringing their huge two-handed hammers to bear, but the creatures are so vast they barely register the blows.

'We can't leave Boreas behind,' says Castamon, and I nod.

'You can. Lead the army to the far side.'

As ever, Zarax knows my mind better than I do and, before I can command it, she races back towards my brother.

We've gone no more than a few yards when the lava erupts again, spewing another howling ghorgon from its depths. As it attacks, I notice that it's trailing a mass of chains and cords.

Zarax leaps clear as the monster smashes through the bones, splintering the fossilised spine with an explosion of cracking sounds.

I cling to her back as a ghorgon dives in our direction, smashing a hole in the bridge.

My army has been split in two. The bulk of my retinues are gathered on one side of the break, watching in dismay as Zarax and I are forced back towards Boreas and the others.

The ghorgon has torn a twenty-foot hole in the bridge of bones. Even if Castamon wished to lead his Liberators back to me, they could never leap the gap.

I look the other way and have to stifle a cry of outrage. Where Boreas and the others were standing, there is only a cloud of spinning bone fragments and embers. I see Boreas pounding his hammer furiously against the snorting monsters, but dozens of Retributors have already been thrown into the lava, and are in their agonised death throes. Moments after the paladins sink from view, lighting cracks down from the heavens, connecting with the lake in a blaze of blue fire as Sigmar reclaims his own.

Boreas staggers under a flurry of blows and I spur Zarax on. She leaps into action, hurtling towards him. There's a crash of breaking stone as a ghorgon smashes into view, blocking my way. I'm too furious to think about the size of the monster and I drive Zarax to even greater speed. She slams headfirst into its massive chest and I bring Grius round in a wide arc towards the monster's face.

The warhammer lands between the ox horns with such force that another explosion rocks the fossil. I slump back in my saddle, too dazed to see what's happened. Then I realise that the ghorgon is on its back, pawing at its bloodied face, blinded by my attack.

The fossil groans and snaps. Zarax almost loses her footing, staggering towards the lava. I grasp on to a broken shard of stone and hold us steady seconds before we plunge to our deaths. I'm just inches from the lava and my eyes stream in the heat.

Zarax leaps back to safety and I draw Evora, preparing to attack the ghorgon again.

The monster's legs are thrashing wildly beneath it and it is unable to rise. My blow has crippled it. I behead the beast with single clean swipe of my runeblade.

I take a look back at the way we came and see a breathtaking sight. Boreas stands alone and his golden armour has been torn away in several places. He's swaying like a drunk as ghorgons charge towards him, perched precariously on a single, massive vertebra, only hanging on with one hand and holding his warhammer aloft with the other. His reliquary has gone and there's blood rushing from his skull mask, but he will not yield an inch. I can hear his voice from here, hoarse but defiant, ringing out over the noise of the monster's thrashing limbs. He's surrounded by blinding columns of light as paladins die all around him.

'Drusus!' I howl, scouring the skies for a sight of the Prosecutors. Most of them are gathered at the opposite end of the fossil, defending Castamon and his Liberators as they try to reach the shore, but there is no sign of Drusus' red-plumed helmet.

I cry his name again and look back to Boreas.

A ghorgon lunges with its rusted hooks and Boreas swings his hammer but as he does a staccato blast of lightning explodes along the creature's head. It jolts back from the fossil, letting out a furious howl, and Boreas tumbles from his perch towards the lava.

I curse, but as the blast clears I see a pair of blazing wings and Drusus soars into view, holding Boreas aloft with the aid of another Prosecutor. Others dive into battle, blasting the enemy back into the lava.

A wounded ghorgon prepares to lash out at Boreas and his rescuers, but Zarax gets there first, bounding over a final section of bone and fastening her jaws around the monster's tree trunk throat.

I bring both sword and hammer down into its face.

The afterglow of Drusus' attack is still shimmering over the monster's hide and it ignites my weapons, creating another dazzling blast.

The creature is thrown backwards, towards the lava. I turn to land another blow. A volley of hammer-blows lights up the monster's flank as Drusus and the other Prosecutor swoop by, still clutching Boreas. The final ghorgon drops into the lava but manages to clamber back onto the bridge and slice its hooks into Zarax.

I thrust Evora into one of its eyes and ink-black blood smashes into me with such force that I'm knocked back in my saddle. By the time I rise, the monster has almost vanished back into the lava. The last of its hooks is still buried deep in Zarax's hide.

She staggers and slips towards the edge of the bones, unable to free herself. Almost in the lava, she turns her proud, draconic head and unleashes a bolt of crackling energy into the ghorgon. The light burns with such violence that she becomes a silhouette, haloed by blazing white power.

A final, agonised howl bubbles up from the lava as the sinking ghorgon releases Zarax and she staggers back to safety.

She pauses to steady herself, then pads back towards the shore, majestic and magnificent, smoke trailing from her jaws and lightning sparking between her midnight blue scales.

CHAPTER THIRTEEN

Vourla – High Priestess of the Steppe

'What were they?' I ask, looking up at the sky and not expecting an answer. It is the first time I have crossed Lake Malice, and I've only ever heard rumours of what lies beyond. The ground is an ugly mass of dull black stone, but the scene overhead is breathtaking. Huge shards of masonry hang motionless in the air, defying gravity or explanation. They are carved from flawless white stone and covered with the most beautiful murals and statues – serpentine, mythological creatures that wind around graceful, arched doorways and looping, spiral stairs. They're clearly the product of an elegant, cultured civilization, quite unlike the brutal Chaos architecture that has looked down on my entire life.

But something terrible must have happened. All that remains are these broken, drifting fragments: steps that lead to nowhere and rooms that are open to the elements, revealing sad glimpses of forgotten halls and abandoned terraces. The lowest of the fragments is over thirty feet above the ground and it's hard to gauge the scale, but I can tell the proportions are all wrong. No humans could have lived in these grand chambers. The rooms and doors are ten times the height of a man. This was the abode of giants.

'It was a palace.'

I'm so shocked to get a response that I almost laugh. Since Khorlagh ushered us down onto the lakeshore no one has spoken. We've trudged beneath these ruins for half an hour in silence.

'Whose palace?' I ask.

Hakh looks up at the shards of white stone. The embers in his eyes flicker into life as he studies the floating remnants. 'Can't you see them?' he asks, sounding surprised.

'See who?' I follow his shimmering gaze and think, perhaps, I can see something – a vague flicker of shadows near one of the doorways. But the harder I stare, the more it slips away.

Hakh grunts a laugh. 'For once I see more than you. You're too mortal.'

I stare harder, annoyed that this brute can perceive things that I can't, but it's no use.

He shrugs, still watching the figures I can't see. 'It doesn't matter. They were nothing. Just stupid giants. They refused to kneel so Khorne gave them a gift.'

'The Crucible of Blood,' I stare through the moonlit ruins at the flashes of brass through the gaps in the crumbling walls.

He nods and spares me a proud glance. 'Their magic could not save them – instead it trapped them.' He laughs again. 'Now they die, over and over again, forever.'

The pleasure in his voice hardens my resolve. Whatever guilt I feel over that golden knight is meaningless. All that matters is that Hakh pays. All that matters is destroying him.

'Not far now,' I say, looking further into the ruins.

He nods, but that's clearly all the conversation he can manage.

As we march on beneath the drifting stones, I start to sense their architects even if I can't see them. Somewhere, in the back of my mind, I hear a low, alien cry filled with increasing desperation. At first it is intriguing, but it quickly becomes distressing. The voice sounds tormented. The centuries have done nothing to lessen the pain. It sounds like something forever on the brink of salvation, but unable to quite reach it. I try covering my ears to block out the sound, eliciting an odd look from Hakh, but it's useless – the sounds are all in my mind.

As we reach the centre of the ruined city, the ground starts to become more uneven and slopes up towards the lip of a vast bowl – an enormous crater at least a mile across. At the centre is the thing I've been trying to avoid looking at, but as I reach the edge of the huge pit that cradles it, I'm finally forced to face the destination I've dragged us all to.

Grinning at us in the moonlight is a single brass skull. It's so tall that my eyes struggle to make sense of its design, but I've heard enough to know this is the Crucible of Blood. It gleams a lurid yellow in the predawn light, but its expression is the thing that takes the strength from my legs. Its leering, rictus grin speaks of a bloodlust so full of vigour that I feel as though I'm facing a living beast, a merciless hunter, about to pounce. The eye sockets stare at me, revealing what lies inside – thousands of gallons of human blood, lapping gently at the thick, brass walls. Some kind of sorcery stops the blood pouring through the eye sockets, so it looks as though the skull is watching me with a pair of blind, crimson orbs.

Hakh shoves me aside and glares down into the pit of charred stone. 'Where is he?' he demands, his voice a low snarl.

'What?' I mutter, hypnotised by the skull's bloody stare.

Hakh rounds on me, trembling with rage. 'Where is the golden champion?'

He goes into a kind of spasm and swings his sword. The blade smashes into the ground a couple of feet from me, creating an explosion of black, glinting splinters that knife into my legs.

I cry out in pain and try to back away, but immediately bump into the armoured bulk of Khorlagh. He locks one of his white-skinned hands onto my shoulder and holds me in place.

'He's on his way!' I cry, waving back through the ruins. 'He'll be here within minutes.'

Hakh is too angry to speak for a moment. Veins bulge from his tree trunk neck and he clutches his head.

'Dawn,' he manages to snarl finally, jabbing his sword at the brass skull grinning at us from the bottom of the crater. 'We must be gone by dawn.' He looks up through the ruins at the quickly vanishing stars. 'There's no time.'

I nod eagerly. 'There is time! I've foreseen your victory. There's still an hour before the sun rises and…' I glance at the skull and lose my thread.

'She's lying,' says Khorlagh. His flaccid lips brush against my cheek as he holds me tighter. 'I saw that she was tricking you the moment you arrived.'

Hakh reels away from us, teetering across the lip of the crater, drunk with fury. 'Tricking?'

Khorlagh pulls a long, rusty hook from his belt and presses the point against my trembling stomach. 'We should gut her and leave.'

Hakh grabs one of his horns and starts wrenching his head from side to side, as though trying to shake understanding from his skull. 'Tricking?'

Then he halts and his expression goes slack. For a moment I wonder if his anger has broken his mind, but then he grins and strides towards us, raising his sword.

I struggle to free myself but Khorlagh tightens his grip.

Hakh swings his sword and I find myself lying on the hard rock in a pool of blood. The warm liquid pumps over me, filling my eyes and mouth but, after a few seconds, I realise I'm not in pain. I'm still alive.

I feel my blood-slick throat and find that my head is still attached to it.

I wipe my eyes just in time to see Hakh reaching down to take my hand. He hauls me to my feet and I see Khorlagh's corpse. Hakh's blade has sliced down through the top of his skull and travelled almost to his waist. I find myself wondering at just how much blood can emerge from a single body.

'Another fool,' says Hakh.

I slump in his grip, weak with shock, unable to do anything but slap feebly at my clothes, trying to clear away bits of Khorlagh's insides.

'You didn't lie. Khorlagh did,' continues Hakh.

I've no idea what he's talking about until I see what he's looking at.

Tylos. I didn't dream him. He's here.

CHAPTER FOURTEEN

Lord-Celestant Tylos Stormbound

Boreas lives on at least, even though so many others are lost. He's delirious with pain, muttering and flailing at shadows as though surrounded by ghosts only he can see. He's struggling to walk, too – one of his legs drags awkwardly as we help him across the black rocks. Before we moved on from the lake I asked him if he needed to rest, but he just stared at me in proud silence until we continued our gruelling march.

As we crunch over the blasted basalt, we make a very different sight to the army that crashed down onto the bridge of birds. Along with the warriors dragged skywards by the lunar storm, I must now count those we lost in the battle for the Anvil and the retinues of paladins that were hurled into the lava attempting to defend Boreas. They will all find their way back to Sigmar's halls, but I would have preferred to have them marching at my side. Nearly half of my army is gone and as we near the Nomad City I can't mistake the pale glow of an approaching dawn. Anger simmers in my gut, testing me, daring me to revive my barbaric past. It is as though part of me is still in a vaulted chamber, watched carefully by the God-King himself. I will not fail the test. I suppress my rage and wave Castamon on, leading the lines of Liberators with calm disdain.

As Zarax carries me towards the city, I have the overwhelming sensation that I'm walking into a dream. After all the noise and violence of our crossing, these drifting ruins seem eerily calm. Strange, incongruous sections of rooms hang next to each other like an unsolved puzzle. If the scholars of the Celestial City are right, the ruins were left by a god. The fire of the spheres was still blasting through my bones when they told me the bloody history of this place. It's hard to imagine such violence now, as the warm breeze whistles through the drifting towers, but I can see the skull clearly enough – a vast dome of brazen metal, flickering beyond the lip of the crater, just half a mile into the city. It's so big I can barely comprehend it.

Between us and the realmgate lies our final challenge. Waiting in shadows beneath the city is another host of Khorne worshippers. These aren't the bare-chested rabble that attacked us on the bridge, but lumbering, red-armoured knights, just like the unstoppable killers we faced at the Anvil, and this time they are not on foot but are mounted on horrific steeds that I recognise only from the darkest legends. Juggernauts – massive, hulking beasts, clad in plates of serrated steel and brass. As their riders sit patiently in their saddles, the metal creatures paw at the ground with blood-caked hooves, spewing gouts of steam and oil from the hinges in their flanks.

The lead rider is the largest knight I've yet seen and, even from here, I can tell that he is barely human. He has a pair of low, swooping horns jutting out of his forehead and his eyes burn like a pair of tiny dying suns.

I turn to face my men and draw a deep breath, preparing to

rouse them from weariness and despair. My words fail on my lips, unneeded. They're already preparing for battle, readying their hammers with silent, unshakeable faith. They've watched their brothers be butchered, hurled into the void and boiled alive, and now they face an army more horrific than anything we've yet seen, but not one of them shows any fear. My breath catches in my throat as they raise their shields and form a perfect wall of gleaming sigmarite.

Drusus lands just a few feet away with his remaining Prosecutors and they drop to their knees in silent genuflection.

The faces of my men may be hidden, but their nobility is not.

I sit taller in my saddle and lift my chin. The barbarian in my soul slips away.

'Look at them,' I say, levelling Grius at the red knights. 'How different they are from us. Can you feel their hunger? Their desperation? These aren't men, but animals, scrapping for dominion over a debased pack. They fight for power over their kin and to hold these broken lands for their own. They fight for everything that is meaningless.'

Zarax starts to pace beneath me, pawing at the ground, sensing that the battle is about to begin.

'But you, my sky-born brothers,' I say, raising my voice. 'You fight for truth.'

They bring their hammers down against their shields, filling the night with sparks and noise.

'And for Sigmar!' I roar as we advance.

CHAPTER FIFTEEN

Menuasaraz-Senuamaraz-Kemurzil (Mopus)

'Curse Boreas,' I say, slamming the palm of my hand on my desk. Dead insects tumble away from my fingers and dust fills the air. 'How dare he wait so long to come back here and then try to fill my head with his religious nonsense? After all I taught him, how can he have fallen for a creed? And then try to drag me down with him?'

The Carrion Princes are watching from the shadows as always, and they drift a little closer as I shove back my chair. I try to rise from my desk and collapse onto the floor. Damp, pulpy books soften my fall and I break into a furious, hacking cough.

Skinless finger bones dig into my arms as the princes help me back onto my feet. I cling onto one of them for a moment, trying to stand straight, gripping a cold, dusty humerus as my legs tremble beneath me.

The princes whisper inside my skull. *You need to eat.*

'Food?' I laugh. 'I'm no animal.'

I reach out and rummage through an old cabinet until I find

a vial of sapphire-blue liquid. There are a few flies drifting in it but I pick them out and gulp the philtre down. Warmth rushes through my body and I slowly start to recover.

I shoo the princes away and stagger over to a mirror. It's thick with dust and obscured by a mound of annotated skulls, but once I've cleared a space I manage to see myself for the first time in months. I feel a little calmer – I could almost pass for one of my skeletons. My skull grins out from behind its thin covering of white skin. I'm everything that an ascetic scholar should be. No gaudy gold armour for me, just a few simple robes and enough flesh to keep my mind working. There was a time when Boreas would have understood such asceticism, but not now. Anger and hurt drives me to drink another philtre. My eyes start to burn the same blue as the liquid and my heart pounds an irregular rhythm.

'I always knew Boreas would return,' I say, 'but not like this – not to mock and accuse. How could he throw his lot in with brutish soldiers when I could have shown him the mysteries of the cosmos? How can he believe in Sigmar's ridiculous doctrine?' The more furious my words, the more I know that I'm lying to myself. I'm angry because I'm afraid he might be right, afraid that I've wasted all these years.

I shake my head, trying to rid myself of this infuriating self-doubt. It irks me that I'm not able to continue studying, but I can't banish the memory of his faith. I stumble across the room, barging past the princes and knocking over towers of books. The Kuriat is on my desk, still thudding patiently. I pick it up and stare at its hardened, shrivelled arteries.

'Boreas has been made a fool of. This thing has no power as a weapon. What did he hope to achieve?'

Then why did you take it from him?

'Because the wretched fool cared for it more than anything!

Because I wanted to hurt him.' I realise how small-minded and ridiculous I sound, but it just makes me even more furious. I put the lump of meat back on my desk and try not to think about it.

'If that really is Sigmar's great army,' I continue, 'why would he send them to the Crucible of Blood? Why is the Kharvall Steppe of such importance to him? There are countless other strongholds he should strike first if he means to unseat the Dark Gods.'

I turn to the princes. 'What else do we know of the Crucible of Blood?'

Very little. Your scribes have searched every text. They're all curiously quiet on the subject. One of the princes waves at the gruesome illustration of daemons boiling in blood. *We know nothing more than that.*

'There must be more. Something is happening here. This is all significant. I know that Boreas is not *really* a fool. I taught him too well for that. There must be something I'm missing.'

What about Giraldus?

'Giraldus?' I frown with distaste as I recall the pompous old bloodsucker. 'He's a third-rate scholar and a first-rate fool.' I picture the deluded vampire as I last saw him, parading around Nagash's court in the ornate, decorative armour of a grand noble. 'He claims to be a king, but he behaves more like a spoiled little prince.'

As a mortal, he dwelled on the Kharvall Steppe. He was indeed a king. He was not always Nagash's puppet. When he ruled, there was still a city where the Crucible of Blood now stands.

It annoys me that I didn't know this myself, but I mainly feel relief. I can't abide not having a thread with which to unpick a puzzle. My mind whirls with thoughts of Boreas, daemon-filled skulls and gleaming, noble armies.

'Ready our legions,' I say suddenly, looking around for some clothes. 'Prepare the Coven Throne.'

They reply at once, filling my head with panicked questions. I can't help but laugh. 'Yes, my old friends. I may lack Boreas' martial zeal, but I know when I need to act. Whatever's happening at the Crucible of Blood needs to be stopped, or at least controlled. I can feel it as surely as I feel Boreas' knife in my back. Giraldus will tell us what he knows and he will lend me his swords.' I grab my rune-inscribed staff from beneath a moth-eaten fur. 'And then I'll make sure we can continue our work here in peace. I won't let Boreas or his soldiers ruin everything with their wretched ideologies and faith. I will *not* have war thrust upon me by Sigmar.'

I stagger through the fane, clambering over my wonderful collections and starting to warm to my task. My purpose has always been to cheat death, but if I need to deal a little of it out, then so be it.

By the time I emerge into the drizzle my army is already mustered. I can't help but smile when I think of Boreas' boasts. *This* is an army. The power of the philtre pounds in my chest as I survey it. The entire valley has been painted white by the gleaming, fleshless skulls of my long-dead spearmen. While my enemies thought I was sleeping, I summoned a host that lesser scholars could only dream of. Countless thousands of warriors stare back at me in unflinching silence, bound by the impenetrable wards tattooed on my skin. Every one of them clutches a rusting, prehistoric weapon and wears fascinating scraps of armour. Their shields and hauberks display the design of myriad cultures. This is archaeology in the form of a lethal, fearless host.

Pacing before them is my greatest prize, a morghast – a winged giant of bone and metal, bleeding light from its armoured ribcage. I stole it at great risk from my supposed regent, Nagash, and it makes an incredible sight. It towers over the spearmen at eight or nine feet tall and it holds a pair of enormous, machete-like swords that predate even the fane. Its fleshless bones are lit up by screaming, tormented spirits. In fact, the entire host is shrouded in a pale green ocean of swirling figures, all bound to me by the same tattooed glyphs. For many years we kept a head count, but recently it has become impossible. Even my hordes of scribes and clerks cannot record the vast numbers arrayed before me. My army numbers in the tens of thousands; that's all that matters. Has anyone ever assembled such a host? I can't believe they have.

The princes materialise from the mist, hauling my chariot behind them – the Coven Throne, a relic of an ancient race, charged with the life force of their countless victims. It billows towards me on a storm of death-magic, drawn by diaphanous horses and a tempest of spirits. Ghosts lift me up like an offering and present me to the chariot. The blazing tumult envelops me and, as I take my seat, it turns to face the numberless hordes below. I hold my staff aloft and spirits whirl upwards, filling the valley with noise and light. The ranks of skeletons say nothing as the Coven Throne lifts me over their heads, but, as I give the order to advance, the sound of their feet falling is like the boom of thunder.

CHAPTER SIXTEEN

Menuasaraz-Senuamaraz-Kemurzil (Mopus)

Shyish: the realm of ageless, boundless, grandeur. What became of you? There was a time when every one of the underworlds contained wonders beyond the imagination of the living. Now they are a collection of broken shells. The iron-clad boot of Chaos has crushed the wonder from my home. I have been hidden away for so long in the fane that it shocks me to see how far Khorne's reach has extended. The horizon is a spine of bristling towers.

Your studies have served you well, say the princes, looking back at me from their skeleton steeds at the head of the chariot.

I nod. 'There are few left who still have knowledge of the back ways through these lifeless groves.' Just a few hundred feet from the flanks of my army, Khorne's armour-clad monsters are scouring the landscape for something, anything to destroy.

They are blind to your passing.

I feel a swell of pride as I hear the respect in the spirits' voices.

'An open mind is hard to suppress.' I grimace at the lumbering brutes that are trying to crush all the wonder from my world. 'And a closed mind is easily confused.' I glance at my pale legions of spearmen. 'We'll show our face once we reach Giraldus, but not a moment before. And, as long as he sees sense, we'll be gone before they know we were there.'

Giraldus always had a penchant for grand displays of power but now, as we approach his fortress, I see how he has been diminished. His fortress was once a mountain of iron-hard bone, warped into solid, squatting towers and thick, hunched buttresses, but the sight that greets me now is far less impressive. The walls have been shattered by countless assaults and the colossal gargoyles are slumped and broken. His vampiric sentries still man the walls, wearing their distinctive winged helmets, but they're a tiny fraction of the army that once marched beneath Giraldus' banner. Still, I can't help but feel a little respect. Almost every inch of this land has been flattened by Khorne's armies, but Giraldus stands defiant.

'How has he survived?' I ask, turning to the princes.

Sorcery and courage. At the first sign of Khorne's armies he severed his link with the land. His fortress is here today but tomorrow it will be gone. He stays long enough to strike a quick blow, then leaves. His luck can't hold out much longer though. The spirits hesitate. They say he is very proud. What if he refuses to help?

I scowl. 'He may only be here for today but that would be long enough for me to teach him a little humility.' I wave my staff at my army. 'That ruin could not withstand this for an hour. Still, I have no desire to waste my energy fighting Giraldus. I will find a better way to convince him.'

I give an order and the morghast lifts into the sky, filling the night with a cry torn from beneath the rain-drenched sod.

As my army pours from the shadowy hills, the full size of it is revealed. I wonder what Giraldus must be thinking as this dread host surrounds his crumbling walls. I nod to the princes and they pull my Coven Throne down towards the palace's towering gates.

They open before we reach them, revealing a ridiculous fanfare of gaudy, fluttering banners and a column of ornately armoured knights. They're all long dead, of course, even Giraldus himself, but they're dressed as lordly, mortal knights. Their black armour is polished to a dazzling sheen and their rictus grins are hidden behind tall, winged helmets. Only Giraldus, riding proudly at the front, has his face on display. A life of murder and unholy pacts has kept his skin intact, but even the thick rouge on his cheeks can't mask his antiquity.

He's one of the few lords who has not fallen to Chaos, whisper the princes.

I'm unimpressed. 'Look at that makeup and finery. Even after so many centuries of life he's not learned to discard the baser pleasures. He could have used all that time devoting himself to study.'

Try to suppress your distaste. This will be so much quicker if you don't have to kill him. Try to at least–

I wave the princes to silence as Giraldus approaches.

'Menuasaraz,' he says, performing an elaborate bow on the back of his horse. As he moves, his armour clatters with icons and medals, filling the night with jaunty music. 'It's rare to see you abroad.' His voice is as inhuman as the cry of the morghast.

He makes no mention of the huge army circling his home but I can hear the outrage in his voice.

I nod in reply. 'You're looking well, Giraldus.'

He recognises the mockery in my voice and lights flicker deep in his hollow eye sockets. 'What brings you to my door?'

I steer the Coven Throne closer and signal for my skeletal honour guard to remain behind.

Giraldus follows my lead and we meet, alone, in the centre of the road. The spirits that haunt my army have filled the night sky with vaporous robes and, as we dismount and approach each other, we're bathed in green light.

'I seek your advice,' I say.

His expression remains wary as he studies me. 'From what I hear, there can't be many questions you can't answer by looking in your own library. What has dragged you from the fane?' He narrows his eyes. 'Perhaps I'm not the only one who's been hearing strange rumours.'

'Yes, I've heard rumours, Giraldus – rumours of golden knights purporting to carry the might of Sigmar in their hammers.' I feel my irritation growing as I say it out loud. 'An army come to rid us of Chaos.'

'It's more than that,' he replies. 'They say these knights are fragments of Sigmar himself – avatars of his will.'

There's a flicker of excitement in his eyes and I can't hide my disbelief. I wave at the ruined landscape. 'Giraldus, you've been trying to throw off this yoke for centuries and look where it's got you. Do you really think a few gold hammers will turn back the legions of the Dark Gods? And if they did, what love do you think they would have for us? True wisdom means nothing to religious zealots. They'd probably see us as tomb robbers and necromancers.'

Giraldus grips the gilded handle of his sword. 'What did you want to ask me?'

I curse my lack of control as I realise he's almost as much of a zealot as Boreas.

'What do you know about the Nomad City?' I ask.

He laughs, surprised by my change of tack. 'The Nomad City? What makes you ask me that?'

Before I can reply he draws back his shoulders. 'No matter.

I'm not ashamed of my past. Yes, necromancer, I was born on the Kharvall Steppe, your books have not misled you. I lived in the shadow of the Nomad City, but that was long ages ago. Have you really braved this journey to ask me about the adventures of my youth?'

'Sigmar's knights are heading for the Nomad City. That's where they mean to strike – there's a shrine of some kind, a brass skull called the Crucible of Blood. Of all the places they could attack, why choose that particular site?'

At the mention of the crucible he looks so pained that I think he might turn and leave. Then he shakes his head. 'Forgive me. I have no love for the Blood God, Menuasaraz. If you've found a way to hurt him, I would be glad to help. What do you want to know?'

'I want to know what the crucible is.'

'It's a monument to a tragedy, Menuasaraz. You have unearthed a great pain in uttering that name in front of me.' He closes his eyes for a moment, then continues. 'When Khorne's legions began spreading across the steppe, the lords of the Nomad City demanded that we stand together against them. They said that it was crucial that their city didn't fall.' I notice a hint of emotion in his voice – shame perhaps.

'But you didn't aid them?'

He glares at me. 'I'm no coward, but I'd been studying the obscure arts for a long time by then. I was consumed by my desire to uncover the secrets of Shyish. I was so obsessed by my studies that I barely registered what was happening to my kingdom.' He waves at the bone-clad peaks that surround us. 'I knew there was a finer, less transient world than my own and I could think of nothing but reaching it. Some of my subjects tried to save the Nomad City, but I paid them no heed – I had my eyes on something greater.'

I nod. 'To survive and continue learning is an honourable goal.'

'So I thought.' He sounds either angry or ashamed.

'What is the Crucible of Blood? Why would Sigmar care about it? Why would he send his army there, rather than to one of the great Chaos strongholds? Or some other shrine?'

'Because it's more than just a shrine. I know because I witnessed its creation. I was almost ready to leave when Khorne grew tired of the Nomad City's insolence. He sent a powerful general…' His voice becomes unsteady. 'A being from Khorne's own realm. It was like an army trapped in a single body. It dwarfed even the giants who guarded the Nomad City, but it couldn't defeat them. Even from the very edge of the steppe I could see the battle. It raged across the heavens – three times the daemon attempted to level the city, smashing the walls with an axe as big as the watchtowers, and three times it failed. The titans wouldn't yield. I realised then that I should have gone to help them, but it was too late.'

He shakes his head, and I get the sense he's forgotten me. The emotion in his voice is now unmistakable – a potent mixture of rage and regret. 'The daemon was called Khurnac. Its rage was so great that the ground bled in pain. The *ground*. The giants of the Nomad City had bound their city with powerful wards though, and their walls refused to fall.'

He's speaking quietly now and I have to step closer to hear. 'After the third attack failed, Khorne arrived to take matters into his own hands.'

'You saw a god?'

Giraldus stares into the darkness. 'After a fashion, yes. My rites were finished and I was already leaving, but I caught a glimpse. Gods spare me, I caught a glimpse.'

I find myself caught up in his story. I can almost imagine I'm there with him, witnessing the fury of Khorne himself.

'My body was free,' he continues. 'Only a shadow of my being was there when the Nomad City fell, otherwise I doubt my sanity could have endured. Even now I don't know exactly what I saw – a crimson thunderhead, perhaps, filling the horizon. My memory has spared me the details. I didn't look directly, of course, and I was miles away, but Khorne was in my mind, of that I'm sure. As I slipped away, I saw a figure. It drew a brass skull from the storm, a skull as large as a mountain, and hammered it down into the Nomad City, destroying it utterly.'

He looks me in the eye, returning to the present. 'The skull has since been named the Crucible of Blood and it stands there to this day, surrounded by the ruins of the Nomad City. The giants had poured so much magic into those walls that they'll never crumble. They're still there, hanging in the clouds – a reminder of Khorne's wrath. For a long time I used to hunt down every record of those places I could find. The thought of that skull's existence, even in the form of books or art, troubled me.'

'You destroyed all that knowledge without studying any of it?'

'I studied it – even when I would rather not. I can tell you what I know. I found out why the titans were so desperate to defend their home. The Nomad City was a doorway between worlds – a realmgate. The giants had been tasked with guarding it and they knew what would happen if Khorne seized control. Their worst fears came to pass – the brass skull claimed the realmgate for Khorne's legions.'

I nod as all the pieces fall into place. 'And Sigmar's knights mean to take the realmgate back.'

He shrugs. 'Perhaps. If they took control of the realmgate, they could travel from world to world. They could attack wherever they wish.'

Finally, I grasp the nameless fear that has been looming at the edge of my thoughts. 'And they could attack *whomever* they wish.'

Giraldus frowns. I continue.

'Don't you see? Sigmar is the warrior-god. He won't stop at defeating Khorne. He won't stop until every realm is back under his golden boot. He has no love for necromancy.' I laugh. 'Imagine what kind of fate he will have in store for kings who abandoned their subjects and refused to aid those who tried to fight?'

Giraldus gives me a look of cold disdain. 'I fear no mortal foe.'

'Sigmar *is* no mortal foe. But if fear is not a reason to act then think what it would mean if we could seize the realmgate for our own.'

Giraldus looks past my Coven Throne to the army gathered behind me. His white lips roll back from long, curved incisors. It's a chilling sight to see him smile.

He grips his sword again. 'I would give a lot to have the upper hand, Menuasaraz, for one last time. I grow tired of this slow, pitiful defeat.'

'Think what we could do together,' I say, waving at the army behind me and the figures watching from the walls of his fortress.

He keeps smiling and rests a death-cold hand on my shoulder. 'You're more of a man than I realised, necromancer.'

There's something odd about his smile. I get the impression that he's holding something back from me – that he has different plans to my own. I decide that I don't care, as long as he adds his army to mine.

I point at my army. 'We have real power here, Giraldus. We could seize the realmgate for our own and use it to uncover the secrets of countless realms. And we would garner such power that we could keep all of those bickering gods from our doors. We could finally be rid of them – as long as we get there before Sigmar's knights.'

He nods slowly. 'But Sigmar is a step ahead of us. You said he has already sent his armies to the skull.'

'But they were delayed. Somebody sent them astray. They are only now nearing their goal. There's still time.'

Giraldus nods. 'When dawn comes the daemon returns. Khorne bound it to the skull as a punishment. Khurnac's rage is unimaginable, and it grows every year. From sunrise until nightfall it rages and thrashes at its chain, and as it tries to break free, other daemons pour from its bath of blood, born of its rage. They're thrown everywhere: other kingdoms, other worlds, other wars, but many of them simply flood out onto the steppe. The region becomes a mirror of Khorne's own realm. Nothing survives the slaughter that follows.'

CHAPTER SEVENTEEN

Lord-Celestant Tylos Stormbound

I keep Zarax on a tight rein as we approach the ruins. The Chaos knights wait patiently on their grunting steeds and I count them as we march. There are at least as many as we faced in the Anvil. There will be no skeleton monster to rise up and save us this time and the thought makes me smile. We will finish this alone. I can feel the determination of my men beating down on my back, Sigmar's light, blazing through their mirrored amour. It will not dim until we have broken through every line of red and brass that comes before us.

The Crucible of Blood is visible, jutting out of the crater beyond us. Our prize is so close now.

As we pass beneath the first of the drifting ruins my head fills with the sound of a roaring, anguished voice. The words hammer against my mind like a choir of lunatics, all wailing in a different key. It's an agonised, inhuman cry and it's impossibly deep. It sounds as though the rocks themselves are crying out in pain.

'What is it?' I gasp, looking back.

My men hear it too. Several are clutching at their golden helmets, trying to drown out the horrible din. Some of them have even dropped their shields and fallen to their knees.

I look back at the Chaos knights and see that they're now riding slowly towards us. They were waiting for this to happen. The world shakes beneath the weight of their snorting juggernauts.

'Boreas!' I cry, scouring the crowds of staggering Liberators for a sign of the Lord-Relictor.

He emerges from the rabble, walking better and no longer clinging to a Liberator's shield for support.

'It's the ghosts of the city!' he shouts over the din. 'They're trapped here.'

Boreas sounds like he's in agony, but he's more awake than I've seen him since we reached the lakeshore.

'They're reliving their defeat,' he continues, staring up at the massive shards of rock. 'Can you see them?'

I follow his gaze and realise, to my amazement, that I can. What I took for flickering shadows are towering, humanoid figures charging into battle. They're as faint and insubstantial as the moonlight glancing off my armour, but their pain is all too palpable. For a while, I can only stare in wonder at their massive forms, pounding into a fight that was lost before my ancestors were born. The longer I look, the less human they become. Their anatomy is similar to that of a man, if ten times the size, but their heads are strangely broad and sunk low in their shoulders and what little I can see of their ghostly faces shows brutal, exaggerated proportions – like crudely chiselled statues.

'Lord-Celestant,' gasps Boreas as he finally reaches my side. 'The enemy.'

I drag my thoughts back to the present. The Chaos knights are moments away from us. I can see the face of the lead rider now, the lord with the swooping horns. This must be Hakh. His eyes are blazing with mirth as he watches my front ranks stumble. The Liberators are struggling to raise their shields as the war cries of the giants boom in their helmets. They look like a rabble.

'Stand proud!' I cry. 'You are Stormcast Eternals.'

The Liberators manage to raise their shields and form ranks, but the sound is growing louder all the time.

'Don't they hear it?' I ask, staring at the crimson-clad riders.

'They're revelling in it,' replies Boreas. The sound of the giants' pain only adds to the knights' bloodlust. Their juggernauts are unhinged – snapping their great, bestial heads from side to side as their riders hold them to a slow trot.

The pain in my mind increases but I clench my jaw and bite down hard, determined not to cry out before my men.

I grab my Honour Scrolls and recite my oath. *Pain may be my flesh. Death may be my fate. But victory is my name.*

I shout with all my might and, as the sound leaves my throat, I wrap it around the words of a hymn. The song springs from somewhere deep in my subconscious; I haven't sung it since I was a child, but the words ring out of me with all the force of my forging. It's a hymn to Sigmar and I roar it like a curse. Behind me, hundreds of other voices pick up the tune.

Boreas raises his sepulchral tones in harmony and, together, we drown out the sound of fallen giants and thundering hooves. The louder I sing the more powerful I become. I start to picture the halls of Azyr soaring up around me – gleaming statues of star drakes and mythical heroes rising from the shadows as I sing louder, driving the noise from my mind.

I lift Grius over my head and give the signal for a shield wall.

The phalanx closes ranks seconds before the juggernauts smash into us.

Hakh leads from the front, his blazing eyes locked on me, and his steed hits us like a boulder. Shields judder beneath the force of the massive beast and, as the front line of Liberators stumbles, Hakh lunges at me from his saddle, swinging his great, two-handed sword. Zarax rears to defend me and the blade sinks deep into her face.

She falls backwards, crushing more rows of blue and gold shields as she lands. Lightning envelops her body as she dies. It spears through the battle, silhouetting us all in white heat.

I tumble, blinded by the detonation, but Sigmar is with me. As my vision clears I see that that I've landed near Hakh and he's reeling from the blast, swaying in his saddle.

'Victory is my name!' I cry, grasping Grius in both hands and slamming it into Hakh's chest.

Lightning flashes a second time, ignited by my blow. The crush of armour and weapons falls away and Hakh topples from view, surrounded by a red cloud of his own blood. Bodies slam into me and I'm driven to my knees. Grius is torn from my grip and I howl in frustration.

I draw Evora and she is singing before she has even left the scabbard. Her eerie tones cut through the cacophony and fill me with strength. The red knights may revel in the pain of the ghosts overhead, but Evora's voice is another matter. They falter in their saddles, confused, giving Castamon and his Liberators in the front line the chance to drive them back and smash some of them from their steeds.

There's a flash of golden sigmarite and I haul Grius from the carnage with relief. It's only then that I see Boreas, trapped beneath a fallen juggernaut and thrashing in silent pain.

I try to reach him but our lines are battered and reeling under the weight of the juggernauts' attack. I see flashes of gold as Liberators throw themselves at the brazen horrors, pounding their sacred hammers into fume-shrouded snouts and plates of jagged metal. The shield wall has held. My god-born brothers have dug their feet into the rock, thrown their shoulders against their shields, and held back the weight of a landslide.

'Zarax,' I whisper, in belated recognition of her death. These blasphemous curs can have committed no greater crime than ending such a proud life.

Hakh's juggernaut tears through the crush. Hammers fall and flash but the monster is unstoppable. It may have lost its rider but it is clearly still set on my destruction as it charges straight for me. Its head is down and its speed shocking but I feint to one side, drop the other way, grab its horn and swing myself up onto its back.

Infernal heat pours up through my armour and my mind recoils at being so close to a creature spat from the Blood God's own realm. It bucks and leaps beneath me, but I hold fast and ride the monster as it careers through the phalanx and takes me out into the enemy ranks.

Suddenly I'm surrounded by jagged, blood-coloured iron rather than gleaming gold sigmarite.

The juggernaut is driven to a frenzy by my presence on its back and it tramples several of Hakh's knights as it circles and stomps, trying to shake me off, but then the daemon steed collides with a force equal to its own, and reels backwards.

When I manage to focus I see a glorious sight – a wall of implacable, towering paladins: the last of my Retributors.

They barrel into the monster, pounding it with their shimmering, two-handed lightning hammers.

Their weapons blaze and the monster staggers, then prepares to launch itself at them with renewed force.

I take my chance and let go of the juggernaut's iron saddle, grasp Evora in both hands and drive the runeblade between its metal shoulder plates.

Evora's voice soars as she sinks up to her hilt.

Flames spout from the wound and the monster bucks even more violently, throwing me clear. I roll aside as the beast tries to pulverise me with its thundering hooves and, as I lurch to my feet, the paladins strike again, bringing their warhammers to bear.

Their aim is true and the creature explodes, firing shards of metal through the air. When the blast clears, they pound across the rock towards me.

'Lord-Celestant,' one of them says as they form a protective circle around me. 'Perhaps we should rejoin the others.' His hammer is still sparking and crackling with power but his voice is a laid-back drawl.

I look around and see that we're on the enemy's flank and a line of them is already hauling their enormous steeds around to face us.

'Celadon,' I say, recalling his name. 'We must find Hakh.' I glance at the pale line of silver spreading across the horizon. 'We have to end this quickly.'

As I stride on, the paladins throw their colossal bulk towards the oncoming charge, smashing and pounding into the bellowing juggernauts. Even their paladin armour can't easily withstand such an onslaught and several of them are ridden to the ground before they can strike, crushed beneath iron-clad hooves. Retributor Celadon fights at my side, swinging his great warhammer in broad, easy swipes, cracking plates of iron like porcelain.

After a few moments the others have all fallen behind, mired in the enemy ranks, but Celadon keeps pace with me. As we smash our way into the heart of the enemy lines, splitting skulls and cracking limbs, he joins me in song, bellowing out the hymn like a benediction. His voice is ragged with fury.

Celadon is swinging his hammer with such force that when

he reaches a wall of white rock he smashes through it without pause, surrounding us both in dust and rubble. Only then does he finally stumble, not from the impact but from an unexpected lack of resistance. Beyond the wall is an opening in the fighting and, with nothing to crash into, Celadon drops to his knees with a resounding clang.

I almost fall too as I stagger past him. The Chaos knights have backed away to create a circle and none of them raise their axes as I stumble into view. The ground is oddly shaped and, as I look around, I see that we have smashed our way onto the palm of a huge, outstretched hand. It is sculpted from the same white stone as the ruins overhead and I realise that some of the city has fallen. It must have landed with incredible force as it is embedded deep in the basalt. I look back and see that we have been separated from the rest of Celadon's paladins. They're lit up by white fire as they try to smash their way to us but, for the moment, we are alone.

I turn on the spot, Grius and Evora before me, expecting attack, but I hear words instead.

'So this is the one,' comes a low growl from the far side of the stone hand.

Standing a few feet away from me, at the base of a crumbling thumb, is Hakh. His pale, horned head is unmistakeable. His powerful frame dwarfs even his heavily armoured knights and he's carrying a jagged, two-handed sword that simmers and hisses as though heated from within. His serrated armour is still scorched and smoking from the death of Zarax, and his low, jutting horns make him seem more animal than man.

'He's the one,' confirms a woman standing next to him.

Her ordinary appearance is almost as shocking as Hakh's mutation. The sight of a mere human, standing at the centre of such a dreadful scene, is quite surreal. She's dressed in a filthy, matted fur but she has the penetrating eyes of a scholar or seer.

I straighten my back and stride towards them, wiping the gore from my armour. Now, as I stand before this dog, I realise that my Reforging is complete. I may not have been born a noble, but I have been lifted far from my humble birth. I draw back my shoulders, plant my feet firmly on the black rocks and level my hammer at Hakh's head.

Some of the knights jeer and mock me, but Hakh and the woman remain silent. Hakh raises a hand to silence his men. Retributor Celadon steps to my side and casually plants the head of his hammer on the ground beneath his feet, resting his gauntleted hands on the handle.

Hakh locks his gaze on me. 'Dawn is almost here,' he grunts, nodding at the fading stars overhead. 'Let's end this.'

I nod and order Celadon to back away.

Hakh's eyes burn brighter as he lifts his sword and steps into the circle.

The giants' roar resounds through my helmet so I start singing again as I raise Grius and drop into a fighting stance.

The circle of knights burst into laughter again when they hear my simple melody, but the woman's eyes open in surprise. Something about my song drains the colour from her face.

'Leave!' she hisses, when Hakh is just a few paces away from me. 'It's impossible. You're too late. You can't reach the skull before dawn.'

Hakh turns to face her and she lowers her head, too afraid of him to say more.

The warlord grins, takes a deep breath, and charges.

CHAPTER EIGHTEEN

Lord-Relictor Boreas Undying

'Hold the line!' I cry, reeling back from the carnage.

The phalanx is still intact but even a wall of sigmarite will eventually buckle under such ferocity. The Liberators have thrown all their weight against each other, still singing my brother's hymn as they shudder under the impact of the juggernauts. Where they can, they unseat the red knights with spring-heeled lunges, pounding their hammers into the enemy and then dropping back behind their shields.

The remaining Judicators are sheltered by the shield wall, loosing volley after volley at the enemy. Arrows blaze as they punch through Khornate armour, toppling some of the riders but leaving others hunched in their saddles, inured to the pain by their unholy rage.

I can no longer see Tylos or Retributor Celadon. I strain to look over the smoke-snorting heads of the juggernauts but it is useless. They had reached Hakh's honour guard and marched calmly into the circle. I have to trust him. I have to believe Tylos can reach the Crucible of Blood or this will all have been for nothing.

Another charge crashes into the phalanx and, finally, the shields start to give.

'Hold the line!' I roar, and we surge back at them with a storm of hammers and arrows.

I slip back through the ranks and grasp my honour scrolls. My heart pounds as I consider what I'm about to attempt. My body is broken and my mind is close behind.

I look ahead and see, briefly, the horned figure of Hakh. He is flying towards Tylos, swinging a great two-handed sword. Tylos has proven his courage, but he can't defeat them all alone. We need to reach him.

The Liberators' song falters as another wave of juggernauts crash into us. They can't hold out much longer. The Stormcasts are greater than any mortal foe, but the daemonic steeds are stealing our precious remaining minutes. Dawn is almost upon us. We have to get Tylos to the crucible.

I start to pray, reading from the mass of scrolls that trail down from my armour, and immediately, my gauntlets begin to spark and flicker.

I recite the final words and power jolts through my body. Before I have chance to register the pain, I point my hammer at the storm clouds and channel the power of the heavens, calling down Sigmar's wrath. Lightning connects with my hammer and splays out over the heads of the Liberators, turning the night into a fierce, colourless dawn. It hits me with such force that I'm hurled backwards across the ground.

Blows falter as both armies pause to watch. For a brief moment, the clouds become silver, shimmering peaks. My prayer flashes across the sky and then hurtles back towards the ground, reborn as a thick column of lighting. The air rips apart as it slams to the earth. It lands in the heart of Hakh's army like a comet from the heavens.

While the others stare in wonder, I'm already running. I ignore the pain of my wounds and stagger through the stunned crowds of warriors.

The column of lightning doubles and redoubles, lashing and arcing its way through the enemy warriors. It's incredible, so beautiful that even the Chaos knights pause to watch, before being blasted apart.

As the column of light reaches the juggernauts it slices neatly through the daemon steeds. The blades of light leave smoking, butchered corpses in their wake.

Some of the knights manage to howl in rage, but most are simply thrown from their mounts and left in bleeding heaps of smouldering metal. As the lightning's power grows, more of the juggernauts are dissected, spilling scarlet flames as their unholy bodies fall apart. Even the ground starts to rupture and crack, spewing gouts of lava from beneath its black, splintering crust.

'Charge!' I cry, weaving through the crowds of Liberators. 'Make for the crucible! Find the Lord-Celestant – the night is almost done!'

As I run across the cracking earth, dodging jets of lava, the tower of lightning begins to slowly rotate, trailing twitching limbs of electricity that tear apart even more of the Chaos steeds. The red-armoured knights are so busy trying to control their bucking mounts that I stagger half way through their ranks before they even notice. Even then, they find it hard to place me in the blinding glare.

One of them manages to bar my way and attack. He's lost his weapon so he simply dives headfirst through the inferno of spinning lights. I sidestep his clumsy lunge and pound him into the ground with my warhammer. Without breaking my stride I race into the heart of Sigmar's fire. It's so fierce I can barely see and my armour begins to ripple with heat, but I can't falter. I will not let Tylos fail.

The warriors of Khorne have fled the blast and I stumble through the blaze alone. The arcs of power are still passing over me, rather than slicing me open, but my armour is starting to buckle and boil. The heat is incredible. I'm still a few feet from the core when my damaged leg gives way. The wound I sustained at the lake explodes with pain and I crash heavily to the ground. I crawl on but the light is growing more ferocious with every second. I take a breath that's nothing but fire and agony blossoms in my chest. The pain is horrific, beyond even the pain of my Reforging.

As the lightning crashes down around me, the earth cracks and judders again. I crawl up a shifting ledge of rock, trying to see if the army is with me. After staring into the light, I realise I'm trapped. The lightning has left me surrounded by a circle of angry, spitting lava. I stagger from side to side, trying to find a way through, but wherever I go I'm met by more lava. There's no way through. I shout, but the roaring of lightning drowns out my cries.

CHAPTER NINETEEN

Prosecutor-Prime Drusus Unbound

It's like dropping into the sun. As I plunge into the Lord-Relictor's storm his howl of pain rings out and I pound my wings faster.

I order the rest of the retinue clear, sending them back towards the brass skull. Some of them falter, unwilling to desert me and unnerved by Boreas' cries.

'Lord Tylos ordered us to wait for him at the realmgate! Do as your Lord-Celestant commands or risk his wrath!'

Reluctantly, they swoop and sail back through the clouds. I turn back to the lights below. This is it. I can feel it clearly. This is my chance to erase the past.

I fold my wings and dive with greater speed than I have yet attempted. The descent is dizzying and exhilarating but the light burns into me like acid.

I have seconds at most.

The ground rushes towards me but it's impossible to see anything clearly. The world is a maelstrom of white, celestial heat.

I realise, too late, how low I am, and only pound my wings

seconds before crashing into the rocky earth. Agony jolts through me and I roll, howling, through the blaze.

The incredible heat drives me back to my feet and I see Boreas lying with his hand outstretched towards the centre of the lightning. His armour is warped out of shape and he's struggling to move. I stagger to his side and lift his head. Blood pours from the eye sockets of his mask, but he manages to speak.

'Tylos,' he grunts through shredded vocal cords.

The heat is beyond anything I have experienced and I topple away from him, unable to breathe.

I reach out and my hand locks around a ball of agony. I see that I've plunged my fist into the magma. I draw back my ruined limb and realise a new wall of lava has sheared up from the ground, separating me from Boreas. I'm so close to death that it fills me with rage – I cannot die until Boreas is safe.

I throw myself through the curtain of lava, grab Boreas and fly with a fury I have never braved before. As the lava eats into me I soar upwards, surrounded by a spinning halo of light.

The pain grows and I realise my armour is collapsing.

I beat my wings harder, holding Boreas as tightly as I can.

I'm flying so fast that I can't breathe. This is no mortal strength I can feel in my wings. This is the strength of a god.

The lightning falls away, the smoke fades, and soon all that lies ahead of me is the night.

My armour peels away and my skin runs like water. Slowly, my insides boil and break apart.

I die as I land, letting out a final roar, not of pain, but of victory. Boreas is safe. We will not fail. It is not my flesh but my past that I can feel burning away, my madness that's dripping from my limbs. Finally, I am worthy of my name. Finally, I am Drusus Unbound.

As Boreas leans over me, reciting the Oath of Passing, I see the God-King, waiting for me in the blaze. He raises his hammer as he welcomes me home.

CHAPTER TWENTY

Lord-Celestant Tylos Stormbound

The Blood Creed roar as Hakh swings his sword at my face.

I plant my left heel in the ground and bring Grius up to meet his blade.

As I am hurled back across the stone hand, I realise I've underestimated him. My arm sings with agony as I roll and stumble back to my feet. His strange, bestial features crease into a leer as he swaggers after me, drawing back the huge sword for another strike. The lumbering colossus should not be able to wield that sword with such ferocious power – the Blood God is in his flesh. Khorne is battling me through the body of this snarling ape.

The thought only adds to my pride. To stand alone, bearing Sigmar's honour. It is not the fate I imagined for myself.

He swings again, but this time I'm ready. Rather than parry I roll towards him, leap forwards and bring Grius down between his obscene horns.

There's a dull crunch as his skull gives way.

The force of the blow sends him reeling into the circle of onlookers.

I stride after him, raising Grius for another blow, but Hakh's honourless warriors crowd around him, blocking my way with a wall of weapons and curses.

They hold me at bay as their lord climbs slowly to his feet. His thick brow has collapsed, giving his face an even more misshapen appearance. He shows no sign of weakening, however, as he turns on his own men. He's clearly furious that they thought he needed help, and he butchers anyone within reach. Only when there is a circle of twitching warriors lying around him does he turn and face me again. He reaches up to his broken head and laughs.

'Not enough,' he growls, as he charges back into our impromptu arena.

I take a deep breath and lift Grius. This is going to take more time than I have.

Before he reaches me, light floods the sky and I realise to my horror that day is upon us.

Hakh and I both turn to look. It's immediately apparent that this is no natural sunlight. A few hundred feet away, not far from my embattled Liberators, a column of light has burst from the ground. It's pouring up into the storm clouds, coruscating and sparking as it lights up the ruins.

Hakh recovers from his shock and takes the opportunity to attack, bringing his sword round in a low strike at my stomach.

I bring Grius down in time to block the blow, but my mind is only half on the fight. As I back away from him, clutching Grius in both hands, I see that the shaft of light is having a devastating effect on the monsters attacking my army. It is spewing buttresses of energy that blast apart the juggernauts when they collide, creating spectacular eruptions of flame and armour.

'Boreas,' I mutter, recognising the power of my brother.

Hakh staggers to a halt and lowers his sword, staring at the scene beyond the edge of the stone hand. He howls in outrage at what follows. As the column of light turns, its radiance slices through the daemon-steeds and tears up the ground, leaving Hakh's knights floundering in a swamp of lava, blood and body parts.

My men are still locked in formation and as their attackers falter they surge forwards, lowering their shields and unleashing a flurry of hammer and sword blows.

Hakh forgets me and races to the edge of the hand, still growling.

The light grows brighter and a fierce heat washes over the plain.

My Stormcast Eternals blaze like a constellation of stars as they smash through the enemy, but the heat is so great that they start to falter. Even Hakh's knights, denizens of this hellish realm, recoil from the blaze, shielding their eyes as the night burns white.

The light grows so fierce that I'm soon unable to see even Hakh, who's standing just a few feet away from me. I hear him raging and cursing as he tries to find my position. Is this dawn after all? Have I failed? Is the Crucible of Blood about to open its gates?

I climb along one of the hand's crumbling fingers, feeling my way, trying to peer through the light.

My mind whirls as I see that it is fading.

As the glare dims, my vision starts to return. Hakh and his knights are still gathered in our makeshift arena, staggered by the display, but Celadon is striding towards me, clutching his great, two-handed hammer.

Blessed night floods back over the steppe, leaving just a single point of brightness, racing through the sky. It briefly becomes a golden, twin-tailed comet before crashing to the ground.

'The God-King is with us,' I whisper, as I see that my army is now free to advance.

'Lord-Celestant,' says Retributor Celadon, raising his hammer and drawing my attention back to Hakh. The Chaos lord turns his mangled face back in my direction, and I see the doubt in his eyes.

In the wake of Sigmar's lightning, my men are now charging across the steppe towards the stone hand. The lightning has filled them with unimaginable fervour. I can hear their voices from here, still roaring the hymn as they smash, pummel and hack their way through the reeling knights.

Hakh looks from the butchery of his men to me and Celadon, fury written across his face. He throws himself at me like a bull, horns lowered. The ferocity of the attack gives him incredible speed and neither Celadon nor I have time to block it.

His horns crunch into my armour and we roll back across the palm of the hand.

Hakh's men charge past us as we stagger to our feet, rushing to attack as my golden Liberators pour up over the rock, so incandescent with faith that even I can barely look at them.

Battle explodes all around me. Sigmarite pounds against brass and swords bite into flesh as a huge tumult of figures surge across the stone hand.

I haul myself to my feet and see that my armour is dented but not punctured.

Hakh lunges again. I block him but the impact knocks the breath from my lungs.

'They will not save you!' cries Hakh as he wades after me.

As I stagger backwards, clutching my chest, he draws back his sword to strike again.

He never stands a chance. Sigmar is everywhere. He's in the

sky, blazing through the cosmos. He's in the song that's roaring from my throat. And he's in the hammer that I smash into Hakh's slobbering jaws.

I swing Grius with such force that the front half of Hakh's head shears away. There's an explosion of red and he's thrown several feet through the air, landing in a broken, lifeless heap.

'Lord Tylos,' shouts Retributor Celadon. He's standing just a few feet behind me over a pile of broken bodies and I realise he's been guarding my back while I dealt with Hakh. The red knights fight with a deranged fury as they're driven back but Celadon pounds through them with fluid, easy blows.

'We must reach the skull now!' I cry, struggling to be heard over the din of tormented spirits, hymns and war cries.

The steady, unremitting blows of my men are smashing Hakh's army apart. We're still outnumbered but the storm summoned by Boreas has wiped out half of Hakh's army, and his sacrifice has turned the survivors into a desperate rabble. In a few more moments we'll have broken them and be on our way to the Crucible of Blood.

I rally my men and drive them in a surge to the far side of the hand. From there it's just a few hundred yards through the drifting ruins and we'll be at the lip of the crater.

At my command, they redouble their attack with a blinding wave of hammer-blows. We force the dazed knights back to the edge of the hand, where many stagger and fall onto the black rocks, dying beneath the shadows of the floating city.

Daylight is moments away, but moments are all I need. I shoulder my way through the lines until I reach the heart of the fighting.

Some of the knights recognise me as the man who killed their lord. They growl and charge, but Celadon is still with me. The first of them crumples beneath a blow from Grius, the second reels away headless, devoured by Evora, and the third is driven into the ground by the force of Celadon's hammer.

Without pausing, I vault over the tumbling bodies and smash my way through the enemy ranks, making my way towards the centre of the Nomad City and the crater at its core.

The Liberators explode into action behind me, summoning up a final, furious push. The red knights collapse before us and we reach the lip of the crater with a victorious roar.

I raise Grius aloft and I look at our prize.

The Crucible of Blood grins back at me – the hideous creation of a brutal god. It soars overhead – thousands of tons of brass, cast by hellish sorcery in a realm of daemons. The top is open to the sky, and with dawn only minutes away, the lake of blood it contains is already starting to bubble and steam. Deep within its cloying depths, an obscenity is forming, preparing to spew madness across the steppe. The sight of it hits me like a physical blow – such a vast act of violence wrought against the landscape makes my breath catch. The bowl of charred rock that surrounds the skull still seems to be smouldering in memory of that ancient wound. Steam or smoke is rippling over the blast hole, but I stride on, feeling the seconds slipping away.

It's only as I enter the crater that I realise that it is not steam that's rippling across the ground – the rock itself is rolling and heaving.

'What *is* this?' asks Celadon, stamping on the shifting ground.

I shake my head and wave him on. There's no time left to think, we just have to act.

We've only taken a few steps when Celadon's question is answered.

As the rock cracks and opens, fleshless, gleaming bones begin hauling themselves from the ground. This is the vision I saw when Boreas healed my eye – this was the nightmarish scene that Sigmar poured into my mind. I pause and mutter an oath as a leering, sword-wielding skeleton climbs into view.

CHAPTER TWENTY-ONE

Menuasaraz-Senuamaraz-Kemurzil (Mopus)

Returning to the Kharvall Steppe is even worse than I remember. The air is so hot and sulphurous that I'm wracked by a violent coughing fit. When I wipe the spittle from my face there are a few withered molars lying in my palm and I curse Sigmar for dragging me up here. I warned Boreas against playing war games and now look what's happened. My stomach lurches again, but I manage to steady it with a quick draft of my philtre. My head is full of metallic buzzing, and energy is fizzing over my skin.

Giraldus is riding as close to my Coven Throne as he can. A tempest of souls separates us, but I can still see his outrage at what has been done to his former kingdom.

Behind us, our fleshless host is clawing itself up into the moonlight. I ignore Giraldus and study the army we have created. Despite my misgivings, I can't help swelling with pride as my morghast heaves its huge frame from the blackened stone as I form the crowds of skeletons into orderly ranks. We're in a fume-filled crater that must be a mile wide but we've filled it with revenants and cadavers from every realm. Such a horde could lay waste to anything the gods have to offer. Death is the great leveller, after all.

'There it is,' says Giraldus, his voice tight with anger.

I turn back and see that the fumes have rolled away to reveal a soaring wall of brass. It's stained with centuries of dried blood and I steer my chariot backwards, unable to take it all in. I can make out the jawbone of a skull but the rest of the brass idol reaches so high that it seems to support the clouds. This is the source of the energy that's rattling my teeth and humming over my skin. Rage is pouring from the bloodstained metal, rippling the air and churning my shrivelled guts.

I hold a hand in front of my face as though blocking the sun.

'We'll have to be fast,' I say. I turn to Giraldus. 'How do we enter? Tell me that you learned that much before destroying anyone else's chance of gaining knowledge about this place.'

He's too furious to notice my harsh tone. 'There are steps to the mouth. We enter through the teeth.'

'Of course we do,' I grimace, steering the Coven Throne towards the jaw. I deploy most of the army around the perimeter of the crater, but I take a few hundred skeletons with me, to keep an eye on Giraldus as much as anything else.

As we approach the skull, the power spilling from it becomes almost overwhelming. There's a deafening grinding sound in the air and my bones ache as the throne lurches and sways above the black rocks. Even the spectral steeds that are drawing my chariot twist and writhe before the wrath of the skull, but I do not allow the princes to pause. I have no desire to be here when Khurnac awakes. I want to be travelling through the realms by then, raiding the mausoleums of a hundred cities and plundering wells of long forgotten learning. Or perhaps just back in the fane, safe in the knowledge that I control a route between worlds. The thought drives me on through the pain and we finally reach the wall of metal. The sound here is deafening and there are streams of energy billowing over the brass.

'Over here!' yells Giraldus, leading the way, and I drive my throne after him. My heart is pounding furiously now, as though I'm being charged by the skull. I shout at the princes until they pull the Coven Throne faster, speeding past Giraldus.

A few minutes later I see the steps. They're wide enough to front a great palace and we race up them, the spirits of my chariot rolling tendril-like across the brass.

Khorne's rancour rises through my seat and eats into my flesh. I can feel my skin starting to blister and burn, but I ignore the pain. My mind whirls with visions of greatness. The higher we go, the grander my visions become. Why stop at merely accruing knowledge? With this army and passage to other worlds, might I not use my scholarship for something greater? I could become the wisest lord who ever walked the realms. Everything starts to make sense. As I travel faster up the steps, I see that I was born for this. It is my destiny to rule with a wise and just hand; bringing the realms into the kind of unity that others have failed to do. And all those who deny my right to rule will face the wrath of the greatest host ever to emerge from the underworlds. If Nagash can no longer protect his kingdom, perhaps it is time that the undead had a new master? If I control the realmgates, who could stand against me?

I'm vomiting now and blood is rushing from my nose, but the spirits struggle on and haul the throne up the last few steps.

I notice that Giraldus and my army are no longer with me, but there's no time to wait. I ride the chariot towards an opening between the skull's enormous brass teeth. The doorway towers over me and I see that it's framed by a huge portico wrought from the same bloodstained brass and forged to resemble snarling, reptilian hounds clawing and tearing at each other. It's an unnerving sight but I drive the chariot on and, as it hurtles down the passage, I see that there is no door – just a wall of rippling blood, rising hundreds of feet over my head.

'Now what?' I try to ask, but my words come out as muffled gibberish.

I look back and see that Giraldus is dragging himself up the last few steps towards me. His sorcery has failed him and his face has assumed its true form. He looks like a reanimated cadaver, smeared with gaudy makeup. His shrivelled flesh has fallen away from his mouth, revealing long, inhuman teeth.

He tries to say something, but I can't hear him over the roaring sound that is pouring through the brass.

He jabs his finger at the crimson wall, shaking his head. He looks to be in horrible pain.

Of course. He's afraid of the power I will hold over him, but he need not be. I will be a benevolent, wise ruler. All my centuries of learning will inure me to the folly that has left Nagash battling to preserve his own domain. I turn to face the wall of blood that fills the doorway and try to ride closer, but the power flooding out is like a physical wall.

I kick the base of the throne and it lurches forwards. We're still several feet away, but the chariot's moving with slow, spasmodic bursts, as though wading through mud.

The closer we get, the more my mind slips away. All I can see is my vast army crushing the realms beneath skeletal feet, with me at their head.

Finally, we reach the wall and I prepare to enter the portal, preparing myself for unimaginable power.

Before I can enter the skull, the visions become even more

violent. I picture myself crowned in the blood of a thousand slaughtered foes. I am standing above a mountain of corpses, screaming words of tribute to my lord as he watches from his throne of skulls.

I look down and see that my robes are drenched in blood, and steaming and shrivelling in the heat. I look like a slaughtered corpse. The sight shocks me and, suddenly, my thoughts seem deranged. I'm no servant of the Blood God – what madness has taken hold of me?

Giraldus hauls himself up the ribcage frame of my Coven Throne and drags my face away from the portal of blood.

'This is *not* the way!' he cries, finally managing to be heard over the din. 'Not for us! We were wrong. All that lies through this gate is damnation.'

The skull's power is smashing through my body with so much force that I think I might be thrown from my chariot. Dazed, I look from Giraldus and down the brass steps to the crater below and our wonderful army. Have I really summoned this host just to create more ruin? Visions of slaughter linger in my head and I'm filled with a growing sense of horror. Is this where all my learning has brought me?

Then I see something else. Racing across the crater towards the skull is a triangle of golden figures. Barely a few hundred of Sigmar's warriors are left, but they make an incredible sight. Vast storm clouds are rolling in their wake and lightning flickers across their shields. There is something so righteous about them, so pure. They could never be consumed by the madness that just filled my thoughts. They are unassailable.

'Boreas,' I whisper, sensing that I might have made a terrible mistake.

The energy pouring from the skull suddenly triples its force. My whole body judders and my teeth begin to clatter against each other.

Giraldus points his sword at the sky and I see that it is grey. Dawn has come.

I look back towards the skull and the sight that greets me makes me collapse back into my throne.

CHAPTER TWENTY-TWO

Lord-Celestant Tylos Stormbound

Sigmar's wrath carries me through an avalanche of bones. Unnumbered hordes of skeletons press around me, crashing, tumbling and rolling in great waves, grasping with their brittle fingers, hacking with rusty swords. I stride on across the crater, leading what remains of my army in a glorious, martial tribute to the God-King. Despite the ivory waves smashing into me, I swing Grius with a grace and serenity I have never achieved before, shattering skull after skull after skull and filling the air with splintered bone.

'We are the exalted!' I cry. 'We are vengeance! We are Stormcast!'

The skeletons topple like mannequins but the onslaught is endless. They are undaunted by my brutal blows. As Grius returns them to dust, hundreds more march into view, as relentless as the storm overhead. They hack at me with a bizarre collection of weapons. Some carry the most incredible swords – things of great workmanship, dragged from the tombs of kings – while others lurch towards me with clubs and broken scythes.

Between the brass skull and me there is now a field of grinning, gibbering faces. We need another way to break through. Dawn is imminent and I could smash these mindless wretches for an age and not reach my goal. There must be thousands of dead souls rising to block our way.

I look back and see that Castamon and his Liberators have almost managed to reach me – a wedge of glinting sigmarite trailing shattered bones as they slice through the host, followed by Celadon and his lumbering ranks of paladins and the last few retinues of Judicators, who have swapped their bows for short swords as they hack through the leering dead.

I raise Grius in tribute then bring the warhammer down, channelling all my rage and frustration. To my shock, a blast of light clears the area ahead of me. The nearest skeletons crumble into dust and dozens more roll away from me. For a moment, I think Grius is responsible but then, as I stride forwards into the gap, I see the truth.

'Drusus!' I cry, looking up at the heavens, delighted to see that he has managed to carry out the order I gave when we crossed the lake. I told him to wait for us near the skull and strike when our need was greatest, but I had started to fear that the Prosecutors must all have perished. They dive from the clouds launching javelins and hammers that blaze as they fall, ripping great holes in the skeleton army. For a moment, my heart races, but I realise that there's no sign of Drusus' plumed helmet. Another winged herald is leading their attacks.

The first ranks of Liberators start to reach my side, still singing as they envelop me with their wall of shields and hammers.

'Where is the the Prosecutor-Prime?' I demand, glancing at Castamon between blows.

The Liberator-Prime shakes his head. 'He fell, Lord-Celestant.'

I glance at him.

He hesitates, sounding pained. 'Lord-Celestant, didn't you see the comet? Drusus braved that inferno so that the Lord-Relictor might live.'

'Boreas?' I feel a flint of pain in my chest but the Liberators are watching me, waiting to hear my response.

'Drusus died with honour.' I look at the sky. 'None of us can ask for more.'

The crowds of skeletons smash into us again, but the Liberators hold their line and we force our way onwards.

'Heralds of Sigmar!' I cry, still staring at the sky. The stars have all vanished from view. The sky is the colour of lead. Morning is moments away. 'Prosecutors!'

What remains of Drusus' retinues sweep back around and tumble from the storm clouds. Some are struggling to fly, held aloft by their brothers as their lightning bladed wings start to falter and dim, but all of them are singing as they snatch lightning from the heavens and form dazzling weapons in their fists.

'We're almost through!' I roar. 'Carve a path!'

They raise their voices in song and dive at the skeletons. Storm-born javelins and hammers fly from their hands as they descend.

'Brace yourselves!' I cry to the Liberators and they drop to their knees.

The ground shudders as a blazing line of explosions tears through the skeletons. A smouldering, white road opens up before us.

'Charge!' I shout, and we race down the shimmering avenue, surrounded by charred, broken bones.

Overhead, the Prosecutors launch another storm of twin-tailed bolts, blasting the path further into the crater. Skeletons are still lurching towards us, but there's now a clear way and we're racing towards our goal through a valley of smoke and glittering embers.

Another series of blasts erupts up ahead and, finally, the brass skull looms before me. I see wide, metal steps leading up to an enormous doorway beneath two of the skull's lower teeth. A metal portico leads to the door, and it's hard to see clearly but I think there are figures at the threshold. Crimson shapes are flowing down to meet us. Khorne's host has arrived.

'Above you!' roars an unfamiliar voice, from somewhere in the crowds of skeletons.

I look up and see a bone colossus dropping through the fumes towards me, borne on vast, skeletal wings.

I drop into a battle stance as it lands and rears over me. It's a revolting construct of sorcery and bone that towers over the fighting. It pounds across the shattered rocks on clawed feet, clutching a pair of great, cleaver-like swords. It seems to be formed from the skeleton of a huge, winged warrior and its bones are clad in the remnants of ancient armour. Emerald light coils beneath its rib cage – luminous viscera wrapped around a collection of broken, human skulls.

I leap forward, whirling Grius around my head.

The bone monster raises one of its swords to parry my blow, but my fury resonates through its hollow limbs, sending it back down the blazing path, its sword spinning away into the melee.

I charge after it, followed by a wave of Liberators but, with a pound of its fleshless wings, the monster launches itself into the air and hacks down at me with its remaining sword.

I smash the blade back and leap again, grasping its legs and hauling myself up over its shimmering torso.

It lurches under my weight but before I can land another blow it grabs me by the throat and swings its falchion.

'No!' cries a female voice and there's a blaze of light as something slams into the monster.

The impact sends the sword strike off target, saving my head, but the bone construct pounds its wings and soars up towards the clouds, with me and the other figure still hanging from its ribs. I realise, to my amazement, that it is the woman I saw with Hakh.

As we fly higher, the creature tightens its grip on my throat and swings again.

This time I'm ready. I smash the blow away with Grius, haul myself higher and pound the warhammer into the thing's giant, bestial skull.

Green light blazes as cracks open up in its snout, but it clearly feels no pain. It pounds its wings again, throwing us through the clouds, away from the Crucible of Blood.

A Prosecutor whirls through the clouds and catches sight of us. He cries out my name and dives towards us. The bone monster lashes out and the blade clangs off the Prosecutor's chest armour. The Stormcast tumbles away, pounding his wings furiously but, as the monster flies higher, I see him soar after us, refusing to let me go. I see the marks on his honour scrolls and recognise him.

'Stay back, Sardicus!' I shout.

Then I see the Crucible of Blood and mutter a curse.

The brass is shimmering in the crimson light of a new sun.

CHAPTER TWENTY-THREE

Menuasaraz-Senuamaraz-Kemurzil (Mopus)

Shapes are forming in the blood. Dear merciful gods, what shapes. These are the malformed things I saw in the painting – hunchbacked daemons wrought of flame and crimson scales. Their heads are like long, snarling anvils and they clutch smouldering blades in their claws.

I order my spearmen to attack and then send the Coven Throne hurtling back down the steps. As I descend, the creatures pour from the wall of blood, spiderlike and frenzied. My spearmen clatter up the steps to meet them and the dead join battle with the damned, levelling a bristling wall of jagged spearheads at the emerging monsters.

'Attack! Attack!' I cry as my Coven Throne reaches the bottom of the steps, and the landscape boils into life as thousands more skeletons race to obey, flooding past me, climbing the steps and swamping the daemons trying to enter the realm.

'Do you see?' cries Giraldus. He's a few feet away from me and back on his dead horse, surrounded by his knights. As the ranks of skeletons charge past him, his knights hold their line and Giraldus points his sword at the line of golden figures on the horizon. 'Do you see now what they are?'

I try to laugh, but I can't. The contrast between the noble, golden knights and my own bloodthirsty visions has left me bewildered. What good is all my learning if I can be so easily led to damnation?

'But what can they do against that?' I wave my staff at the vile daemons smashing into my ranks of spearmen. And yet, as I look back at Sigmar's knights, I find myself wanting to believe. Even from here I can see that they are unlike anything I have ever seen before. They've battled across a world that was long thought lost and they have remained utterly defiant, still trailing their elegant pennants and shimmering with the power of the storm.

As they enter the crater that surrounds the skull, they tear through my army, blasting them back with huge explosions but, rather than feeling enraged, I find myself replaying my conversation with Boreas. *Things have to change, and we have to change them.* Could he be right?

'Could we really turn back Chaos?' I say.

I'm not addressing Giraldus but he hears me. His eyes blaze in their sunken pits. He points past the boiling mass of daemons to the brass skull. 'If Sigmar's army could seize this realmgate, I believe they could. I've heard such tales, Menuasaraz. This army is just one of many. Sigmar did not abandon the realms, he's just been waiting for the right moment to strike.'

We're jolted further down the steps as my spearmen are driven back by the daemons. I look back at the blood portal and see that they're flowing through my skeletons – tearing them apart in their desperation to advance.

'Hold them!' I cry, waving hundreds more of my spearmen up the steps. They advance in cold, fearless lines, but the steps can only handle so many of them; most of my army remains trapped around the base of the skull or spread out across the vast crater.

Giraldus waves his sword at Boreas' army. 'We should help them, not fight them.' He gestures at our combined armies. 'We could hold the daemons here so that Sigmar's knights can reach the skull.'

I look up at the daemons tearing my army apart and shake my head. 'We need to leave, Giraldus. We were fools to come.'

'Where would we go?' he demands. 'Do you think they won't hunt us down? Do you think you can hide in your library forever? They'll find you, Menuasaraz. It's only a question of when. They'll find you, they'll burn your precious books and then they'll mount your head on a spike.'

Suddenly I know this is true. I've tasted the bloodlust that drives these fiends – they will never stop until they have butchered every living being in the realms as a tribute to their furious lord.

I'm about to reply when a series of red shapes slam into my coven throne, causing the spectral steeds to rear and scream.

I howl a curse as a winged daemon hurtles towards me. I lash out with my staff and there's a flash of phosphorous as the magic-charged wood connects.

The daemon screeches and tumbles away from me. The attack was so fast that I only get a brief glimpse of crumpled, bat-like features and black, leathery wings.

It loops around and dives at me again but, before it reaches the Coven Throne, Giraldus cuts it down with his greatsword. There's another blinding flash as the daemon explodes.

More of the furies pour out of the fumes surrounding the base of the brass skull and I raise my staff, crying out a word of summoning, calling my greatest warrior back from the battle, but it's too late. The daemons are seconds away and the morghast will never make it in time.

Giraldus comes to my aid with his knights at his side, hacking down those daemons he can, but dozens more are diving towards me.

Suddenly a blaze of white light envelops the steps. The clouds part, unleashing great columns of lightning. They slam into the daemons, blasting them away and causing my Coven Throne to lurch and judder.

I manage to hang on to the throne and as I do I'm blessed with an incredible vision. As I slump in my chariot, hundreds of winged warriors loop and soar down from the clouds. Their golden armour shines brighter than the dawn and there are javelins of pure energy hurtling from their hands.

Their lightning spears erupt upon landing, engulfing the daemons in holy fire, and Giraldus cries out in delight.

'We have to help them!' he cries. Without waiting for a response, he waves his knights back up the steps. 'Hold the daemons back!' he cries, charging after them.

For a moment, I can do nothing but watch the incredible scene unfolding before me. As the golden figures plummet from the heavens, blasting Khorne's daemons into crimson dust, Giraldus and his knights lead a heroic counter-attack on the gate of blood. It's hopeless and glorious at the same time. The daemons are pouring from the skull in such numbers that nothing could hold them back for long, but the sight of so much defiance in the face of inevitable defeat stirs something in me that I thought long dead.

Giraldus vanishes beneath the avalanche of horrors, but I'm already raising my staff. It's as though someone is speaking through me, someone greater than I thought I could be.

'Hold them back,' I demand, turning to face my grinning, skinless captains and their bristling ranks of spearmen. I turn the Coven Throne around and find myself leading a charge back up the steps. Daemons are now pouring down the walls of the skull in their hundreds. There is no way I can survive but, somehow, I no longer care. I can think of nothing but Boreas and his belief.

'Things have to change,' I whisper as I level my staff at the Chaos creatures and hurl my army at the face of the Blood God.

Daemons crowd onto my chariot, but my staff is charged with more power than I have ever felt before. As I strike them down, the blows crack like thunder and their crimson flesh detonates in a series of spectacular explosions. All the while, Sigmar's tempest is raging overhead, spewing golden knights from its thunderheads. They add their hammer-headed bolts to the carnage, ripping more of the daemons apart.

Countless hundreds of terrible monsters sprint into my ranks of spearmen. For every skeleton they destroy, dozens more rush to fill the gaps, but there's no end to the skull's profane outpourings. Gradually they drive us back down the steps, ripping my army to pieces with the ferocity of their sword blows.

Death is rushing towards me but an incredible vigour fills my limbs. As the white bolts slam down all around me, I blast daemon after daemon back from the Mortal Realms. The princes whirl around the Coven Throne, binding the daemons with death magic and hacking at them with phantom blades. They fight so heroically that none of the horrors can reach me. I look back through the inferno and see Boreas' army hurtling across the crater towards us and my heart swells. They *are* going to make it. Boreas will never know it, but I have bought him the chance he sought.

One by one the princes are devoured and, finally, I am

surrounded by snarling, blood-slick daemons. They pause for a moment, sniggering at my ruined body, then they fall on me with their vicious blades. There is pain, but it is dwarfed by my pride. After all those years cheating death, my final breath is the first taste of life.

CHAPTER TWENTY-FOUR

Lord-Celestant Tylos Stormbound

The morning sun blinds me as we soar higher. We're so high I can now barely see the crater below.

Air explodes from my lungs as we crash into a wall. The woman and I roll across marble steps and the monster spins off through the clouds, dazed by the impact.

I glance around and see that we've smashed into one of the drifting fragments of the Nomad City, a vast, broken wing of white marble, the feathers of which spiral up towards a white, crumbling eagle's neck.

The monster soars away and I charge after it. Pain fills my head, causing me to stumble as I climb the steps. The song of the ghosts is deafening now that I am actually in the ruins. It's as though the soul of the Nomad City is all around me. I stagger and only manage to stop a few inches from the edge of the wing. My stomach turns as I look out over a mile-high drop.

As I back away from the edge, the bone monster dives back towards me with its sword raised.

I draw Evora and, to my relief, the runeblade's otherworldly song eases the agony in my head, drowning out a little of the ghost's pain.

I easily dodge the monster's blade and plunge Evora into its chest as it smashes into me.

The sword passes cleanly through the empty ribcage and I only succeed in jamming the hilt between the bones. We roll across the marble wing, locked together as we clang and clatter towards the precipice.

Seconds from the edge I manage to draw Evora from the monster's chest and bring her round in a wide arc, slicing through one of the monster's shoulder blades and hacking part of its wing off.

The monster opens its weird, bat-like jaws and mouths a silent scream.

I throw all my momentum into a hammer-blow, smashing Grius into its chest and sending the creature tumbling through the clouds in a rain of broken bones.

The bone monster loops and prepares to launch another attack, but before it can, it pauses in midair, beating its wings as it looks down on me from the clouds, suddenly unwilling to attack. For a moment, it hangs there staring at me, then it banks away and dives back towards the battle below.

I stagger to the edge of the ruins and look down across the fighting.

'Now what have you done, Boreas?' I mutter as I see what's happening. The vast army of skeletons is no longer battling my army. They're charging towards the skull instead, rushing to engage the crimson host that is tearing its way into the world. I can only assume this is another sign of my brother's burgeoning power.

As Evora's kill-song dies away, the giant's cries hit me with redoubled force, driving me back to my knees. The pain centres on the eye that Boreas healed, and blood is rushing from my golden mask again.

'Let me help,' says a voice.

I lurch to my feet, readying Grius for another blow, and see Hakh's woman rushing towards me. Her skin is pulsing with sorcery and her eyes are featureless white orbs, but, as before, I sense that she means me no harm.

The lights in her skin fade and the colour returns to her eyes as she reaches my side and places her hands on my mask.

She sings a few quiet words and blessed relief pours through my skull. I can still hear the ghosts' lament, but it's just a sound now. The horrendous pain is gone.

'I'm Vourla,' she says, looking at my scorched, dented armour. Dawn blazes across the metal, dazzling her as she tries to look at me. 'What are *you*?'

I study her in silence.

She backs away from me, looking anxious.

'You need not fear me,' I say, sheathing Evora and holding out a hand. 'You came to my aid. I owe you a debt.'

She looks away, as though in pain. 'You owe me nothing.'

I shake my head, confused, and follow her up the steps of the stone wing.

There's a clatter of metal as Prosecutor Sardicus lands on the ruins. He folds his blazing wings and rushes towards us.

I'm about to greet him when I see a shocking sight. The brass skull is now aflame with morning light, but I'm blind to anything beyond the figure rising from the open top of the cranium. A crimson horror is drawing itself up from the boiling blood. As hundreds of lesser daemons flood from the skull's mouth, a mountain-sized nightmare is rising from its open crown. The world unravels before its unholy power. Colours and shapes tumble into each other, forming a rippling kaleidoscope.

As the daemon, Khurnac, drags itself into the world I see black, canine flesh and vast, blood-red wings. Looking upon such perversion turns my stomach but I refuse to avert my gaze. Such virulent, blasphemous hate cannot be ignored.

'I did this to you,' says Vourla, sounding appalled.

She's sitting on the edge of a crumbling step, paying no attention to the daemons, but staring at me.

'Why did you save me if you despise me so?' I say, managing to shield my thoughts from the abomination forming below us.

She shakes her head. 'I don't hate you. I just didn't believe…' Her words trail off. 'It's only now I see you that I understand.' She stares at me again and her voice fills with panic. 'I never considered that you might actually have a hope.' She rises to her feet, shaking her head furiously. '*I* sent your storm astray. I did this to you. I still had a remnant of power in me and I saw a chance to use it before I died. I thought that you were doomed whatever happened, so why not use you before you met the same fate as all the others?'

Rage jolts through me as I realise what she's saying. 'You delayed us?' I glance at the skull. Khurnac is beginning to thrash and grow. The blood that spews from its movements forms limbs and jaws as it drops. The hordes of the Blood God are here.

'I couldn't let Hakh live,' she replies, talking to herself rather than me. 'Not after so much pain, so much cruelty.'

'So you used me as your executioner? And delayed Sigmar's vengeance?'

My body is shaking with fury and I see that Sardicus is the same. I draw Evora as we walk towards the dazed woman.

Vourla makes no attempt to flee, she just nods her head in shame, waiting for my blade.

The runeblade lifts its voice in reply to my bloodlust. I'm hardly conscious of raising it but, as I near the priestess, I see myself reflected in her terrified eyes and pause. I look like every other monster in this pitiful ruin of a world. I look like the man I was long ago.

'No.' I lower the sword and back away. Not that. Of all the ways I could fail Sigmar, I would not become the thing he sent me to kill. I sense that this is the power of the skull at work. It's twisting my thoughts.

'I won't harm you,' I say, turning my back on the Crucible of Blood. 'I'm here to save you.'

She looks up at me, her eyes full of tears and confusion. 'But can't you see?' She nods at the scene below. 'There's nothing to save. It's too late.'

Khurnac is wrenching its brimstone flesh from side to side, straining against an enormous chain that binds it to the rim around the skull's open crown. An axe has formed in its claws – a weapon that must be thirty or forty feet long. As the daemon thrashes around it slams the axe against the walls of the skull, consumed by an immemorial fury, attempting to hack itself free. Every blow sends out a dull, tuneless *clang* and each one heralds the arrival of hundreds more daemons. They're flowing from the skull in a crimson tide and pouring into the crater below. Through gaps in the clouds I see them scampering and sprinting into the ranks of skeletons. Nothing can stand against them. The undead crumble like kindling and, wherever my Stormcast Eternals are, I know that even their sigmarite shields will not stand against this. Clang after clang tolls out and the torrent becomes a storm. The writhing, ephemeral shapes become a vast wall of hate, pounding down into the crater.

I grab my honour scrolls and recite the runes. *Pain may be my flesh. Death may be my fate. But victory is my name.*

I know that Sigmar would not send me here without hope. I just need to look harder. I need to find Sigmar's face in the darkness. I need to hear his voice. *His voice…* I remember the ghostly cry still circling my head and finally recognise something that has been at the edge of my consciousness since we reached the Nomad City. The dead titan is not howling in pain, but frustration. He sounds as though he is forever trapped in sight of a prize that's just out of reach. It's like he's calling me to witness something.

I look around, trying to locate the source of the cries, and my eyes settle on the white tower at the top of the stone wing – the soaring, graceful neck of marble that rises away from me into the clouds.

Vourla's still staring at me and follows my gaze to the tower.

'It's too late,' she says, sounding almost angry at my persistence. 'I've murdered you.'

I place a hand on her shoulder. 'You're no murderer.'

She closes her eyes, holding back tears. 'Why did you come?'

'The Crucible of Blood is a gate between two worlds. It leads to the heart of Khorne's realm. It leads to the birthplace of his whole empire. This skull feeds his armies. Every dawn, when Khurnac pounds that axe, he sends fresh legions. We have to–'

My words are interrupted as Khurnac strikes the skull again, vomiting more daemons onto the already swamped skeletons. I start to imagine what must have become of my men, then crush the thought before it can take hold. I'll grieve when the realmgate is sealed.

'We have to close it,' I say, I racing up the steps towards the tower with Vourla and Sardicus rushing after me.

'Lord-Celestant!' cries Sardicus. 'What about the Kuriat? The Lord-Relictor has the key to the realmgate and he's still on the far side of the crater. If he's even alive, daemons and the dead lie between him and us.'

I look back at him and shake my head. 'The heart has been lost. Boreas bought our passage through the Anvil with it.'

Sardicus falters. 'Then we will…' His words trail off as he considers the significance of my words.

'We can no longer claim the realmgate for Sigmar.' I lift Grius and turn it so that light plays across the sigmarite. 'But we have one card left to play.'

Sardicus stands proud despite the fear he must be feeling. 'You will not go alone.'

Words will not suffice. I grasp his hand in silence.

He glances down at the boiling ocean of daemons where my army once stood. 'But how will we get to the gates?'

I turn back to the tower, sure that Sigmar is already giving me the answer. The voice of the dead titans is so loud here that I can feel it buffeting against me. The more I listen, the more sure I am that this is a message from the God-King.

The tower is a stone shell, with no stairs and, as I step inside, I see that it's open to the sky. Sunlight beats down on me through vast, serpentine windows, blinding me.

I hold Grius up to block the light and, as my vision clears, I look back through the centuries into the Age of Myth.

Overhead, one of the giant ghosts is clearly visible, frozen in the midst of a heroic dive; preserved at the moment of his death. The sunlight beats through his vaporous flesh and I can see clouds through his billowing spear, but his eyes are as fierce and vital as my own. They're locked on something below, something on the Crucible of Blood. He's showing me something; calling to me.

'Carry me,' I say.

Sardicus spreads his wings, flooding the ruins with light.

I place my hand on Vourla's arm. 'The time has come. Rise up and reclaim your home.'

'Me?' She looks from me to Sardicus, baffled.

'You stood face to face with the enemy, Vourla, and you still found a way to fight. Find others and teach them to do the same. We didn't come simply to close a gate. We came to start a landslide.'

She laughs in disbelief, but I can see a fire starting to kindle in her eyes. I've done enough.

The tower whirls around us as Sardicus lifts me up through the ruins, surrounding us with images. I see faces in the marble, heroic and proud, beings born in an age free of monsters like Hakh. They seem at once distant and recognisable. I see the same fire in their eyes that I saw in Vourla's. Centuries of brutal oppression have not dampened it.

'Lord-Celestant,' says Sardicus, and I realise that my mind has been wandering. There's something hypnotic about these ruins and the cry of the ghost.

Sardicus draws my attention to the figure looming overhead. We've almost reached the spectre of the dead titan. His cries are heartbreaking in their desperation. Wisps of armour trail around his gargantuan form and he roars as he tries, endlessly, to launch his spear.

'Closer!' I shout, struggling to be heard over the ghost's cries. 'Take me closer.'

Sardicus hurls us into the miasma of the giant's flesh.

The effect is instant, and shocking. The crumbling ruins vanish, replaced by a dazzling array of colours and shapes. I'm seeing the Nomad City through the eyes of the ghost. The walls are covered with beautiful murals of gold and ochre and the rooms are capped with ornate ceilings. Enormous pieces of furniture are all around me, gilded and gleaming, and the air smells clean and pure. It's no idyll though. Hundreds of titans are tumbling backwards past me, roaring in anger and fury, swarming with vicious, crimson daemons. They're being devoured by a host of hunched, scaled monstrosities with anvil-shaped heads and gaping jaws. The giants are attempting to defend themselves, but it's clear that the battle is already lost. Their strange, inhuman faces are tormented by fear and anger as the daemons flood over them in uncountable numbers, clawing and devouring like a plague of locusts.

Even over the din of battle, I can hear the voice of my host-spirit. His language is strange and incoherent, but I can feel the dreadful urgency in his cries. As I look out from his mind I finally see what he's been trying to reach for all these centuries. As the daemons tear him apart, shredding his flesh with frantic, snarling mouths, the giant's gaze is fixed on a goal he'll never reach.

Of course.

My heart quickens as I see what I must do.

CHAPTER TWENTY-FIVE

Lord-Celestant Tylos Stormbound

The stink of charred flesh greets me as I return. I feel Sardicus struggling to hold me aloft as we fly up through the top of the ruined tower and out into the clouds.

Beneath us, the crater is a seething mass of red shapes but the skull has not finished its work yet. Blood-red figures are pouring over the lip at the skull's crown, from its nose and from the doorway beneath its teeth. There must be thousands of daemons, tumbling over the rocks and charging to war. Some of them resemble the things I saw through the eyes of the titan, but others assume forms I cannot even describe – mongrel things that combine the canine and the reptile into something obscene.

And, over all of this pandemonium, Khurnac still rages, smashing its colossal axe against the walls of its brass prison and roaring in fury. Every blow spews another glut of daemons from the crucible and, as they tumble into the world, Khurnac turns its fury on its own kind, tearing apart anything it can lay its claws on, cramming visions of madness between its slavering jaws.

Reality has given up trying to contain such overwhelming corruption. The world beyond the daemon is like a tattered curtain, revealing glimpses of a landscape even more tormented than the Kharvall Steppe. This is now my destination – the Blood God's foothold in the Mortal Realms.

Sardicus pounds his wings, struggling to stay aloft as I steel myself for what I must do.

'Take me as close as you can,' I call out.

'Close to what?' he cries.

'Drop me on the rim of the skull, as near to the daemon as you can!'

Sardicus shakes his head, horrified.

'Do you trust me?' I cry.

'But what can you do against that?'

'That's where darkness is deepest. That's where I'll find Sigmar waiting.'

Sardicus keeps shaking his head, but he flies down through the clouds nonetheless.

Daemons hurtle to greet us. They're no bigger than dogs, but they have ragged wings, long, revolting snouts and mouths full of dagger-like incisors. They swoop towards us, screaming like demented gulls and reaching out with grasping talons.

I slam Grius into the first of them, crushing its head between its shoulders and sending it spinning back towards the skull.

The other manages to latch onto me, but I fling it off with a roar and, as it swings round to attack again, Sardicus blasts it from the sky.

'More,' gasps Sardicus, pointing at countless red shapes that are lifting up from the crush of battle to attack us.

'Faster!' I cry, jabbing Grius at the brass skull.

Sardicus dives with stomach-churning speed, plunging us towards the Crucible of Blood.

Before the smaller daemons can reach us, I leap free and land on the crown of the brass skull. Nausea-inducing pain rushes up through my legs. The whole skull is seething with power.

'Go!' I cry, glancing at Sardicus as I climb to my feet.

He hesitates, watching the mountain-sized horror thrashing through the lake of blood behind me. Then crimson-fleshed figures burst through the clouds, screaming as they attack him.

Sardicus launches Sigmar's fury at them, but, as I rush to help him, I feel a wave of incredible power smashing into my back. I topple to my knees, clattering across the brass rim of the skull, and my head fills with dizzying visions of slaughter and bloodshed.

'Lord-Celestant!' cries Sardicus, from somewhere outside my pain.

I stagger back to my feet, just in time to see the source of the hateful energy that's crippling me.

The daemon rises over me – a monumental fortress of scale and fire, blocking out the sky with leathery, tattered wings and raising its immense axe. I can't meet its gaze but the hate in its eyes burns through my armour, scorching my flesh.

I dive clear just as the axe smashes into the brass wall. The force of the blow rocks the whole skull and I'm thrown from my feet.

The daemon roars and at such close quarters the sound fills my head with agony, but along with the pain comes outrage. This monstrous creation is everything I was born to destroy.

As Khurnac draws back its axe for another blow, I spit blood from my helmet and turn to face it, standing defiant before the flaming goliath with my hammer gripped firmly in both hands.

I swing Grius and the warhammer connects squarely with

the daemon's colossal axe. There's a blinding flash and sickening power jolts through my body, hurling me through the air. I manage to roll as I land and, as I break into a sprint, I see my target no more than thirty feet away.

The daemon laughs as it sees that I have no escape. It doesn't realise that I don't seek to run away.

Waves of blood boom against the walls of the skull as Khurnac wades slowly after me, drawing back its axe for the final blow.

My lungs are burning and I'm drowning in my own blood. The fury pouring up through the brass is starting to cook me from the inside out; I can feel my innards burning and twisting. I have nothing left in me but one, final attack.

'My name. Is. Victory,' I whisper, launching myself at the object I saw through the eyes of the ghost: a thick ring of brass that locks the daemon's chain to the wall of the skull.

I leap, hammer raised, and cry out an oath as I swing Grius.

The air ignites. I'm thrown for a third time, this time by the thunderclap force of my own strike. For a moment I'm blinded by the afterimage of the detonation. When my vision clears, I see what I've done.

Khurnac has waded deep into the lake of blood and is staring at its broken chain. It lets out a final roar of exquisite relief as it realises I've freed it from its centuries-old bonds. I have unleashed one of Khorne's most powerful servants.

But instead the daemon's flesh begins breaking apart and drifting into the sky, like a swarm of insects leaving a nest. Khurnac reels back and forth through the gore, grunting and bellowing as its physical form collapses. Finally, there is a brittle cracking sound as its form dissipates completely. Then the daemon is gone. I have done what the giants of the Nomad City have long dreamt of – I have severed Khurnac's link to the Mortal Realms and sent it home to its master.

Immediately, the blood ceases to boil and the violent power stops blasting through my body. All I'm left with is exhaustion and the pain of my wounds. I drop to my knees and groan.

From the top of the skull I see that the lesser daemons remain below. I had hoped that vanquishing their wretched progenitor might banish them too, but they're still pouring across the landscape.

I climb unsteadily to my feet and study my surroundings. Standing up here, at the summit of the huge skull, I feel like I'm already dead, watching the death of the Mortal Realms from a lofty, god-like perch. Far below, I see where I need to be – the gateway between the skull's teeth.

I whisper a prayer of thanks for Sardicus' disobedience as I see him swooping towards me, still blasting daemons from the air despite terrible, bloodstained rents in his armour. One of his wings has been badly damaged. The blades of light have lost their lustre and they're flickering and failing. He's flying in lurching, drunken arcs, barely keeping aloft, but when he lands on the skull, he extends a hand towards me.

We fall rather than fly towards the earth, a dead leaf spinning from a tree, but Sardicus summons final reserves of strength as we near the ground, thrashing his one good wing just before we crash onto the steps. The impact still jars through me but we both manage to stand.

As we climb to our feet, the daemons swarm around us, loping across the brass on their cloven hooves and raising their swords. They're wiry, crook-backed things, knots of scaly muscle that reek of death.

Sardicus launches a volley of hammers, filling the air with crackling energy and dazzling explosions. Dozens of the daemons fall, but dozens more vault the blasts and throw themselves at me.

My strength is all but gone. As their snarling faces speed towards me I drag Grius up to meet them. The warhammer lends me its vigour. It's as though it can sense the proximity of its goal. I bring the slab of sigmarite down again and again, barging through their smouldering ranks as I try to reach the entrance up ahead. Sardicus lifts himself overhead and surrounds me with thundering, furious blasts of god-fire.

Our assault draws the attention of the whole host and I see countless hundreds of the daemons racing back up the steps towards us, gripping flaming swords.

I see a wall of blood up ahead of me and I realise I'm moments from victory.

Dozens more crash into me as I try to climb the last few steps. They tear my armour and flesh. I'm aflame with agony, but the pain only drives me on. I pound and lunge but it's no good. My body is broken. I can barely stand. The opening is still ten feet or so away but the daemons are pouring over me in such frantic waves that I can't fight through.

Finally, the weight of them drives me to my knees.

I try to fight on, but it's impossible. They swarm over me like rats and I can't find the strength to shrug them off.

'Sigmar!' I howl, turning to face the heaving throng. Where is my lord? He *must* be here. I've looked deeper into the darkness than any man. Where is the face of the God-King?

Sardicus swoops overhead, but his lightning is useless against such numbers, and I see that he's as ruined as me. He's on the verge of dropping into their waiting talons.

'Sigmar!' I try to shout, but my lungs are full of ash and nothing emerges but a croak.

And then I see him.

Crashing up the steps, ploughing through the ranks of daemons and piles of broken skeletons, comes a golden triangle of shields. They're dented, scorched and bloody, as are the men behind them, but they do not stop.

My army lives. Despite everything, it lives. There are no more than a hundred or so left from the vast host that set out, but they have fought, tirelessly across this valley of madness to reach me. What valour is bound into those bones? I see Boreas staggering at their head, drenched in blood, followed by Retributor Celadon and others I recognise but, above all, in their gleaming forms, I see the face of Sigmar.

'For the God-King,' I cry, driven to my feet by the glory of it, raising Grius in tribute, shrugging off mounds of daemons as I stand.

They hesitate.

Boreas speeds up at the sight of me, powering through the crush, hurling entire rows of daemons aside in his determination to reach my side. Behind him, the Liberators finally lower their shields and charge, crushing daemons beneath a storm of golden boots.

They reach me. Despite everything Khorne has thrown at them, they reach me. I feel dozens of hands grasping my ruined body and hauling me towards the doorway.

I cry out, seconds before we leave the steppe. 'Victory!'

Then we cross the threshold and step into a wall of blood.

CHAPTER TWENTY-SIX

Lord-Celestant Tylos Stormbound

The clamour of the daemons dies away and blood envelops us. The liquid is hot and cloying, flooding my armour and filling my mouth, but after the vision on the steps, nothing could stop me. I hurl myself through the curtain of gore and burst into a new kind of hell. As I leave the wall of blood, the sudden lack of resistance throws me forwards and I crash to the ground. No, not the ground – a pile of glistening skulls.

I clamber to my feet and look around as Boreas and the others emerge behind me. I can't help but laugh. We're standing on an endless, sunless plain of skulls, lit only by violent gouts of fire scattered across the landscape as though supporting the tormented heavens. In every direction, the plain is walled by brutal, brass fortresses, bristling with spines. Talon-crowned towers soar out of sight and comprehension, making me stumble as I try to study them. They're huge in a way that staggers the mind. The horizon seems to sag under their weight.

Above the towers there's no sky, only an endless, rolling storm of daemons. Countless thousands of them, billowing and heaving like blood spiralling in water, lit up by the blooming columns of fire.

Circling the plain of skulls are vast, roaming packs of daemon-hounds trailing smoke from their ruby eyes and howling at the tumult overhead. And wading between the hounds is a loathsome, thrice-damned multitude. Every form of debased soul that ever worshipped the Blood God is here: towering troll-like monstrosities, winged, bull-faced daemons and snorting, armour-clad knights, all locked in battle for their master's enjoyment, all clashing in endless, pointless, war.

'Lord-Celestant,' says Boreas, wiping blood from his broken armour. My brother's hammer is gone and his skull mask has been warped into a nightmarish grin, but he sounds as calm as ever. 'The Crucible of Blood is still open.'

I grip his shoulder in gratitude then stagger back towards the portal. Crimson daylight is still pouring through the doorway and I can just make out the portico beyond. On this side the realmgate is surprisingly tangible – a tall stone arch, carved with brutal images of slaughter and war.

I heft Grius into my hands, savouring its weight; savouring its purity. No amount of blood could stain such a weapon.

'There can be no return,' I say, turning back to my men.

They nod in silence, wearing their wounds like medals, facing me with unshakeable pride.

I turn back to the stone arch and swing with all the strength I can muster.

I'm half dead with exhaustion and pain, but a greater force than me throws the blow. It smashes into the stone and sends thick, silver lightning up from the metal, splitting the clouds of daemons; drenching us all in holy light.

The archway collapses and the world beyond it vanishes from view. The realmgate that has stood for countless ages is no more. Now there is only the plain of skulls, grinning mercilessly at us from every direction.

'Victory comes in many forms,' I say, staring at the pile of smouldering rubble.

I turn back to my men and as the lightning dies away we're plunged into the fitful darkness. The world starts to shake as a furious roar booms out from the towers. Khorne's legions cease their games as they see what I've done – what I've taken from them.

They charge – a tsunami of daemons, monsters and killers, flooding across the plain.

As the damned hurtle towards us from every direction, remnants of lightning play across our golden armour, so that we resemble a tiny, polished coin set adrift in a lake of tar.

I feel no fear. No doubt. Only pride.

At my command, shield walls form around me and I hold Grius aloft.

The host crashes into us.

The hammer falls.

SCION OF THE STORM

C L Werner

CHAPTER ONE

What use the weapon forged without the hand to wield it? It needs more than a mighty weapon to make a mighty warrior! Even if the metal is strong, how shall it prevail if the flesh that bears it is unready? By the fire of tribulation and ordeal is the spirit tempered; in the clamour of battle is valour proven.

The realms burn in the havoc of Chaos. Hour by hour their substance, their very essence, is degraded and corrupted. The powers of darkness assert their ascendancy, ready and eager to consume all. Never has there been greater need for Ghal Maraz.

Though the weapon is ready, the warrior must be proven. Haste in battle is oft as disastrous as over-caution. The cries of the numberless multitudes who languish in the chains of Chaos, whose lands and lives are despoiled by the Ruinous Powers, sear through my being like fiery daggers, urging me to throw aside all caution and descend in a mighty storm upon the enemy. Such recklessness would please the foe. The atrocities their creatures inflict are bait to draw me out, to stir my wrath that I may forget the greater purpose of war: liberation of the realms from the darkness that would devour them.

No, they will not goad me into foolish action. I will wait to loose Ghal Maraz into the greater war. I will wait until he who will bear it, he who will be my champion, is ready to fulfil his purpose.

Flesh, mind and spirit – tempered and tested until they have become as unstoppable and unopposable as Ghal Maraz itself, until the Hammer of Sigmar is ready for my war.

Such is the decree I, Sigmar, make now!

The crack of thunder boomed across the swamps of Krahl, sending flocks of hairy fen-hawks winging away from their nests among the dagger-leafed spineferns. An entire stand of the trees with their scaly, armoured trunks was obliterated as a blazing lance of lightning hurtled downward, smashing into it with volcanic fury. Embers and ash were sent flying across the swamp, splattering the sluggish streams and murky lagoons. A ribbon of smoke steamed upwards from the scorched crater.

Amid the wreckage of the thunderstrike, something stirred that was not smoke or ash. A figure climbed out from the charred hole. Towering in stature, he was of more than merely human proportion. The armour that encased him was a thing of wondrous craft and fearsome design, forged from sigmarite, with a nimbus of gold secured to the top of the backplate to provide a permanent halo framing the warrior's metal helm, a helm cast in the shape of a human visage frozen in a scowl of perpetual and inexorable judgement. Mighty wings stretched outwards from the figure's back, endowed with dazzling purity and a starry lustre. Upon the heavy pauldrons that shielded the warrior's upper arms and shoulders was emblazoned the shape of a twin-tailed comet, sacred symbol of the God-King himself. Hanging from a loop on his belt was a golden sceptre cast in the same shape.

An even greater symbol of the God-King was gripped in the warrior's hands. Crackling with ancient enchantments and the energies of Azyr, the Celestial Realm, the great warhammer was of such massive size that even in the grip of this formidable warrior it looked gigantic. Jewels shone from its golden haft and upon the broad and brutal head were inscribed runes that had been old even in the Age of Myth.

The blast of the thunderstrike was still echoing across the land as the crackling blaze dissipated from the warrior's eyes and his vision resolved itself to take in the savage tableau. He had descended upon a primordial scene, sluggish streams of silvery muck that were neither liquid nor metal flowing past islands of rusty earth peppered with black spineferns and predatory leechpines. Jagged spires of raw, twisted iron stabbed up from the creeks, scratching at the murky sky. There was a hot, heavy quality to the air, foetid and stifling with a dull coppery reek.

The grisly environment was far from deserted. All around him the warrior could see feral, savage figures. Two great packs of barbarous fighters had converged upon a broad lagoon of the semi-metal swamp muck. Hideously mangled bodies floated downstream, their flesh sundered by claw and blade. Some of the bodies were human, though of a brutish and monstrous aspect. Other carcasses were those of horned beasts, their frames covered in matted fur and cabalistic brands. Man or monster, even in death the things carried the stench of cruelty and depravity.

More numerous than the slain were the living: horned creatures armed with axes fashioned from bone and stone and hulking men, their brawny frames draped in skins and scraps of armour. The combatants drew apart, stunned and bewildered by the warrior's sudden appearance.

Beyond the brutish tribes, lumbering through the morass, two colossal horrors of muscle and sinew gave battle to a third monstrosity. The pair had the rough semblance of human form, though swollen and twisted with primordial ferocity. The foe of these monstrous giants was still more hideous. Squat and bloated, the thing was like some mammoth toad. One of the ox-headed giants wrapped its arms about an iron spur, wrenching it from side to side and trying to rip it free. While the creature was engaged, the other giant kept the abomination busy, swatting at it with the uprooted length of a spinefern. Blows that would have pulverized a man struck the toad-thing's side, slamming against its shifting skin, splitting the slimy surface and drawing syrupy blood from the monster.

A mighty shout pierced the air, arresting the battle. The golden warrior could feel the black sorcery that leant the words forcefulness and command. Every creature turned, compelled to attend. Even the warrior felt his eyes drawn to the grotesque sorcerer who marched across the swamp. The mystic was a gangrel figure, draped in a feathered cloak, hands encased in gauntlets of black steel, head locked within a faceless helm of obsidian tipped with spiralling horns.

Another shout came, less forbidding and imperious than the first, and the mystic raised one of its armoured hands. The warrior could feel the fell energies rush out at him. He saw a tangle of leechpines between himself and the sorcerer wilt and crumble. Then the malefic magic was searing across his body. The dire power of the spell dissipated in a crackling nimbus of darkling sparks as it crashed against sigmarite armour. Unharmed, the warrior strode through the arcane residue and pointed his hammer in challenge at the horned enchanter.

Memories rushed through the warrior's mind, images and imperatives that thrust themselves upon him. He had descended upon this realm to confront the Prismatic King, to bring an end to the tyrant's sorceries. Such was his mission, his purpose, the duty stamped upon his very soul. Was this horned magician the fiend he sought?

The sorcerer cried out again, waving its armoured hands in an imperious gesture. Barbarians and beastmen alike responded to that call, roused from their shock by the command. Howling with bloodlust, braying with animalistic savagery, they rallied and surged towards the golden figure.

The warrior didn't wait to meet the charge of his foes. Stretching his wings wide, he soared up into the misty sky to come diving down upon them. He arrowed into the midst of the horde. His warhammer cracked against the breastplate of a barbarian fighter, collapsing the man's chest and tossing his broken body back into his bestial comrades. A goat-headed gor was next, its pelvis splintered by the crushing force of the golden hammer and its neck broken beneath the golden warrior's boot as he trampled it underfoot.

The unearthly figure charged, striking left and right. With every blow, another of the Chaos creatures was struck down, their mangled bodies slipping away in the semi-silver lagoon. A hulking beastlord toppled into the muck with its horned skull split in half. A barbarian chieftain thrashed in the sludge with his side caved in. Packs of snarling gors were smashed aside, gangs of howling marauders beaten into the mire. Scores of the enemy dead lay strewn in his path, yet none had landed a blow. As unstoppable as an avalanche, he thundered through the horde, drawing closer to the horned sorcerer.

The Prismatic King. That title banged through the winged warrior's thoughts as he smashed aside the brutish fighters. To vanquish that tyrant was his cause, yet with every step that took him nearer to the sorcerer, the more his mind made him question. Disconnected memories and images rose up, impressions of shadowy courtyards and mirrored halls, foggy battlements and moats of boiling fire.

A sweep of his warhammer spilled the wreckage of a dozen furred beastmen into the muck. King or minion, it was sufficient for the moment to know that the sorcerer was his foe.

The sorcerer fell back, hurling its magic at the oncoming avenger. Its conjurations, growing rapidly more desperate, pelted against the golden plates of its adversary. Spells that should have melted organs, enchantments that could pulverize stone: these sorceries simply dissipated as they drew near the warrior, fading away like smoke.

The barrage of sorcery swelled into a storm of destruction. Raging clouds of flame immolated packs of marauders as the sorcerer loosed his power against the winged avenger. Crackling spears of black lightning seared through herds of beastmen, yet whatever havoc the magic wrought against incidental victims caught in its path, upon the warrior himself they lost their terrible potency.

A fierce bellow boomed over the lagoon. The golden avenger swung around in time to face the charging one-eyed giant. With a great leap he flung himself into the sky and away from the brute's path, leaving his enemies to be crushed beneath the cyclopean titan's hooves and impaled upon its bovine horns. The great beast turned, stamping and braying in frustration, furious at missing its prey. Angrily, it tore the still writhing bodies of men and monsters from its horns, rending them in its enormous claws.

The warrior hovered in the air above the ox-headed giant. Before he could dive down upon the savage colossus, he was struck from a different quarter. Without warning, a slimy mass coiled about his leg, plucking him from the sky. He could see the obscene bulk of the toad-creature, its tentacle-like tongues lashing about its fanged mouth. One of these noxious appendages had latched onto him, dragging him back into the mire and towards the abomination's maw.

Instead of struggling against the ropy tongue, the warrior propelled himself downwards, diving upon the toad-monster with meteoric fury. The obscenity reared up, its clawed forelimbs raking the air as it tried to swat its winged prey.

Nimbly, the warrior dived between those flailing claws. Uttering a mighty shout, he brought his warhammer crashing against the nearest of the toad-beast's legs. The impact of the golden weapon sent a shudder pulsing through the swamp, causing the spineferns to shiver on their tiny islands and flakes of iron to crumble from the oxidized pillars. The reptilian brute reared back on its grisly hind legs, pawing at the sky with one of its forelimbs while the other quivered as a mess of torn flesh and broken bone.

The warrior scowled at the beast. The hammer should have wrought still greater destruction. He could feel the might of the weapon throbbing through his being, calling to him, urging him to loose its full power against the foe: to visit in truth the vengeance of Sigmar upon the spawn of Chaos.

The warrior raised his weapon to shatter the toad's ribs with a second blow of the warhammer. Instead he was nearly bludgeoned by the monstrous tail of the creature. Arcing over the beast's back, driven by some dull instinct rather than any actual awareness, the mace-like tail struck again and again at the mire, blindly trying to destroy the one who had hurt it. The warrior dodged the first strike, ducked beneath the crushing sweep of the second.

On the third swing of the tail, the warrior met the spiked bludgeon with the divine might of his own weapon. Sacred energies crackled across the hammerhead as he brought it slamming into the tail. A sickening tearing sound, the meaty pop of severed tendons and torn sinew, screamed across the swamp. The toad-thing howled anew as the weapon was ripped free and sent spinning back at the creature, slamming into its side and sinking its spikes deep into the slimy flesh. A fountain of blood sprayed from the broken tail as it whipped through the air in a spasm of pain.

The warrior noticed a tremor ripple through the sludge around him just before the giant came charging back to the attack. This time the brute attacked not with hoof and horn, but with a pair of spineferns it had torn from one of the islands. Wrathfully it brought one club slamming down with enough force to crack a mountain, sending a wide sheet of the silver muck streaming upwards in an uncannily sluggish wave. The second club gouged a crater in the bottom of the lagoon.

Instead of retreating before the giant's assault, the warrior charged forwards. Exploiting the beast's rage, the warrior was in motion the instant the clubs were swinging downwards. While the one-eyed monster obliterated the spot its adversary had occupied a moment before, mighty wings propelled the warrior beneath the massive cudgels. He darted past the giant's assault, taking advantage of its graceless might to attack it.

A deafening howl of torment roared from the giant's jaws as the warrior cracked his great warhammer against the beast's leg. From ankle to knee, the bone was pulverized. The leg collapsed, knee sinking down to slam into the hoof beneath it. Crippled, the giant toppled forwards, slamming face-first in the sludge. It howled again as it pulled its head up out of the muck, streams of silver dripping from its mane and across its eye.

Soaring up into the air, the golden warrior glared at the stricken brute. 'So fall all that bow to Chaos,' he snarled at the toppled giant. Swooping down, he brought the warhammer crashing into the monster's skull, splintering bone and brain. A crimson glaze of blood spilled across the cyclopean eye as the slaughtered beast slumped back into the mire.

A host of bloodreavers and gors advanced upon the warrior. In droves they charged at him, but with each sweep of his hammer, the winged avenger cut them down, hurling broken bodies into the ranks behind, flinging shattered chieftains into the faces of their followers. The silvery sheen of the sludge vanished beneath a patina of gore and still they came, too proud to admit a lone warrior could defeat them, too afraid of their Dark Gods to confess that a lone warrior *had* defeated them.

The warrior's golden halo shimmered above the carnage, a beacon that drew the enraged minions of Chaos to it. A great hunk of jagged iron came hurtling towards that beacon, flung through the air by a titanic force. Taking wing, the warrior flew from the descending missile, leaving dozens of his foes to be crushed beneath it. From his vantage, he could see the second giant stalking away from the severed stump of an iron spur and making towards another of the oxidized pillars.

New determination gripped the warrior. Diving down, he fell upon the gors and bloodreavers once more. The ferocity of his attacks became too great for even them to bear. First by ones and twos, then by the score, his enemies began to flee. They had learned there were other things than the Ruinous Powers that they should hold in fear. Overhead, the celestial storm that had brought the thunderstrike and the golden warrior continued to rage, crashing and crackling with the God-King's wrath.

The last of the routed marauders were obliterated beneath another of the iron pillars, crushed as it came hurtling downwards. Again, the missile failed to smash its intended prey as the winged warrior soared from its path. He had used the giant's ungainly throw, exploiting the beast's brutality to inflict further destruction against the mass of beastmen and bloodreavers. As he gazed upon the smashed bodies, the warrior felt outrage swell within his heart.

To fail in his duty would be a dishonour almost unthinkable, but to be crushed like a crawling insect was too much for his pride to bear. 'The hour of Sigmar is come, beast!' the warrior cried out. 'The hour of your doom is here!'

Flying through the mist, the warrior could see the giant trudging towards another of the iron pillars. Snorting and braying, the brute turned to glare at him with its blemished eye. The beast seized the metal spire, rocking the pillar from side to side, seeking to rip it free as it had done to the others.

'For Sigmar!' the warrior cried as he hurtled down to the attack. His great warhammer didn't crack against the bones of the giant, but instead slammed into the opposite side of the pillar the creature had weakened. A grinding, metallic shriek rose from the spur as it was sundered. Unprepared for the abruptly loosened mass, the giant found the full weight of the pillar crashing down upon it. It was borne down, smashed under tons of metal, its head crushed beneath the iron mass.

The warrior regarded the dead giant with a cold gaze. This was the ignominious end the brute had intended for him. Instead it was the beast that had perished. Surely the hand of Sigmar was visible in such irony.

Turning from the giant, the warrior surveyed the battlefield around him. Amidst the wreckage of beasts, men and monsters, he looked for any sign of the sorcerer who had united them against him. There was no trace of his enemy. Unlike its savage followers, the sorcerer had wit enough to abandon the field ahead of disaster. The winged figure could only hope that the fiend wasn't able to rally other tribes of Chaos to further obstruct him.

The thought made the warrior pause. He could recall little enough, whispers and fragments that stirred through his mind. The Prismatic King, an enemy to overcome. Yet there was more.

He was certain of that. Hints and suggestions tugged at the edge of his consciousness, slipping away whenever he tried to grasp them.

Only one certainty was firm in his mind. That was the nature of the weapon he carried. He'd felt the thrill of the warhammer's power, the awesome potential lurking within it. A sense of abject reverence flowed through him as he reflected upon the great honour that had been entrusted to him. In his hands he held Ghal Maraz itself, the godhammer of Sigmar! He could feel that truth in every mote of his soul, every speck of his essence.

Such then was his purpose. More than warrior or hero, he was Sigmar's champion. The duty entrusted to him was bestowed by the God-King himself.

If only he could remember what that duty was.

CHAPTER TWO

The light was nearly spent before the warrior reached the edge of the swamp. Rising up from the silvery streams and islands of spineferns was scrubland. Clumps of ugly grey bushes with branches like wire and gaudy flowers of turquoise and emerald lay strewn about the plain. Here and there heaps of boulders and mounds of rock lay piled, each stone exhibiting a riotous range of colours in the swirls and whorls that marked them.

The warrior hesitated as he climbed out of the swamp. Carefully he studied the terrain before him. A weird sense of familiarity nagged at him, but nothing that resonated with conviction. Perhaps if his eyes could pierce the cloying mists that swept across the horizon in great undulations, then he might find his way.

Gazing into the dingy sky, the warrior shook his head. The temptation to take wing, to soar above the bleak landscape, was great, but so too was the appreciation of the danger such course would invite. From such a lofty vantage he would see leagues across the scrubland, perhaps even past the veil of mists. But he would likewise be seen by such loathsome things as inhabited the plain.

'Mighty Sigmar, lend me your holy wisdom,' the warrior prayed. 'Guide my steps upon the path you have set for me. Show me the way to fulfil the purpose I have been chosen for.' His hand tightened about the haft of Ghal Maraz, feeling the holy weapon's power rippling through him. The relic was a connection between himself and his god, a compact between servant and master that resonated through the warrior's very being. In battle, the powers of Ghal Maraz had asserted themselves with a primacy that was almost instinctual. He had felt the potential of the godhammer, felt rather than known how to evoke the relic's might. It was a knowledge imprinted not upon his mind, but within his soul itself, something that transcended thought.

The warrior bowed his head in submission. That was the God-King's answer. Not a mighty roar, not an imperious command writ in letters of fire, but a subtlety etched upon the soul. It was left to him to choose whether to submit or resist, to obey or refuse. If he quietened his thoughts, if he let himself feel rather than question, then he would find the way.

'I have faith in you, Great Sigmar,' the warrior declared. 'I will trust you to lead me, for I understand that doubt is the first chink in the armour of righteousness.' The curious impulses and inexplicable certainties that rose within him had yet to deceive him. He had to trust that they would continue to lead him true.

The warrior marched across the misty plain, his stride assuming the mile-eating jog of the soldier on campaign. Past windswept spires of crystal and around deep crevices billowing with strange vapours and stranger energies, he pursued the fading light. A dull luminance behind the shroud of mist, a lessening of the gloom that choked the sky, the unseen sun drew him after it like some celestial lodestone. Only the feathered lizards that crawled upon the rocks and the diamond-winged scavenger-flies that buzzed about the grey bushes attended his passing, skittering away as he drew near.

Darkness settled across the plain, the mist blotting out whatever light might be shining from moon and star. Still the warrior kept on, warier in the gloom, vigilant for observers more malignant than lizards and flies. Three times he had been set upon by the scrubland's monstrous denizens in violent encounters of blood and carnage. The warrior drew no satisfaction from such skirmishes, recognizing them as naught but obstructions between himself and the purpose that drew him on.

Reaching one of the jumbled heaps of stone, the warrior spread his wings and rose into the sky. Keeping close to the jagged mound, he used the crumbling peaks to hide his presence. By staying close to the rocks, however, he exposed himself to unexpected danger. Sudden downdraughts buffeted him, seeking to sweep him into the knife-edged stones. He could see great polypus shapes wedged among the rocks, obscene growths that were at once both fungal and mineral. Like huge bladders, the growths expanded and contracted, sucking in great draughts, drawing nourishment from the air.

The warrior struggled against the pull of the fungal growths. A confusion of currents weakened his resistance. Opposing the draw of one cluster of growths would send him spiralling into the drag of another. His armour rang as it glanced across jagged heaps, sending trickles of broken rocks rumbling down the cliff.

Folding his wings against his back, the warrior caught hold of the rocks. If he couldn't soar above the heap, then he would climb over it. Clawing handholds, he defied the dragging suction of the fungus and pulled himself across the face of the cliff.

As he climbed, the warrior's keen senses caught the patter of dislodged rocks somewhere below him. He lingered, waiting for any new sound that might betray the presence of a pursuer. When none came after several minutes, he pressed on. Whatever was following him might reasonably suspect that the warrior had decided the betraying sounds were mere imagination or some caprice of the wind being drawn down into the fungal growths.

The warrior was content to lull his stalker into such belief. He knew what he'd heard and he knew what it meant. As he descended the other side of the crag, he kept his senses trained on the rise, waiting for anything that would expose the approach of his hunter. For just an instant, from the corner of his eye, he saw the drift of shadow among the rocks, a shape that had started forwards and then furtively withdrawn.

Just as suddenly as the shadow withdrew back into the rocks, a cry of anguish rang out. There was terror and despair in that cry, but there was something more, something that caused the warrior below to spread his wings and dare the dragging currents of the rock-fungus.

The cry had been human.

Reaching a height above the ridge, the warrior's keen gaze pierced the shadows below. He saw a lean figure draped in a wispy cloak of grey languishing upon a plateau. The shape was caught in the grip of a squamous, monstrous thing. It seemed kindred to the fungal growths, yet endowed with a ghastly animation. Great stalks of squirming, fibrous material undulated from the mass, coiling around the cloaked figure in a constricting mesh of tendrils. Inch by inch, the horror's tentacles were drawing its captive towards a slavering maw.

The imprisoned figure struggled to free itself. It gave a wail of frustration and despair.

The warrior didn't delay. Folding his wings at his sides, he powered down towards the tableau in a dive. The might of Ghal

Maraz blazed forth as he brought the relic slamming down against the horror. The obscenity burst apart in a splash of purplish ichor and pulp, its tendrils falling slack as the monster's vitality evaporated.

The figure quickly pulled away, flinging the remains aside in disgust. Beneath the wispy web-like cloak there was a man, lean and lanky, yet with a hardness and firmness that suggested considerable strength and endurance. The face that stared from beneath the threads of his hood was thin and drawn with deepset eyes that shone with the brilliance of gemstones. His expression was one of resignation, of utter despair, uncountable worries etched into the wrinkled brow.

The man looked anxiously at the splattered husk of the horror that had seized him, then focussed upon the armoured visage of his rescuer. Folding his hands across his chest, he prostrated himself. 'Glory to you, noble hero, that you should redeem the life of one so wretched.'

The warrior stared down at the cloaked man, studying him with a penetrating gaze.

'Who are you and why do you follow me?' he demanded.

'Peace mighty master!' the reply came. 'I mean you no ill! No ill at all!'

'Then answer me,' the warrior said. 'To survive in lands such as these you must either have a dangerously cunning mind or powers not apparent to the eye.'

An almost embarrassed look fell upon the man's lean face. 'Mind and powers wouldn't have saved me this day.' He pointed at the splattered husk. 'A moment of incaution is all it needs to draw the attention of the Prismatic King.'

The warrior felt a tremor of hate boil inside him at the mention of the tyrant, the foe he knew he'd come here to vanquish. 'You are an enemy of the Prismatic King?'

'I am Throl of Shaard,' the man said. Despite his fear and the quiver in his voice, there was pride when he spoke the name Shaard.

'Shaard?' the warrior repeated, finding the name strangely familiar.

Throl gestured to the misty scrubland around them. 'All of this was the indomitable nation of Shaard, with its crystal palaces and golden cities. Towers of diamond and ruby that soared up to the heavens themselves. Roads of alabaster upon which were borne the treasures of discovery and the glories of empire.' He shook his head, closing eyes that were suddenly watery. 'Lost now,' he whispered. 'Torn down by the destroyers. All the wonder and all the beauty, all the craft and art crushed beneath the talons of our conquerors.'

The warrior nodded in sympathy. It was a tale that might be heard throughout the realms. Mighty kingdoms and great nations reduced to ash by the coming of Chaos. The despoilers left nothing in their wake, the corruption of the Dark Gods transforming the land itself into an unrecognizable horror.

'I am all that is left of my people now,' the man declared. 'Throl of the Malachite Throne, greatest wizard of the empire. Once potentates and viziers grovelled before me, offering fortunes for my enchantments. My palace was more glorious than the sun – thousands of pilgrims would journey hundreds of leagues simply to gaze upon its splendour before they died. Princesses from a dozen kingdoms attended me...' Throl waved his arms in an expression of helplessness. 'Now I lurk in the swamps among the newts and vipers, living on a diet of rats and snails, hiding from those who are the new masters of the land.'

'You saw the storm?' the warrior asked.

Throl nodded. 'The thunderstrike echoed throughout the swamps of Krahl. To me, its import could not be mistaken. I have seen such warriors before, descending upon Chamon from the realms beyond.'

At mention of others, a memory stirred deep within the warrior's mind. There were others. Yes, others who he had been sent to find. Others who had fought against the Prismatic King.

'You have seen the Thriceblessed?' he asked, giving voice to the name as it emerged from the fog of memory.

'A golden host wrapt in splendour and glory,' Throl said. 'But even they couldn't prevail against the Prismatic King.'

Anger flared within the warrior's heart. His eyes glared from behind his golden mask. 'Yet somehow you have managed to succeed where the Stormcast Eternals have failed?'

Bitter laughter rose from the wizard. 'You call this success?' he scoffed. 'I have magic enough to reflect his power. It is how I have remained as the last echo of my nation, the last shadow of my people. Yet what good does it serve? The Prismatic King's power flows from his Eyrie of Illusion, contaminating the lands of Shaard. Nothing in these lands has been spared the touch of the Soulshriver. He is the lord of this blight. From his stronghold his corruption ebbs and flows like the tides of damnation, polluting all. Only I have remained unchanged.'

Throl pointed his finger at the warhammer. 'My spirit is yet pure enough to recognize the energies that course through that weapon. Merely to gaze upon such a force would pain any creature of the Prismatic King.'

The warrior lifted the hammer high. Even in the misty darkness, there was a gleam of light reflecting from its golden surface.

'Ghal Maraz,' he declared.

'The godhammer of Sigmar.' The words came to the wizard in an awed gasp. 'I had thought the relic lost, vanished into the mists of legend. It is spoken of in the oldest myths of my people, but never did I dare dream the stories to be true.' He turned his eyes from the hammer to the man who bore it. 'Now I understand how a lone warrior could decimate so many of the Prismatic King's creatures. It pains me that I did not see your battle, only the aftermath. I had thought an entire warhost had wrought such havoc upon the enemy. I was confused to find the trail leading only to you. Tell me, who is this great hero who bears the godhammer to the very doorstep of the enemy?'

The question gave the warrior pause. Throl asked him for his name, yet there was none he could give the wizard. Perhaps there wasn't an answer. Perhaps no name had been bestowed upon him. Perhaps it was something he had yet to earn. He looked down at the hammer he bore, at the ancient script etched into the golden metal. Here was all he needed to know. Here was all the identity necessary to him.

'I am the Celestant-Prime,' he declared, sensing the title buried deep within him. He looked at the holy relic in his hand. 'But if you must name me, call me by the name of the weapon I bear. Ghal Maraz.'

'There is power in names,' Throl said. 'Names are things to be guarded, especially in the domain of the Prismatic King. I will call you Ghal Maraz, for there is a name even the lords of Chaos fear to utter.'

'You spoke of seeing my brothers? Others like me?' the Celestant-Prime asked.

'They descended upon Shaard in a rain of lightning,' Throl recalled. 'They were a glorious warhost, so vibrant and strong. The legions of the Prismatic King fell before them like wheat before the scythe. Man, daemon or monster, none could prevail against the golden warriors. Through the storm I could see a great gilded lord holding his hammer aloft in triumph, leading his army forth across my ruined homeland. In their wake they left the wreckage of the Prismatic King's legions strewn about the plain. Such battles they must have fought as they pressed deeper into his blighted domain.'

The wizard sank down upon the ground sadly. The wonder left his voice, replaced by a mournful bitterness. 'I dared to hope my people would finally be avenged, but it was not to be. I followed the path of their march from the swamps of Krahl to the hills of Zehnthi and the gates of the Maze of Reflection. And that is where their journey must have ended, and where my hope died.'

The Celestant-Prime shook his head. 'It is impossible that the Thriceblessed could have been destroyed,' he said.

'There are things worse than death that await the enemies of the Prismatic King,' Throl declared. 'The Maze of Reflection is a trap that has claimed many who would oppose the tyrant. It was raised when he first brought his legions against Shaard. A great treasure is hidden in the maze, something of such power that it could break the Soulshriver's magic. In the early days of his invasion, the knights of Shaard tried to breech the maze and seize the treasure, but none were ever seen again. Mighty wizards and cunning thieves matched their prowess against the maze, but never emerged. Dragons and giants, even rebellious warlords from the Prismatic King's legions, have sought to seize the treasure.' Throl waved his hands in a gesture of futility.

The Celestant-Prime was silent, wondering what manner of fate had claimed the Thriceblessed. If they'd been defeated in battle, then they would have been Reforged in Sigmaron, yet such had not been the case. That meant they were still here, lost within the Prismatic King's maze.

The Celestant-Prime let his hand fall to the Cometstrike Sceptre hanging from his belt, feeling the destructive potential woven within its enchantments, the might to devastate armies. To depose the Prismatic King was his purpose, of that he was certain. He could feel that imperative echoing in his very bones.

Yet to leave his brothers, to leave the Thriceblessed locked within the tyrant's trap for even a moment longer, was something that sickened his spirit. His first duty was to his fellow warriors, to free them from the doom that had claimed them.

'This maze,' the Celestant-Prime said. 'You can lead me to it?'

'To what purpose?' Throl asked. 'That you can join the others in the Prismatic King's trap? There is no defeating him. He is too devious, too cunning to overcome. This land is lost to him.'

The warrior glared down at the wizard. 'Those are the words of a coward.'

'No, they are the words of one who has clung to hope too long,' Throl replied. 'Hope can only cheat a man for so long before he understands that it is naught but a cruel illusion. It is the fool and the dreamer who refuses to abandon hope when it has abandoned him.' He turned his head, staring out into the misty scrubland. 'When I saw the warhost march against the Prismatic King I had hope. Forgive me if I have none left to spare for you, Ghal Maraz.' He thrust his arm towards the south. 'If you would find the Maze of Reflection, seek it there beyond the fires of Uthyr.'

The Celestant-Prime gazed off towards the south. 'A guide would speed my journey,' he said. 'I do not ask you to brave the maze, only to show me the way.'

'That would draw me nearer to the Prismatic King's Eyrie,' Throl said. 'It is a fool who tempts fate too far.'

'What of the debt you owe me?' Ghal Maraz asked. He pointed at the fungal husk. 'Were the men of Shaard a people with honour? Or were they no better than the beasts that have claimed their lands?'

The wizard glowered at the golden warrior. 'You save my life only to throw it away again,' he stated. 'You would march into the heart of the Prismatic King's domain.'

'Is a life spent hiding in swamps and eating snails so precious to you?' the Celestant-Prime wondered.

'A man doesn't choose his life, only the manner of his death,' Throl said.

Ghal Maraz nodded. 'There is wisdom in those words, wizard, but you are too afraid to recognize it.'

Throl stamped his foot against one of the tendrils lying on the plateau, grinding it beneath his heel. 'You would shame me into following you,' he said.

'I need your knowledge of these lands,' the Celestant-Prime told him. 'Shame and dignity are riddles for your own conscience to decide.'

The wizard bowed his head in defeat. 'Very well,' he said. 'I am weary of lurking in the shadows. Whether to doom or glory, I cannot say, but I will lead you to whatever fate has decreed.'

CHAPTER THREE

The bleak scrubland of the plain rose into crystalline hills of chromatic splendour. Eerie nimbuses of light spilled from each facet, forming into broad strands of phantasmal substance, as transient and fragile as cobwebs. Hulking growths, neither tree nor stone but a riotous assemblage of both, thrust their way up through the rainbow webs. Pulpy fruit swayed from the craggy branches of the treestones, dropping to the ground in explosive displays of flame and smoke, gouging deep fissures in the crystal mounds.

Throl was able to steer the Celestant-Prime away from the more dangerous treestones, his magic giving him warning when the explosive fruit was ripe and ready to fall. The vapours that billowed up from the fissures, however, were a hazard that couldn't be predicted. Several times the wizard had been forced to evoke a hasty spell to send the caustic emanations back into the crystalline depths.

'The bloodreavers used to collect the fruit of the treestones,'

Throl explained, 'but the gasses from below made them stop.' He pointed at several curious spurs of crystal scattered about the edges of the fissure. 'Those were men who tarried too long among the vapour. If you draw too near to them, you can still hear their moans.'

The Celestant-Prime shook his head. For expediency he had told Throl to lead him by the most direct route to the Maze of Reflection, but to guide him by such paths as the minions of the Prismatic King were unlikely to frequent. He didn't fear battle with the hordes of Chaos, but he couldn't accept the delay such combat would cause. It was why he continued to march rather than take to the sky and betray his presence.

Yet for all that, the hostility of this corrupted terrain made the Celestant-Prime wonder if the dangers of this course outweighed the potential gain. Throl had led him through canyons of porous bronze inhabited by birds with beaks of ice. They'd trekked through a desert where the sand was iron and the sky a bilious green, with vast slug-like behemoths surging through the desolation to feast upon creeks of molten glass.

The warrior wondered what this region had been like before the Prismatic King focused the corruption of Chaos upon it. The Realm of Chamon and all its many lands were known for strange transmutations, the alloying of substances into something new. How firm had Shaard's grip upon permanence been? How transitory had been the essence of that vanquished empire?

'This domain has no limit to its horrors,' the Celestant-Prime remarked, nodding to one of the crystalline statues, a groan of anguish whispering from its frozen face. 'How dear your thirst for vengeance must be. I pity you, Throl, for your memories of what these lands once were.'

Throl paused, staring out towards the horizon, across the shimmering expanse of hills.

'Memory fades,' he said. 'It retreats into shadow, becoming naught but an echo after a time.' His eyes were solemn as he looked to his companion. 'When it is buried deeply enough, memory becomes confused with imagination.' The wizard pointed his finger at the most distant of the hills. 'Did the vineyards of the Brothers Kaltos stretch there once, or perhaps it was the fastness of the Knights Ebon? Perhaps there was nothing. Maybe what I think to have been never was at all.' He kicked his foot against the crystalline ground, tiny flakes crackling beneath his toes. 'Of what consequence is it to remember? It can't change what is.'

The Celestant-Prime looked at the hills, trying to imagine grapes and castles as Throl described. He pondered his own sense of familiarity with the lands of Shaard.

'No,' he conceded after a time, 'memory may not change things back to what they were. But memory can kindle the flame that avenges what was. If you didn't have your memories of a vanquished people and a vanished home, would you have the courage to guide me? Do not belittle the power of remembering.'

The wizard bowed his head. 'There is wisdom in your words,' he said. 'I will reflect upon what you have said.' Throl tapped the side of his head. 'For now, I fear we must test the limits of memory. Beyond these hills I think we should find the Daemon's Hopyard.'

As he heard the name, the Celestant-Prime felt an inexplicable familiarity. His mind was filled with an image of strange columns of wind-carved rock and great mesas of basalt and onyx. He could almost hear the eerie whistle of winged rock-rats gliding from the cliffs and smell the pungent tang of flowering weeds rising from the loamy earth.

'Something troubles you?' Throl asked, noting the change that had stolen upon his companion.

'Lead me to the Hopyard,' the Celestant-Prime said. 'I might know better then what it is that troubles me.'

With the crystalline hills behind them, the Celestant-Prime found that Throl needn't have worried about the accuracy of his memory. The loamy earth, grey with its gritty, spore-like vegetation, rippled around great black mesas of volcanic rock that loomed hundreds of feet into a greasy sky of shining purple and gibbous silver.

As the Celestant-Prime circled a towering plateau of basalt and onyx, the sense of familiarity became overwhelming. He stared at the side of the mesa, trying to recall the memory. Almost without conscious volition, he strode towards the rocky base. Here the basalt was scorched and burned; there the onyx was disfigured and splintered. He looked down at his feet and saw something lying half-hidden beneath the crumbled rock and grubby spores. Brushing the debris away, he exposed a helm of blackened steel, its mask cast in the semblance of a grinning skull. The helm was cracked, a great gouge snaking from crown to chin.

A battle had been fought here, fierce and terrible. Gazing up at the mesa he could envision tattooed marauders howling as they poured semi-molten boulders down from the heights. He could smell the foul reek of daemonic things as they slithered down the cliffs. He could hear the booming challenge of an armoured warlord in blackened mail and, again, the clamour of conflict.

No. The sounds of battle weren't in his mind. He could hear the crash of steel, the cries of warriors. Amidst the foul shrieks of beasts the Celestant-Prime could hear the shouts of men, voices raised in a cry that sent fire pouring through his veins.

'For Sigmar!' The war cry was repeated, ringing out above the din of battle. Leaving Throl behind, the Celestant-Prime hastened towards the sounds, running around the base of the plateau and on to all the eerie rock hoodoos that peppered the valley beyond.

Among the bizarre stone formations raged a bloody fray. Hundreds of gors armed with crude stone axes and clubs of bone charged up from burrows gouged into the valley floor. The beastmen swarmed around a tight knot of figures with locked shields, foes clad in golden armour who struck at the creatures with sword and hammer.

The Celestant-Prime recognized the cast of their armour and the emblem adorning their pauldrons. These were warriors of the Thriceblessed. For all his despair and bitterness, Throl had been wrong. At least these men had escaped the Maze of Reflection.

'For Sigmar!' the Celestant-Prime roared as he charged into the battle. The first blow from his warhammer sent lightning crackling across the body of a gor he struck, flinging the creature into one of the stone hoodoos and splitting the rock with the ferocity of its impact. More of the monsters turned to confront this sudden attack on their flank. A second strike from the hammer sent a dozen of the beastmen tumbling into the dirt, their bones shattered by the hammer's might.

The Thriceblessed, ringed on every side by the gors, now broke out from behind their shieldwall and flung themselves full into the enemy. The confusion wrought by the Celestant-Prime's sudden assault against their flank was now redoubled as the Stormcasts took to the offensive. Horned brutes broke before crushing blows from sigmarite hammers while others bleated and squirmed upon the blades of swords. Yard by yard, the warriors pushed the beastmen back, strewing the ground with inhuman bodies.

The Celestant-Prime fought with the cold determination of righteousness, smashing enemies at every step as he forced his way towards the Thriceblessed. A blow from his hammer splattered a bull-headed chieftain's body across the rocks. Another strike and a pack of gors was reduced to a pile of carrion. Carnage was the hero's herald, horrible and magnificent. Each yard he pressed into the valley was littered with the mangled carcasses of his foes.

The combined valour of the Celestant-Prime and the resurgent Stormcasts finally broke the savagery of the gors. Whining like whipped curs, the creatures gave up the fight, fleeing back down into their burrows. The Thriceblessed pursued the routed monsters, slaughtering many of them before they could withdraw into the subterranean darkness.

Only when the last of the beasts was gone did the Thriceblessed turn to regard the warrior whose aid had delivered them. They numbered less than a score, their armour scarred and stained with the filth of many ordeals. Liberators with their warhammers and swords, a pair of Judicators with their skybolt bows and a single Retributor with his immense lightning hammer clenched in both hands. The Celestant-Prime could feel the uncertainty as the men approached him.

'Is he real or another trick of the Prismatic King?' one of the Stormcasts asked his comrades, armoured fingers drumming menacingly against the blade of his sword.

Another warrior shook his head. 'No, Othmar, he is real enough. Can't you see he carries the Cometstrike Sceptre? Can you not see Sigmar's hammer!'

'Are you certain, Deucius?' Othmar wondered aloud. 'That could be a trick too.'

The Celestant-Prime held the warhammer towards them, pointing the runeweapon at each man in turn. 'I could doubt you as well,' he said. 'Each of you bears the emblem of the Thriceblessed, yet they have been accounted lost. I have been told the chamber was caught within the Prismatic King's Maze of Reflection. How then is it that you eluded the trap that claimed your brothers?'

Deucius shook his head and pointed at the weapon the Celestant-Prime bore. 'I cannot doubt the God-King's hammer. Only Ghal Maraz could wreak such carnage upon the foe. Only Sigmar's hammer could make me feel such awe. No thing of Chaos, mortal or daemon, could bear the weapon you carry. Only one favoured by Sigmar could do so and only one mighty in his service could evoke the hammer's power.' Deucius bowed to his knees and removed his helm. He stared up at the hero. 'No thing of the enemy can withstand the touch of the godhammer. Let it touch me and you will know I am truly Stormcast.'

Casting his gaze across the other warriors, the Celestant-Prime raised Deucius to his feet. 'It is by faith that men prove themselves,' he said. 'It is through trust that men are made brothers.'

Othmar let his fingers be still. Slowly he too bowed. 'Forgive our doubt, but we have come to question all that our senses tell us.' He glanced at their surroundings, at the strange sky and eerie hoodoos. 'In this place, nothing is what it seems to be. It comes hard to trust anything.'

'It is in doubt that the seed of defeat is sown,' Deucius said. 'A Stormcast Eternal can have no room for doubt. His mind must hold room only for duty and honour. There is no place for doubt in the righteous.' The warriors nodded, reflecting upon the catechism Deucius quoted.

The Celestant-Prime approached Othmar, laying his hand on the warrior's shoulder. 'Hardship can sap even the most stalwart faith. There is no shame in such caution.' He looked across the other Stormcasts. 'For myself, to find brothers in this desolation brings me too much joy to question it. Triumph and glory ring hollow without comrades to share it.'

'We found no triumph and little glory when we challenged the Maze of Reflection,' Deucius declared, lowering his face in contrition. 'Devyndus Thriceblessed led us into the very heart of the enemy. But we were unequal to the test. We failed our Lord-Celestant and we failed great Sigmar.'

'Even in failure there is room for redemption,' the Celestant-Prime said. The words came to his tongue with a sense of humility, a feeling that they came not from himself but from something greater. A conviction that they were meant not only for the Thriceblessed but also for himself.

Deucius met the Celestant-Prime's gaze. There was an almost reverent glow in the Liberator's eyes now. 'The wisdom of the *Deus Sigmar* brings both comfort and challenge.' He turned and darted a triumphant look at Othmar. 'Would a trick of the Prismatic King quote Sigmar's holy scriptures?'

Othmar spread his arms wide in a gesture of submission. 'I have already conceded the field, brother,' he said. Bowing once more to the Celestant-Prime, he apologized to the winged hero. 'You must indulge Deucius. He has enough devotion in him to balance the faults of all the Thriceblessed.'

'If that were true,' Deucius said, 'then we should have conquered the maze and captured the Pillar of Whispers.'

The Celestant-Prime swung around, his eyes locking upon Deucius. 'The Pillar of Whispers?' he hissed, feeling the name resonating within him, blazing through his mind like a ravening firestorm.

'It is the realmgate we were charged to capture,' Othmar said. 'A portal seized by the Prismatic King and hidden within the maze. Lord-Celestant Devyndus believed that by securing the Pillar of Whispers we would sever the Prismatic King's source of power. We could begin to reclaim the lands of Shaard without the threat of new enemy legions being drawn through the realmgate.'

'We never even came within sight of it,' Deucius stated. 'The sorcery of the maze overwhelmed us before we could threaten the enemy's treasure.'

The Celestant-Prime could see the shame and remorse these warriors felt at their failure. It was an illness coiled about their hearts, slowly eating away at their valour, making them less than what they were. Boldly, he raised Ghal Maraz, compelling the eyes of every Stormcast to the relic. 'Here is the key that will unlock the maze,' he declared. 'What sorcery can endure the God-King's hammer?'

Many of the Thriceblessed fell to one knee, seized by their awe of the relic and their belief in its indomitable power. Othmar remained standing however, his tone dour when he spoke. 'I know Ghal Maraz is mighty,' he said. 'But I have also seen the power of the maze. All of us have... except you, my lord.'

'Tell me of the maze,' the Celestant-Prime ordered. 'Tell me of this power that makes you question the might of Sigmar.'

Othmar shook his head. 'It is a thing beyond words. Something past sight and sound and feeling – at once all and none of these things. We marched into a place of nothingness, an emptiness where there was only ourselves. An emptiness that stretched on forever, without limit or end.'

'Othmar found a flaw in the maze,' one of the other warriors declared. 'A crack in the cage of nothingness that held us.'

'Only we few were able to slip free before the crack closed,' Deucius explained. 'But of what consequence has our freedom been? We're too few to assail the Prismatic King's Eyrie and we lack the secrets of the maze to seize the realmgate or rescue our brethren.'

'Then it is well you have found Ghal Maraz.' The Thriceblessed swung around, reaching for their weapons as the voice carried to them. Stalking out from the shadow cast by the plateau was the lean little wizard Throl. The man nodded respectfully to the armoured warriors as he hastened towards the champion.

'Such do I call him, for his is the burden of the godhammer,' Throl boasted. 'If Ghal Maraz cannot break the power of the maze, then there is no force that can!'

The Celestant-Prime gazed down at the little man. 'You took your time joining us.'

Throl plucked at his ragged cloak and slapped his lean legs. 'You might have tarried a bit and given me a chance to catch up. I am hardly so spry as once I was.'

'My lord, who is this man?' Deucius asked.

'Throl of Shaard,' Ghal Maraz answered. 'Last of his people and our ally.'

Throl bobbed his head in agreement. 'My magic is too weak to oppose the Prismatic King, but I have been able to spy upon him. I know the secret paths that lead to the Maze of Reflection, ways hidden from even his most loyal servants.'

Othmar approached the little wizard, towering over the cloaked man.

'And what of the Maze? Do you know its secrets too? Can you lead us through the trap? Can you help us redeem ourselves?' The Liberator shook his head. 'How can this wretch bring victory where the Thriceblessed have found only failure,' he scoffed.

'There is a time for valour and strength and a time for cunning,' the Celestant-Prime reminded Othmar. 'Pride is a poor substitute for strategy.'

'I only want to redeem the shame we have all suffered,' Othmar explained. 'This is a burden that belongs to the Thriceblessed.'

'Your zeal does you credit,' the Celestant-Prime told him, 'but it is presumptuous to think the burden is yours alone. All who oppose Chaos have a stake in the Great Battle.' The winged hero turned back to the wizard. 'You say you know the way to the maze, but what of the Prismatic King's Eyrie?'

Throl took a step backwards, almost tripping over himself in shock at the question. 'You can't mean to attack the Prismatic King's stronghold.'

'It isn't my place to question one chosen to bear the godhammer, but shouldn't we overcome the maze before we take on the Prismatic King?' Othmar asked.

'The maze has been challenged before,' Ghal Maraz declared. 'If courage alone was sufficient to overcome its magic then the Thriceblessed would have prevailed. No, there is a secret behind the maze. None of us here knows that secret, but we know where to find the one who does.'

'The Eyrie of Illumination is guarded by the most infernal of the Prismatic King's legions,' Othmar said. 'When our chamber came here, we knew that only by capturing the realmgate and securing it could we prevail against the Eyrie. If our warhost was insufficient for the task, how can a mere handful triumph?'

'You forget that we have the might of Ghal Maraz now,' Deucius declared. 'What army can stand against the power of the godhammer?'

'It isn't necessary to capture the Eyrie,' the Celestant-Prime explained. 'For that, we would need the strength of numbers. But our purpose isn't to seize the fortress, only to find its master. To that end, a small group is better. Let the Prismatic King underestimate his peril, let him believe we are naught but a nuisance to be swatted aside. He will hesitate to commit his legions if he believes they are unnecessary.' The hero turned from the Stormcasts and again regarded the cloaked wizard. 'Do you know a way into the Eyrie?'

Throl smiled. 'The Prismatic King moves his Eyrie whenever it suits him. Sometimes it is in the plains, sometimes the mountains. But always it must return to the fields of Uthyr where he first raised it from the fire. At dawn and dusk, the inbetween times when the borders of existence are at their thinnest, that is when the stronghold must return to its foundations.'

'Then guide us to the fields of Uthyr,' the Celestant-Prime told the wizard. 'Do this, Throl, and know that you will have done your part to avenge your people.'

CHAPTER FOUR

The fields of Uthyr could be felt long before they were seen. Their stifling heat spilled across the domain like a blast of dragonfire. Only the hardiest of creatures braved the desolation surrounding the region: steely weeds that nestled in the shelter of rocks and ugly lice-like bugs that burrowed beneath the hot sands.

The Thriceblessed marched across this blighted expanse, their armoured boots digging deep furrows in the parched land. Throl trotted along behind the warriors, pausing every now and again to renew the spells that enabled him to endure the ghastly heat.

'Does it never rain in this hell?' Othmar growled, fingers twitching on his sword.

Throl chuckled darkly. 'None that would quench your thirst,' he said. 'The storms of Uthyr are things of boiling lead and ash. If you want water, we must stray far from our course.'

Othmar turned to glower at the wizard. 'If you can endure, then so can I,' he declared.

The wizard smiled at Othmar. 'If I told you that the clouds

you see on the horizon are simply fumes rising from the flames of Uthyr, would that cheer you?'

Othmar looked at the black expanse stretching across the sky. 'Not particularly,' he grumbled as he pressed on.

Deucius shook his head and waved his hand at the smoke. 'It seems the worst is yet to come. It is hard to imagine a blaze that could create such smoke.'

'The fires of Uthyr have been burning since the founding of Shaard,' Throl said, his eyes gleaming with the memory of his vanished nation. 'Even the Prismatic King could do little to tame this part of his domain.'

The Celestant-Prime laid his hand reverently against the head of Ghal Maraz. 'The sorcerer may have failed to overcome this land, but the power of the God-King will overcome him. He will atone for his evils and confess his secrets. With the threat of Ghal Maraz before him, even a sorcerer might reveal the truth.'

A scowl formed on Throl's face. 'So long as he doesn't confess his secrets too easily,' he grumbled. 'It has been a long walk from the swamp to be cheated of watching the Prismatic King suffer.'

Against all hope, the heat grew worse when the Stormcasts reached Uthyr itself. Each breath they drew felt as though it must sear their lungs. A mortal warrior would have cooked within his armour before he could begin the climb out from the sandy waste and onto the fields. A lesser metal than sigmarite would have become blisteringly hot from the mephitic atmosphere that surrounded them.

The fields of Uthyr were a scorched morass of cinder and ash, gutted and scarred by streams of molten lead and boiling copper. Geysers of volcanic fumes exploded from yawning pits, dancing in fiery gyrations as they billowed upwards. Great pinnacles of pumice, their faces carved into the tormented shapes of the damned, thrust themselves up from the hellish terrain, piercing the smothering miasma of smoke.

Thrusting its way through the fire and slag, supported upon ethereal peaks of shimmering heat, was a great tunnel of volcanic glass. Rippling with strange colours, exuding weird harmonics that wailed across the bubbling din of the fields around them, the glassy channel cut across the fiery terrain. The shifting intensity of the heat that supported it caused the tunnel to pitch and roll, undulating like some vast serpent.

'There,' Throl declared, pointing into the tunnel. 'That is the foundation upon which the Prismatic King raised his Eyrie. That is the place to which his fortress must return!'

The Celestant-Prime gazed into the cavernous passage. Navigating it seemed impossible, an insurmountable obstacle. Yet he remained undaunted. The Prismatic King held the key to both the realmgate and the missing Thriceblessed. Whatever obstacles the lands of Shaard put in his way, he would achieve Sigmar's purpose and confront the disciple of Tzeentch.

'Then that is where our path leads us,' the Celestant-Prime declared. He cast his gaze across the Stormcasts. 'Have courage, brothers. However arduous the task, know that if it is Sigmar's will that we succeed, then only our own lack of faith can bring us to ruin.'

Deucius bowed his head. 'By the grace of the God-King, let none of us be found unworthy,' he said.

'Can we be certain that the Eyrie will appear where the wizard claims it will?' Othmar asked. 'It is only by his word that…'

'His word has led us this far,' the Celestant-Prime reminded him. 'It is late to doubt him now.' As he spoke, he turned and nodded to Throl. At every step, the wizard's advice had *felt* right in a manner more compelling than conventional logic or wisdom. In a way he couldn't explain, he knew they weren't being led astray. Perhaps it was the wizard's fierce desire for revenge, perhaps it was the hand of Sigmar upon the Stormcast's soul, perhaps it was something deeper buried within his very essence: he couldn't say – all that he was certain of was that when the dusk came, they would find the Eyrie standing just where Throl had promised them it would appear.

'No mean feat,' Othmar declared, fingers tapping. 'A tunnel of black glass floating in a sea of flame.'

'A simple task for those with a small and simple faith,' Deucius said. 'Cast aside your worry, brother, and rejoice that Sigmar has deemed us worthy of such a trial.'

The Celestant-Prime strode out onto the fields, feeling the burning rock searing at his sigmarite boots. 'Rejoice when we are through the tunnel and the Eyrie stands before us,' he advised.

The Stormcasts followed him out across the scorched crust of Uthyr. The burning rock splintered and cracked beneath their armoured weight, fraying and splitting with every step they took. At times ugly holes would appear, vomiting toxic vapours in a spray of steam. Once a great fissure opened as Deucius advanced across the field, nearly swallowing the warrior as the surface crumbled away. The Celestant-Prime flew to the Liberator's side and pulled the imperilled warrior back from the edge, hurling him back with a display of his prodigious strength. The champion stared down at the roiling river of glowing magma that yawned below, appreciating how utterly the molten fire would have consumed his comrade.

'The ground is too treacherous,' Othmar cursed. 'We will never reach the tunnel.'

Throl hurried towards the Celestant-Prime. Lacking the armour and superhuman vitality of the Stormcasts, the wizard depended upon his magic to guard him from the hostility of Uthyr. As he sprinted across the blackened ground, patches of rock disintegrated under even his comparatively light tread. 'My spells can show you the way!' Throl shouted to the hero.

'Then use your magic!' Deucius ordered the man.

Throl shook his head. 'It isn't so simple,' he warned. Shifting his gaze back to the Celestant-Prime, he hurried to explain. 'Only my magic protects me from the fire and heat. If I turn my mind to a new conjuration, I will lose my focus. The spells that protect me will dissipate.'

The Celestant-Prime nodded towards the magma flowing at the bottom of the fissure. 'Without a safe path, many of us may be lost before we gain the stair. It may be that Sigmar has sent you to us to overcome this obstacle.' He looked across the flames at the sinister tunnel. It seemed as distant as when they had first set out across the fields. 'If one of us were to carry you, would you be able to turn your mind to the magic that will show us a safe path?'

The wizard scratched at his chin. His gem-like eyes blazed as he considered the Celestant-Prime's words. 'Maybe the God-King did allow our paths to cross,' he mused. 'Maybe it is fate that has cast us together. Yes, I think if you were to carry me across I could focus my energies on exposing a safe path through the fields.'

Deucius came between Throl and Ghal Maraz. 'You are the bearer of the godhammer,' he told the Celestant-Prime. 'It is unseemly that you should be asked to carry the wizard alongside the holiest of holies. Let me carry Throl across the fields.'

The Celestant-Prime let his hand brush across the golden head of his hammer, feeling its sacred power crackle under his fingers.

'It will be as you say, Deucius,' the hero decided. He fixed his eyes on Throl. 'Begin your conjurations, wizard. We must be through the passage before twilight.'

Deucius reached down and lifted Throl from the rocks. As

soon as his feet were clear of the burning ground, Throl closed his eyes and began to murmur to himself, strange incantations whispering across his lips. The Celestant-Prime could see tendrils of aethyric energy being drawn into the wizard's body, dancing and writhing about him in ropy coils of light. At the same time, he could see luminous patches blaze into life all across the fields.

'Where the light shines the ground is firm,' Throl spat the words in a hurried gasp, then quickly resumed his incantation.

The Celestant-Prime raised the godhammer overhead, fixing the attention of every Stormcast upon him. 'Follow the light. Make for the shining ground and keep to its path.'

Balancing haste against caution, the Thriceblessed picked their way across the fields of Uthyr. Stretches of blackened earth separated the patches of safe ground revealed by Throl's magic. Here the rock splintered and crumbled beneath the warriors, threatening them with immolation as jets of hot gas spewed up from the ground or pits of magma were exposed. Despite the promise of an excruciating death, the men pressed on, moving from one expanse of stable ground to the next.

CHAPTER FIVE

At last the tunnel of volcanic glass came within reach. Othmar was the first to gain the eerie passage, climbing into the blackened corridor, feeling the heat of the glass billowing around him. Deucius was among the last. As the Stormcasts neared the entrance, he caught hold of Throl and flung the wizard into the arms of the Stormcast who had already entered the corridor. Then Deucius lunged at the undulating mouth of the passage, his hands sliding on the smooth glass as he fought to gain a grip on the edge of the opening. Before he could drop away, his comrades reached down and caught hold of him, dragging him back from the edge of oblivion.

The Celestant-Prime braced himself as he saw the tunnel dipping along the surface of the fiery pits. Holding back to aid any of the Stormcasts, the champion found himself the last remaining on the scorched field. The ground around him was splintering and cracking, sloughing away in a widening crater. Tongues of volcanic fury blasted upwards, searing the air with their fiery rage. What had been a patch of illuminated ground lost its enchantment, fading to the same charred hue as the rest of the fields. The meaning was clear: this ground was no longer safe and so Throl's magic no longer shone upon it.

Feeling the earth beneath him trembling, the Celestant-Prime knew he couldn't wait for the tunnel to rise back to a more advantageous position. Mustering all the strength in his mighty frame, the hero dived for the sinking passage, mighty wings propelling him into the yawning mouth as it skirted the surface of the flaming sea. The Celestant-Prime's body hurtled through the narrow gap between tunnel and sea, fire licking about him as the thermal current smashed his body against the glassy roof of the corridor. Shards of glass from the fractured roof clattered around him as he fell to the scorching floor below. Almost at once, Deucius was beside him, helping the Celestant-Prime back to his feet.

'As you said, my lord,' Deucius stated. 'We have come too far to falter now.'

'With farther yet to go,' the Celestant-Prime observed. Before them, the tunnel stretched away, writhing and whipping about in mad gyrations. The floor was broken, split into great slab-like sections with menacing gaps between them that opened into the molten sea beneath. What magic kept the fire from bubbling up through the openings, he didn't know, but whatever its nature he was grateful for it. Gaps in the roof overhead let a patina of ash rain down from the smoky sky above.

'The land itself fights us,' Othmar cursed, wiping his gauntlet across the face of his helm to clear the scum of soot that was already gathering there.

'The Prismatic King guesses your purpose,' Throl said. 'He unleashes the elements to defy you. He seeks to break your spirit and cast you down in defeat.'

The Celestant-Prime tightened his hold upon the godhammer, feeling the power pulsing within the weapon. 'What better proof that the enemy fears us than these sorcerer's tricks? He thinks he can break us with his magic, believes he can overwhelm us with his spells. He can't understand our strength or imagine the fastness of our faith. He denies the power of Sigmar and the conviction of those who serve the God-King!'

The Stormcasts echoed the passion of their Celestant-Prime in a mighty shout, howling the name of Sigmar down the grim tunnel, defying the elements raging all about them. Boldly they followed the champion's lead as he charged down the passage and hurled himself across the first gap in the floor. With a sea of fire blazing up at them, the warriors leapt across the gap, slamming down onto the undulating surface of the slab beyond.

As soon as the Stormcasts had crossed one gap they were running towards the next. They didn't hesitate as the slab began to pitch, making their footing treacherous. They ignored the threat of disaster, the promise of burning death that awaited them below. For them there was only the objective ahead. Where the Celestant-Prime led, they would follow.

Throl matched the tremendous pace set by the mighty Stormcasts, the wizard's lean body crackling with the magics he wove around himself to meet the demands of Sigmar's chosen. Despite the taxing effort, he maintained the pace, confronting each hazard with the same fortitude as the warriors of Azyr. Only when they had leapt across the eighth gap in the floor did Throl hesitate. Throwing his arms wide, the wizard gave voice to a jubilant cry.

'The ninth breach!' he shouted. 'Behold, the Eyrie manifests itself beyond the ninth breach!'

The roof of the tunnel and the smoky sky of Uthyr made it impossible to judge the disposition of the sun. Twilight, it seemed, had stolen upon the land without warning. As the wizard cried out to them, the Stormcasts stared at the far end of the tunnel. There they saw a deepening and thickening of the darkness that hovered above the fires of Uthyr. With each heartbeat, the blackness became a bit more solid, losing more of its nebulous appearance. Before their eyes, the Prismatic King's palace was drawing shape and substance to itself.

The Eyrie of Illusion was built not from brick and stone, but seemed woven from shadows and echoes. It was a great pinnacle of darkness that drew all light into itself, making it stand stark and abominable against Uthyr's fiery sea. Polished panels of darkling glass glimmered amidst the tower's nebulous walls, pulsating with weird reflections and uncanny echoes. Twisted spires contorted away from the main bulk of the fortress, thrusting out in every direction like the thorns of some fecund growth. They would fade and distort even as the eye tried to fix them upon the map of memory, in one instant extending outwards a hundred feet and more, while in the next dissipating down to a mere nub protruding from the black walls.

The Celestant-Prime looked upon the Eyrie and felt his flesh crawl. It wasn't fear that unsettled him, it was revulsion, the innate repugnance experienced by any mortal creature when faced with the infernal manifestations of powers profane and damned. It was a blight against the very concepts of reason and order – madness endowed with the most tenuous suggestions of shape and form, the most fleeting mockery of existence and substance. Only the most depraved and degenerate of Tzeentch's minions could suffer such a blasphemy to be his abode, and only the bravest, most steadfast of men would dare to confront such a fiend within his obscene lair.

'Thriceblessed!' the Celestant-Prime cried out to the Stormcasts, raising the godhammer high, so that all his comrades might see the holy weapon and be bolstered by the relic's sacred presence. 'The enemy is before us. He thinks himself safe within his castle of nightmares. Now let us show him that from the Stormcasts, no pawn of Chaos can ever count himself safe.'

The Celestant-Prime rushed to the edge of the gap and flew across the span to the slab where the Eyrie had appeared. He drifted across the gulf and onto the narrow lip between the shadowy walls and the edge of the floating island. As soon as his feet touched the ground he was moving, circling around the fortress to make room for the warriors following him.

A piercing shriek shuddered through the cavernous tunnel, pulsing outwards from the very walls of the Eyrie. Ghoulish lights throbbed from deep within the fortress, glowing behind the veil of shadows. The Stormcasts locked their shields, Judicators taking position behind the defences of the Liberators, ready to loose their skybolts into whatever foe responded to the alarm.

'Guard yourselves, brothers,' the Celestant-Prime told the Stormcasts.

As he spoke, he saw shapes forming within the walls. The glowing lights were rising through the shadows, growing more distinct with each passing breath. It was like watching a swarm of kraken rising from the depths of a black sea, their outlines slowly taking form as they drew nearer the surface. At last the glowing forms began to bleed out from the walls themselves, a kaleidoscope of pulsing lights and undulating sounds. The defenders of the Eyrie had emerged to defy the Stormcasts, sallying from the fortress without either gate or door to mark their passage.

The creatures scuttled out from the walls: loathsome assemblages of madness, discordant fusions of flesh and bone, insane alchemies of claws and tentacles. Some were squat monstrosities with gaping maws and snapping beaks, ropey arms with clawed hands protruding from their bodies without pattern or symmetry. Others were boiling stumps of obscene flesh supported upon a single broad foot festooned with fang-like growths, the arms that grew from their wiry shoulders ending in mouth-like paws that drooled smoke and eldritch fire. Above these gabbling atrocities, sleek long-tailed beings soared into the smoky air, their bodies rippling with wordless screams and coronas of gibbous light.

'Faith is my valour,' Deucius snarled as he swung his hammer into the leering visage of a creature clawing its way out of the wall beside him. The pink-skinned abomination split apart under his blow, bursting in an incandescent display of flickering lights and crackling energy. The shattered energies coalesced into two smaller manifestations, blue obscenities that giggled to themselves as they surged towards the Stormcasts.

'Thriceblessed of Sigmar, do not falter!' the Celestant-Prime shouted to his comrades. He swung the godhammer in a murderous sweep, pitching a clutch of fanged daemons down into the gap. Their splitting shapes dwindled as they plummeted into the fires of Uthyr raging below.

A blast of aethyric fury seared past the champion's shoulder, immolating one of the screaming fliers as it dived towards the Celestant-Prime's back. Caught in the magical flame, the airborne daemon became frayed and tattered, dissipating in puffs of colour and sound. The warrior glanced aside, and saw Throl crouched between two of the Stormcasts, his fingers still aglow with the magic he was unleashing against the Eyrie's defenders.

'There are too many of them,' Throl cried. 'We cannot hope to prevail.' The wizard spun around, a cascade of blazing light leaping from his palm to annihilate a clutch of daemons pushing themselves out from the shadowy walls.

The Celestant-Prime brought his hammer slamming down

against the slab itself, cracking a piece of the ledge and sending it hurtling into the cauldron below, a score of daemons carried down with it to fiery oblivion.

'Where there is faith, there is always hope,' he told the wizard. As he spoke, a crackling daemon bounded towards him upon its stalk-like body, blue flames billowing out from the mouths at the ends of its pulpy arms. The Celestant-Prime stood within the fiery blast, the hammer held before his body.

In the next instant, the daemonic flames dissipated, broken apart before the holy power of the godhammer. The weapon crackled with energy as he held it before him, unharmed. The spirits of the watching Stormcasts soared as they saw the hero advance upon the daemon. With a single blow of his weapon, the Celestant-Prime burst the fiend into a spray of flickering cinders and wailing steam.

Inspired, the Thriceblessed pressed their attack, shields locked in an impenetrable formation as they advanced upon the reeling daemons. The great hammer of the Retributor swatted capering fiends from the slab down into the fiery sea. Arrows from the Judicators felled soaring abominations. And all the while the hammers and swords of the Liberators took a toll on the creatures spilling from the Eyrie's walls.

'Faith is the armour no daemon can pierce!' the Celestant-Prime thundered as he strode across the ashy residue of his vanquished foe. A flock of the airborne monstrosities swooped down upon him, their ray-like bodies slithering through the blizzard of soot falling from the clouds. The daemons shrieked and wailed as they drew near the hero, the gash-like mouths that yawned across the bottom of their bodies gnashing their fangs in greedy anticipation of rending his flesh.

Before the daemons could strike, the Celestant-Prime swung the godhammer at them in a nimbus of crackling energy.

Somewhere deep within the recesses of his soul, he understood how to evoke the relic's awesome might. As the flyers descended, the energies billowing out from the godhammer rose to meet them. The hungry wails of the monsters became anguished howls as their profane substance struck the wave of holy power. The daemons wilted in the purity of Ghal Maraz's aura, shrivelling like slugs under a hot sun. The withered, desiccated things fell from the air, the residue of their wing-like lobes fluttering uselessly as they sank into the fires of Uthyr.

Around him, the Celestant-Prime could see the other Stormcasts fending off the daemonic host, knocking squealing horrors into the gap or skewering flame-spitting blasphemies on their swords. Othmar struck down a beak-faced creature, splitting its skull with his sword, splattering the walls of the Eyrie with its ichor. Deucius struggled in the clasp of a ray-winged beast, his hands pushing against the edge of its fanged maw to keep it from snapping at his face. Before the daemon could prevail, a bolt of magic from Throl pierced its side and sent it floundering into the fires below.

The Celestant-Prime scowled within his helm as he saw more daemons pushing out from the walls of the Eyrie. They could stand here and fight the fiends forever, but doing so wouldn't get them inside the fortress. There could be no confrontation with the Prismatic King while the Stormcasts were kept fighting on the palace's threshold. How long would it be before the moment passed and the Eyrie was free to slip clean of its temporal foundations?

He couldn't risk such potential disaster. Firming his grip upon the hammer, he brought the weapon crashing against the shadowy wall of the Eyrie. If the Prismatic King didn't see fit to offer a door into his fortress then he would make his own.

A dolorous boom sounded as the godhammer struck the

skein of shadow. Lances of light streamed away from the hammer, crackling through the ebon substance of the Eyrie. When the Celestant-Prime drew his weapon back, tendrils of shadow clung to it, dripping from the golden metal like rivulets of black blood. Where he had struck the wall, he could see that the web of darkness was fractured.

'For Sigmar!' the Celestant-Prime cried as he brought the weapon slamming against the already weakened section of wall. This time, when the godhammer's blazing aura struck the shadows it did far more than simply crack them. The phantom material disintegrated, evaporating in black tatters of ash. Where it had been, an opening was exposed, a gaping wound in the side of the Eyrie.

'Stormbrothers! With me!' the Celestant-Prime shouted to his fellow warriors, charging through the fissure he'd opened. Ahead all he could see was a grey dinginess, like a cloud of dust. The foggy greyness clung to him as he rushed into the breech. Then he was through, past the walls of the fortress and inside the palace proper.

What he saw was a deranged confusion of angles and distorted perspectives, stairways of marble that folded in upon themselves or merged with alabaster ceilings or flowed both into and out of topaz floors. Corners were at once convex and concave, defying the senses with the insanity of their violations. Crystal fountains bubbled from the roof, the chromatic liquid flowing from them arcing about in gravity-defying spectacles that mocked every effort to define them.

The Celestant-Prime forced himself to confine his focus to only that which was immediately before him. Something inside him warned that if he tried to contemplate the infernal manipulations of the palace's confines then the barrage against his senses would break his mind. Only by restraining his awareness could he defy the discordant architecture of the Eyrie and the transforming sorceries of the Prismatic King.

'By the thunder of Azyr!' Deucius gasped as the warrior joined the Celestant-Prime within the mad hall. As each of the Thriceblessed pressed through the breech in the wall, he felt a similar sensation of wonder and revulsion.

'Do not marvel at the Prismatic King's illusions,' the Celestant-Prime cautioned them. 'Focus upon what is near and tangible. Fix your mind upon what you feel and not what you see.'

'Listen to the wisdom of Ghal Maraz!' Throl echoed the hero. 'If you allow your attention to wander, if you lose your focus, then your mind will abandon itself to the Prismatic King's coils!' The lean wizard looked towards the Celestant-Prime. 'My magic can protect against the worst of his illusions but I worry that any spells I cast here may be corrupted by the sorcerer. To my cost I have learned how much greater his power is than mine.'

'We will protect you, enchanter,' the Celestant-Prime promised.

'Whatever we do, let it be done swiftly!' Deucius cried out. He pointed towards the crazed array of stairways and corridors that opened into the maddening hall. Every passage was swarming with enemies, mortal warriors in grisly armour of bone and chain rushing alongside gibbering daemons and horned beastmen. The Eyrie's garrison was answering the intrusion of the Stormcasts into their master's domain. Lost to the Prismatic King's insanity already, the monstrous horde was accustomed to navigating the chaotic discord of his halls.

Throl closed his eyes, clapping his hands together as he drew upon his own magic. Eldritch energies flashed from his fingers, snaking around his body before stretching outwards.

'Pursue the light,' the wizard hissed through clenched teeth. 'The Prismatic King seeks to usurp my spell. I know not how long I can fend off his sorcery.'

The Celestant-Prime led the Thriceblessed in pursuit of Throl's guiding light. They rushed past gaping doorways that opened into nothingness, hurtled down stairways that descended into the ceiling and dashed around corners that bled back into themselves, racing against the malignity of the sorcerous tower. At every turn, bands of Chaos warriors and packs of shrieking daemons assailed them, seeking to drag them down with blades of steel and talons of iron.

Before them, the hall opened into a great gallery, the walls fashioned from bizarre panels of stained glass, each pane emitting a kaleidoscope of light. Strange scenes unfolded along the translucent walls, frozen images of obscene sorceries and magical atrocities, portraits of maniacs and monsters, each more wicked and obscene that the last.

Billowing up from the centre of the gallery, spreading like a skeletal tree, was a wide stair fashioned from shimmering hoarfrost. Branches of the stair stretched into the glass walls, vanishing through the images locked upon the panes. Other limbs of the stair connected with the raised arcade that ringed the hall, widening into broad platforms of mist and ice. From these platforms and down the arctic branches charged a snarling horde of Chaos knights, their foul armour stained with cabalistic sigils and arcane emblems. The weapons each knight bore were things of fell sorcery and vile ritual – great axes of brass and silver that shrieked as though endowed with monstrous vitality of their own, hideous swords, their blades coruscating with eldritch flames, spears of iron and bone that pulsated with the discordant harmonies of unchained ether, and flails that writhed with the infernal essence of the daemons bound within their steel.

The Stormcasts met the charge of the Chaos knights, and Ghal Maraz tore a path through the armoured fiends. The Celestant-Prime loosed the sacred fury of the godhammer against the degenerate men, shattering their armoured bodies with each blow. By the score he reaped a butcher's toll upon the vassals of the Prismatic King, strewing the gallery with their broken bodies. Yet for each knight he brought down, a dozen more appeared to take their place.

The Thriceblessed locked their shields, letting the charging knights break against them in a wave of rage. Swords stabbed out from between shields to gut the warriors who strove to batter their way past. Skybolts sizzled into the howling guards, piercing corrupt mail to gouge the abominable flesh within. Safe behind their defending brethren, the Judicators were able to measure each shot, loosing only when certain of a killing strike. From the shadow of the Stormcasts, Throl worked his magic, unleashing fingers of flame that licked across the oncoming knights and left their armour scorched and smoking.

The Prismatic King's slaves, however, took their own toll upon the Stormcasts. First the lone Retributor was pulled down, his knee shattered by the impact of a spiked mace, his head crushed beneath the halberd of a horned warrior. Then the Liberator beside Othmar was felled by a spear through his gorget, blood spilling from the mask of his helm as he coughed out his life.

Lightning rumbled through the great gallery as one by one the Thriceblessed were killed by the enraged knights. As life ebbed from the body of each Stormcast, flesh and spirit evaporated in a blast of coruscating brilliance, hurled back through the vastness of space to return to the realm of Azyr and the golden halls of Sigmaron.

Death might not be the end for the Stormcasts, destined to be reforged anew, but the loss of so many comrades pained the Celestant-Prime. They were now only ten. Each fighter lost raised the odds against them all and made the task ahead of them that much greater.

Leaping upwards, powering into the gallery's frosty air on his shimmering wings, the Celestant-Prime drove down upon the stairway. Raising the Cometstrike Sceptre, he unleashed the magic bound within the relic. The head of the sceptre blazed with dazzling energies, a spike of divine power streaking upwards, piercing the profane vaults of the Eyrie. An instant passed, and then the ribbon of holy energy was hurtling down once more, bearing a fiery sphere. A sweep of the sceptre and the Celestant-Prime unleashed the imprisoned comet. His target wasn't the horde of Chaos knights spilling down into the hall – with a thunderous shriek the comet slammed into the stairway. Branches cracked and split, sending howling knights crashing to the floor below. The main trunk of the stair shivered, sagging to one side then another, guards clinging to the swaying balustrades as they lost their footing.

The Stormcasts were quick to exploit the opportunity the Celestant-Prime's attack presented. Breaking their formation, the golden warriors rushed forwards, striking down the stunned knights writhing on the floor, attacking the Chaos warriors who continued to slip free from the swaying trunk. A blow of the godhammer and the stair came crashing down in an avalanche of frost and flailing bodies. The knights caught in the collapse screamed in agony as they were crushed.

The Thriceblessed drew away from the mound of glowing debris, listening to the anguished cries of those being consumed within the frozen heap. The Celestant-Prime swooped along the overlooking platforms, driving back those knights who yet lingered above the gallery.

The mound of frost began to boil, rivulets streaming upwards to reshape themselves in new patterns. The Thriceblessed turned from their extermination of the crippled knights, circling around the shifting frost. The same thought was in each of their minds, the fear that the stair would regenerate and bring fresh waves of knights surging down upon them. The prospect of battle wasn't daunting – it was the worry of failure, the shame lest they should never reach the Prismatic King and wrest from him his dark secrets.

Striking down a clutch of Chaos knights ranged along the platform, the Celestant-Prime turned and started down towards the bubbling geyser of frost. He had smashed the stair once already. To hold the gallery against the Prismatic King's guards, he would do so again.

'Wait, my lord!' Deucius cried out as he saw the Celestant-Prime diving towards the resurgent frost. The Liberator waved his hammer in warning, imploring him to keep back.

The Celestant-Prime noticed what Deucius had seen just as he was raising Ghal Maraz to smash the skein of glowing ice. He pulled out from his dive, swinging away as he gazed in surprise at the billowing mass of frost. What was growing out from the mound wasn't the stairway, but rather had the shape of an enormous door, a mammoth gate of icy spikes. Around the portal burned the magic light of Throl's spell, the shimmer that revealed the path to the Prismatic King.

As the Celestant-Prime flew above the gate, the massive door began to shake and shudder. Folding upon itself, without any manner of substance or solidity behind it, the door swung open to reveal a murky chamber beyond, a room utterly different from the kaleidoscopic gallery.

Before any of the Stormcasts could draw near the uncanny phenomenon, something vast and monstrous erupted from the murk beyond the door. It was a gigantic, brutish horror, a thing of purple scales and leathery blue flesh, black chitinous plates and scarlet membranes that fluttered angrily in the arctic chill. The thing's shape was not unlike that of some gargantuan ape, squat, powerful legs supporting it from behind while great clawed arms dragged its ghastly mass forwards. Twin tails lashed the air behind it, each ending in a slavering mouth filled with dripping fangs. Between its broad shoulders, instead of a head, a far greater maw stretched wide, a scourge of oily tentacles slobbering past its knifelike fangs. A grotesque star-shaped growth bulged from the abomination's back, a baleful flame blazing at its centre, pulsating with arcane energies. Fingers of sorcerous fire seeped out from between the monster's scales, crawling up its hideous bulk to merge with the conflagration at the core of the star.

'The Prismatic King's hound!' Throl wailed. 'Its very touch is annihilation!'

As though to prove the wizard's words, the hulking beast sprang forwards, its great claw snatching one of the Judicators before the archer could loose an arrow. The golden armour sizzled beneath the thing's touch. There was a cracking groan, and the sigmarite mail began to disintegrate, trickling through the horror's claws in a stream of dust. The other Thriceblessed charged forwards to rescue their stricken comrade, striking at the beast with sword and hammer while the arcane lightning of Throl's wizardry crackled across its hideous frame.

The efforts of warriors and wizard alike were hopeless. The slavering monstrosity ignored their assault, instead lashing out with its tails to catch a second Stormcast. The monster started to raise its second victim towards its dripping tentacles when a fierce cry from above caused it to rear back in surprise. Even its maddened bestial brain recognized the might behind that shout and the challenge it proclaimed.

The Celestant-Prime hurtled down upon the huge beast. A blow from the godhammer and one of the ape-like arms was shattered. His blazing hammer crushed the grisly mess of tentacles and fangs between the brute's shoulders. Swinging the hammer on high, he brought it cracking around once more, shattering the weird star-like growth and causing the bubbling mass of arcane fire and eldritch energy at its core to cascade down into the beast's own body. The gigantic creature howled in agony as the vortex consumed it, immolating its mutated frame from the inside.

The Celestant-Prime tore the whip-like tendril from the embattled Stormcast the brute had seized. The first to be caught by the beast was gone, but he lifted the second warrior into the air, bearing him back across the floor to their comrades. Landing beside the Thriceblessed, he watched as the vortex dissolved the Prismatic King's nightmarish pet.

'So dies the hound. Now we go and find its master,' Othmar vowed as the last of the beast was consumed.

Throl pointed to the now undefended gateway. 'The mutalith would not have been set to guard this door unless it was important to the Prismatic King,' he said. 'The tyrant's throne itself may lie beyond it.'

The Celestant-Prime nodded. 'Then let there be no further delay,' he said, leading his remaining comrades through the gate of frost.

The moment they were through the doorway, the Thriceblessed froze, stunned into silence. The Celestant-Prime could feel the dismay of his comrades, could sense the trepidation that threatened to consume them. To his eyes, they had entered a shimmering canyon of glass. Tier upon tier upon tier of mirrored panels, rose far overhead and sank away deep beneath their feet. The floor upon which they walked felt as hard as stone but at the same time had the transparency of spring water, revealing the limitless depths below.

'The Maze of Reflection,' Deucius gave voice to the anxiety

which gripped each of the Thriceblessed. The warriors had been prepared for almost anything when they breached the walls of the Eyrie, but they had hardly expected to find the insidious trap they had managed to escape – a trap that by any law of time and space should be leagues from the fields of Uthyr.

'The Prismatic King!' Throl cursed. 'He has usurped my magic, twisted my spell to draw us all into his trap.'

The Celestant-Prime glared at the tiers of mirrors. The thrill of warning grew more insistent. He felt that if he concentrated, if he plumbed the very depths of his soul, he would understand the nature of the menace they now faced. But to do so would need time, and that was one resource he didn't intend to squander.

'We aren't trapped yet,' Ghal Maraz declared. 'Back away to the door. We'll try to navigate the hall again.' As he turned, however, the Celestant-Prime found that their avenue of retreat was closed to them. Where the door of ice had been there was only a continuance of the mirrored rows. The doorway was gone, vanished after hurling them into the heart of the Maze.

Ghal Maraz looked to the Thriceblessed. 'You broke free of this trap before,' he began.

Deucius shook his head. 'That was a miracle in itself,' he said. 'We managed to find a flaw in our prison.'

'Or so I was allowed to believe,' Othmar scowled. 'Maybe it wasn't fortune that allowed us to leave, but some scheme of the Prismatic King. Maybe he knew we would find the Celestant-Prime and bring him into this trap.'

The Celestant-Prime stared across the canyon, studying the mirrored tiers. As though in response, an eerie shimmer rippled through them. The reflective faces were no longer empty. Bound within them, he could see the armoured figures of Stormcasts. From the iconography that adorned their sigmarite mail, he knew these were the Thriceblessed, the rest of the warrior chamber that had been lost in the campaign against the Prismatic King.

The figures in the mirrors weren't static images. He could see them marching, searching, struggling within the weird limbo behind the mirror. They were trying to find a way out, but their efforts never drew them any closer to the glass. Whatever they attempted, to the observer on the outside the warriors remained the same distance away. From their actions, the Celestant-Prime decided that they couldn't see the glass, much less the world beyond it.

'This is sorcery beyond any mortal,' said Throl, shuddering as he joined the Celestant-Prime and looked upon the mirrors. 'This is the magic of Tzeentch himself. Imperious and incontestable.'

'It can be beaten,' declared the Celestant-Prime. He gestured to the Stormcasts. 'These warriors slipped free of the maze. That means this magic does have a weakness, whether it comes from Tzeentch or simply one of the Deceiver's minions. There is a weakness.'

Even as he spoke, the Celestant-Prime saw the mirrors begin to shift, spinning across the walls, sinking from upper tiers to lower ones, ascending from beneath the floor to take a new position far above. It was a bewildering, disorienting display, like watching the world slide onto its side and then turn itself over again. Deucius staggered, overwhelmed by a sickening revulsion. The rest of the Thriceblessed outside the mirrors fell to their knees as nausea sapped their constitutions as well. The warriors locked within the mirrors gave no sign that they were aware of the rotation, the grey nothingness behind the glass unfazed by the shifting spin of its frame.

The revolving mirrors began to show other shapes now, captives far different from the noble Stormcasts. Behind some of the mirrors loomed the putrescent bulks of gigantic plague daemons, their antlers festooned with decaying carcasses of men and beasts. Lascivious monstrosities with snapping claws and supple bodies leered seductively from their magic prisons. A great rat-like thing with thirteen horns scrabbled against the glass, trying to gnaw at its cell with fangs of iron. Warlords and sorcerers, men and monsters, daemons and the abominable undead, all these had tried to oppose the Prismatic King during his tyrannical reign, and all had been consumed by his Maze of Reflection.

Something caught the Celestant-Prime's eye as it went whirring past, revolving and spinning away amidst the confusion of panels. A bare pane amidst the riot of images assailing his senses, an emptiness that stood stark and clear among the clutter of the maze. A single mirror that didn't have a captive locked behind its glass. Instead there was a jagged crack that snaked down its face. A memory, an impulse, made the Celestant-Prime turn and look to the other wall. Again, there was an empty pane, clear and distinct amidst the turmoil of the maze's reflections. Taking wing, he rose towards the second barren panel. He found the exact same crack running down its glass as the one on the opposite wall. It would have been natural to believe the mirrors to be reflections of one another, but they were too distant from each other for that to be true. They were more than visual echoes of one another. They were more like twins.

An incredible idea rose within the Celestant-Prime's mind, a thought that nagged at him with the persistence of some half-forgotten experience. He focused upon one of the mirrors holding the Thriceblessed and locked every detail in his mind. Swiftly he swung around and faced the opposite wall, eyes roving across the thousands of shifting mirrors to find the one which would further the theory he had formed. At last he spotted it, far overhead, a mirror that exhibited the exact twin of the scene he had memorized from the first one. Again, the two mirrors were too far apart to simply be reflecting the same image. In some way he didn't understand yet, they formed a pair, and within that eldritch symmetry was hidden the secret of the maze.

'Watch the mirrors,' the Celestant-Prime said to Deucius, raising the warrior to his feet. 'I am going to try something.' Deucius nodded, tightening his grip on his weapon. The other Thriceblessed followed his example, ready to lend their own efforts to the Celestant-Prime's plan.

The Celestant-Prime had just begun to soar towards the first of the mirrors, when he sensed an unsettling change in the air. The atmosphere, already tainted with the chill of sorcery and the stink of mutation, now became pregnant with a smouldering hostility. Turning his gaze below, he saw some of the ever-shifting mirrors begin to slow, their gyrations become more focussed. In a blaze of light, two of the mirrors flared outwards, a hideous form emerging from the midst of that light. Verminous and gigantic, the thirteen-horned rat-beast reared back on its clawed legs and chittered a fierce shriek of jubilation. Its yellow eyes glared about the Maze, fixing upon the Thriceblessed. With a snarl of inhuman malignance, the rat-beast was charging towards the armoured warriors.

Other mirrors now blazed with light, disgorging their own captives, loosing clutches of fiendish creatures against the Stormcasts. The Celestant-Prime whirled around, ready to lend his might to his embattled comrades. Before he could descend, however, his attention was caught by the mirror beside him. Here the glass wasn't filled with the image of an imprisoned Stormcast. It was a different kind of captive that glared out from the mirror. A vision of hate and fury, its skull-like head sporting great curled horns, its blood-stained body rippling with thick cords of muscle. Vast bat-like wings erupted from its back. Strips of twisted mail and shattered plate hung from its torso, less as armour and more in the fashion of gruesome trophies. Carved into the beast's forehead was a loathsome symbol, a sign that spoke of havoc and murder throughout the Eight Realms: the rune of Khorne.

The eyes that smouldered within the pits of the daemon's face were unfocused at first, as unaware of the outer world as the Stormcasts. But then a grisly change came upon them. They shifted and fixated upon the Celestant-Prime, the lipless mouth below them spreading in a malicious leer. The creature could see the Celestant-Prime. It was aware of the world beyond the mirror.

The Celestant-Prime looked across to the other wall just as the whirring rotation of mirrors brought the exact opposite of the daemon's glass into place. As the two mirrors now faced one another, a terrible rending sound echoed through the Maze. There was a blinding flash and then the two mirrors were spinning away again – only now the glass was empty. The thing that had been held captive was free, soaring towards the Celestant-Prime on its own wings. At a gesture, its clawed hand erupted into a cataract of bubbling gore. The stream lengthened and thickened, spreading out from the monster's talons. With each heartbeat, the blood coagulated, building successive layers of solidity, assuming the form of a double-headed axe.

The Celestant-Prime darted away as the infernal creature swooped towards him. The thing's axe slashed through the air in a murderous sweep, flecks of sizzling blood streaming from the grotesque blade. The Celestant-Prime retaliated with a swing of Ghal Maraz, the holy weapon causing the daemon's flesh to bubble like molten bronze as it grazed past the fiend's wing.

The daemon threw its head back in a savage howl, pivoting in midair to face its foe. It slashed its axe along its own forearm. Steaming blood dripped from the injury, writhing in a gory rope as it rushed from the wound. Like the axe the beast had formed, the rope quickly thickened, taking on the shape and substance of a barbed whip. The daemon cracked its lash in the air, spattering Ghal Maraz's golden armour with flecks of blood that steamed against the sigmarite mail.

The Celestant-Prime glared back at the skull-faced daemon, ready to match his righteous fury against the beast's murderous rage. Before he could, he was struck from behind, a brutal kick smashing into his back and causing him to plummet downwards. As he spun away, he could see a second Khornate daemon, another of the Blood God's bestial champions, speeding after him, its spiked maul ready to deliver a further treacherous blow.

The first daemon howled, streaking past its comrade to lash at the Celestant-Prime with its whip. The crimson coil wrapped about the hero's arm, snapping taught as it arrested his fall. For an instant, he hung there as the daemon with the maul came rushing at him. The beast flung its weapon at the Celestant-Prime. Only a rapid twist of his body prevented a more solid contact, as the maul ripped sparks from his armour as it scraped past him.

The second daemon was far from disarmed. It uncoiled a black mass of cord from around its wrist, a ghastly whip fashioned from skulls and sinew. It struck at the Celestant-Prime, trying to bind him.

Swinging back and forth like a pendulum, the Celestant-Prime defied the efforts of the daemons to hold him. The first greater daemon was trying to drag him upwards, but even its prodigious strength was no match for that of Sigmar's champion. With the brawn of its twin to assist it, the daemon might have succeeded, but the Celestant-Prime was determined to thwart such ambitions. When the swinging motion of his body brought his feet against one of the mirrors, he pushed himself off with a mighty kick, feeding his momentum into an upward drive.

The daemon was taken utterly by surprise when its enemy arrowed towards it. Soaring upwards, the hero saw the trap the Khornate fiend had intended for him: an empty mirror, stark against the prisons around it. A quick shift of his eyes showed him the mirror's twin waiting on the other side.

Just before he drew parallel with the empty mirrors, the Celestant-Prime arrested his ascent. Seizing the blood-whip in his hand, he wrenched the now slackened lash. The beast's eyes widened with shock as it was jerked downward, tumbling towards the Celestant-Prime and past the empty mirrors.

Again there came the blinding flash. When it faded, the daemon was gone, its image caught in the paired mirrors that now swung about on mismatched courses down the tiers.

The remaining bloodthirster roared and shook its horned head, disgusted that the Celestant-Prime had slipped the trap that had once more claimed its fellow vassal of Khorne. Vengefully, the fiend leapt at the champion, powering its dive with its wings. The hulking brute's lash licked out, the blackened skulls shrieking as they bit towards the Celestant-Prime.

He didn't allow the daemon a second blow, and brought the godhammer slamming down into his enemy's horned visage. The skull-like face shattered under the impact, golden fire from the hammerhead surging through the fiend. Like a weed shrivelling under a hot sun, the daemon's body wilted away, collapsing into a scabby crust that rained down across the floor.

The Celestant-Prime looked down upon his comrades. The carcass of the rat-beast lay twitching, vermin spilling from its wounds. The bodies of plague-ridden warlords and wanton sorceresses lay strewn about the tiny wedge of Stormcasts. The Thriceblessed were holding their ground, but more foes were spilling from the mirrors with each heartbeat.

Glaring at the spinning mirrors, the Celestant-Prime cursed the malignant power that directed the revolutions of the tiers, ensuring only enemies were freed from their prisons. Then his thoughts seized upon a flicker of memory, something that only now did he recognize. The cracked mirror – there had been something familiar about the way the glass had splintered. Seizing upon that sense of familiarity, he flew upwards, sweeping past rows of enchanted glass to find the one panel he sought.

He found it, speeding away among the tiers, spinning and rotating as though desperate to escape. The Celestant-Prime could see now that his memory wasn't wrong. The crack echoed the outline of Ghal Maraz. A conviction he couldn't shake seized the hero. The damage had been wrought by Sigmar's hammer. How, when, he couldn't say, but he was certain he knew why.

With an effort that taxed his mighty wings, the Celestant-Prime chased after the spinning mirror. Swinging Ghal Maraz, he brought the great hammer smashing into the cracked glass, obliterating it in a spiral of glistening fragments and glowing aethryic harmonies. A titanic scream rippled through the Maze, an elemental wail of discord. The revolutions of the mirrors slowed, the tiers sagging downwards as the prisons collapsed one after the other.

The flaw in the maze. It had been found once before, but the opportunity to exploit it had been thwarted. Now, the Celestant-Prime was here to turn that failure into success. All around him, the mirrors were breaking, freeing the captives locked within them. Now it wasn't merely the fiends of Chaos that were at liberty, but all the Stormcasts that had been caught in the Prismatic King's coils.

The monstrous creatures imprisoned in the maze fell upon one another, less willing to make common cause against the Stormcasts than those beasts deliberately freed by the maze's master. The Thriceblessed weren't wracked by such disunity. As they emerged from the aethyric discharge of the mirrors, the golden warriors formed ranks and brought battle to their hideous foes.

Ghal Maraz blazing with holy light in his mailed fist, the Celestant-Prime dived downwards to join his brothers in battle.

CHAPTER SIX

Locked within their prisons for so long, the Thriceblessed were disoriented as they emerged back into the mortal world. Questions of how long they had been trapped were forgotten when they saw the Celestant-Prime and the weapon he carried. The sacred aura of the godhammer swept through them, driving away all sensation but that which stemmed from their devotion to Sigmar. By the God-King they had been tasked to conquer. Now, with the aid of Ghal Maraz, they would accomplish that noble purpose.

The Celestant-Prime looked with pride at the fighters he had freed from the Maze of Reflection. Judicators armed with rune-etched skybolt bows and fearsome boltstorm crossbows. Retributors with great mauls of enchanted sigmarite. Troops of Liberators with their slashing swords and brutal hammers, their shields held proud before them. There were hundreds of the mighty warriors gazing with undisguised reverence at the hero and the weapon for which their Stormhost had been named.

'Celestant-Prime,' Deucius said, bowing to the champion. 'This is Lord-Celestant Devyndus Thriceblessed.'

'It is my honour to stand in the presence of Sigmar's chosen,' Devyndus said. He was a tall, powerfully built man even by the standards of the Stormcasts. The breastplate of his golden armour was fashioned into the image of a twin-tailed comet and from his shoulders there hung a cloak of woven sigmarite, its edges weighted with small hammers cast from the same material. Like the Celestant-Prime, the Lord-Celestant's helm was ringed by a halo of metal, the spikey crown framing his head like the rays of a golden sun.

'All who are reforged upon the Anvil of the Apotheosis are the God-King's chosen,' the Celestant-Prime told Devyndus. 'It is only the bravest and most noble who can meet the rigours of such rebirth.' As he spoke, he could see in his mind the great palace of Sigmar, and himself being remade upon the anvil of the God-King. Who and what he had been before was only a whisper, something just beyond the edge of his memory. What had been wasn't important. It was the here and now, the ordeal before him that was. His role as rescuer of the Thriceblessed was fulfilled. Now it was left to be liberator of the realmgate and vanquisher of the Prismatic King.

Lord-Celestant Devyndus bowed. 'We stand at your command,' he told the hero. 'Give us your orders and it shall be done.'

Throl stepped forwards, lean and miniscule among the mighty Stormcasts. 'If you will forgive my impertinence, Ghal Maraz,' he said, and picked up one of the broken shards from the mirrors. 'The Maze of Reflection's presence here and the fiendishness of the trap laid for you was no accident. We were led here, meant to be drawn to this place. It wasn't mere chance that caused the captive daemons to be loosed against you.' He held up the sliver of glass, turning it from side to side, letting the light play across its surface. 'Everything was being directed by the Prismatic King, his terrible magic both setting the stage and moving the players.'

'The Stormcasts are no puppets to dance for a sorcerer's whim,' Othmar snarled, bringing his foot stamping down on a piece of glass.

Throl bowed in apology. 'No, the warriors of Sigmar aren't so easily manipulated. That is why the Prismatic King's trick failed.'

'But he will try new ways to destroy us,' the Celestant-Prime said. He clenched his mailed fist, glaring at what remained of the broken maze. 'Unless we destroy him first.'

'That is what I propose,' Throl said. Holding the shard of mirror high, he pointed to its gleaming surface. 'The Prismatic King spied upon us through the mirrors. More than simply prisons, they acted as windows for his witchsight. Through the mirrors he could watch those he'd caught and those he intended to catch. That is how he knew the right moment to free the blood daemons and when to shift the mirrors to try and snare Ghal Maraz.'

Othmar picked up one of the broken slivers, glaring at it. 'I hope he's still watching,' he growled, scowling at the glass.

'Is he watching, wizard?' the Celestant-Prime asked.

'The spell should be broken,' Throl said. 'When the mirrors broke, so too should their magic. But they remain things of the Prismatic King. The thread of his enchantment, the trail of his scrying is still there. My own magic may be able to exploit that lingering thread.'

'Exploit it how?' Lord-Celestant Devyndus asked.

Throl gestured expansively at the other shards scattered about the chamber. 'Gather every piece together. Combine them in a great circle.' He turned and looked up at the Celestant-Prime, an imploring look on his face. 'The essence of the Eyrie is the stuff of Chaos – transitory and mutable. It is unfixed and unfinished by the rigours of mortal reality. I can use that shapelessness. My magic can bind itself to the aethyric tether linking the mirrors back to the Prismatic King. I can open a portal that will follow the path right to him.'

The Celestant-Prime nodded. 'If you can do this, then we won't need to fight our way through the Eyrie. You can take us straight to the Prismatic King's throne.' A concern flared through his mind, a worry that howled with warning. 'Won't your magic warn the sorcerer of our coming?'

Throl frowned, the light of vengeance faltering in his eyes. 'His mastery of the black arts is such that there would be no hiding my magic from him. The instant I evoke my spell, the Prismatic King will know we are coming.' The wizard shook his head. 'There is small chance of surprising him if we march through his halls. This way at least you will be brought into the fiend's presence. This way you will at least see the face of your enemy.'

Feeling the heft of Ghal Maraz in his hands, the Celestant-Prime experienced a sensation of righteous wrath. 'Let me get that close to him, and your people will be avenged, Throl. The Prismatic King has mocked Sigmar long enough.' He looked to Devyndus. 'Have the Thriceblessed gather up the shards. Whatever the wizard needs to work his spell, we will render it to him.'

Lord-Celestant Devyndus clasped his hand to his chest in salute and hurried to pass Ghal Maraz's commands on to the other Stormcasts. In a moment, the warriors were picking up the broken pieces of mirror, setting them into a growing circle of glass. Throl walked across the jagged shards, seating himself at the very centre of the ring. Closing his eyes, he began to chant.

The pieces of glass began to shift and shudder, quaking upon the floor. Gradually their reflective surfaces became suffused with a brilliant light, a whirring aura that turned from one hue to the next in rapid rotations. The frigid chill of magic swept through the chamber, the breath of each Stormcast ghosting through his helm.

'The door is open,' Throl declared, his eyes more glassy and gem-like than the Celestant-Prime had ever seen them. Sweat streamed down the wizard's strained face. 'Quickly, while I can still maintain it!'

Devyndus gripped the Celestant-Prime's shoulder as the champion started towards the glowing circle. 'Are you certain of the wizard's magic? Let one of us…'

The Celestant-Prime shook his head. 'I send no man where I fear to lead,' he declared. Holding forward the golden head of Ghal Maraz, he shook the weapon at the magic circle. 'If the godhammer's might is not enough to bear me to victory, then the valour of the Thriceblessed will be for naught. Let me lead the way, Lord-Celestant.' His voice grew low, subdued by the magnitude of emotion boiling inside him. 'This is my trial, and there is none who may lift it from me.'

Without further word, Ghal Maraz strode out into the blinding ring of light. The luminance swirled around him in a coruscating miasma of brilliance, a cascading stream of reflections and echoes that flooded through his senses. With each step he could feel the energies of the broken mirrors engulfing him, blotting out the outside world. He was fading from existence, marching through the passageways between space and time. Where the passage would lead was a matter of faith, not in the magic of Throl, but in the divine power of Sigmar.

A deafening clap of thunder rolled through the Celestant-Prime's skull as he emerged from the nimbus of eldritch light. One instant he was engulfed in the blinding flash, the next he found himself standing in a grand hall of cyclopean proportions. Titanic columns of crystal soared up into an arched ceiling of uncut gemstone. The floor was like a single mosaic of stained glass, its panes depicting the manifold atrocities and conquests of Chaos throughout the Mortal Realms.

Across the gargantuan hall, an enormous seat rose, a throne fashioned from diamonds that blazed with a kaleidoscope of colours smouldering deep within their facets. Upon the throne sat a vulture-headed Lord of Change, its face turned towards the Celestant-Prime as he emerged from Throl's portal. There was amusement in the greater daemon's jewel-like eyes as it sensed the champion's shock when he gazed upon it. The Celestant-Prime had thought the Prismatic King would be a monster of at least mortal birth. Instead he found himself before an infernal steward of Tzeentch, one of the greater daemons who existed as extensions of their twisted god's desire.

Bigger than the one-eyed giants he'd fought in the swamp, the Prismatic King rose from its throne. Possessed of roughly human shape, the Lord of Change adorned itself in a long robe of silks and satins, jewels woven into the pattern to form arcane sigils and sorcerous talismans. The gaunt, starveling body of the daemon was covered in black feathers that faded to a leprous yellow at the tips. The vulturine head leered from atop a bare, scraggly neck, the face dominated in a metallic beak of blackened iron. Upon the horror's talons enormous rings burned with unholy energy. From the Prismatic King's back spread gigantic wings, exhibiting a dazzle of whirling patterns among the rainbow display of coloured feathers. Upon the beast's brow, a mirrored crown reflected the Celestant-Prime's image back at him, but it was a reflection twisted and corrupted by the ruinous essence of the daemon.

'You have come far to seek an audience with me.' The Prismatic King's voice was like the crackling of broken glass and the scrape of steel against stone. 'In all its long existence my court has never entertained an emissary of Azyr.'

The Celestant-Prime felt every syllable the daemon uttered clawing at him, probing around in his mind and spirit for any trace of weakness. However mighty the godhammer was, however resilient his armour of sigmarite, their strength would account for nothing if the Lord of Change found a flaw within the man himself.

Thunder roared through the hall. The Celestant-Prime could feel the Thriceblessed emerge from the portal. Firm in their faith in the champion chosen by their god, the Stormcasts had dutifully followed him through the magical gate. He could feel the shock that swept through each warrior as he gazed upon the hideous enormity of the Prismatic King, but that shock was tempered, subdued by a sensation yet more powerful: the conviction that each Stormcast held that the Celestant-Prime could overcome even this foe.

Strengthened by the faith of his comrades, the Celestant-Prime took a step towards the diamond throne. 'I'm not here as emissary,' he snarled at the daemon. 'I'm here as executioner. I'm here to answer the cries of the innocent you have enslaved and killed. I'm here to avenge the kingdoms and empires you have annihilated. I'm here to defend the worlds you would despoil with your sorcery.' He held Ghal Maraz overhead, letting its holy presence blaze forth in a nimbus of sacred fire. 'Tell me where you have hidden the Pillar of Whispers and earn the mercy of swift destruction.'

The Lord of Change uttered a cackle of withering mirth. 'I whispered in the ears of priests and emperors in the Age of Myth. I set nations aflame in the Age of Chaos. What are you, *Ghal Maraz*? A mortal substituting for a god? A nameless vagabond who calls himself by the trinket he carries? Who are you to contend with me?'

The Celestant-Prime felt the bite of the daemon's words. He

felt too the strength of his own faith. His eyes burned behind the mask of his helm. 'It isn't who I am that matters – it is what I am!' He brought Ghal Maraz slamming into the floor, sending a shockwave through the panes that cracked and splintered the innumerable atrocities of the Prismatic King's glass legions. 'I am your doom, Soulshriver.'

The daemon's enraged howl shrieked across the hall. Translucent membranes slid across the fiend's eyes as it brought its talons together. A surge of crackling magic swept down the gallery, dragging the cracked slivers of the floor into its seething storm. The gale rushed towards the Celestant-Prime and the Thriceblessed, an arcane tornado of boiling sorcery and razored glass.

The Celestant-Prime held his ground, brandishing the god-hammer. In a shriek of elemental violence, the dark magic of the Prismatic King crashed into the faith and devotion of Ghal Maraz. The dark storm frayed, its grisly energies blown apart in splatters of roiling corruption that sizzled against the crystal columns and gem-encrusted ceiling. The slivers of glass dropped back to the floor in a cascade of broken fragments.

'The chosen of Sigmar! The Celestant-Prime!' Deucius raised his voice in a roar of adoration. The cry was taken up by the other Thriceblessed. Their shame at failing to overcome the trickery of Chaos and at their imprisonment in the Maze of Reflection was now fanned into a surge of judgemental wrath. Like an avalanche, they charged across the hall to confront the daemon who had worked its deceit upon them.

The Prismatic King glared contemptuously at the army of Stormcasts. With a gesture of its ensorcelled talons, the arrows of lightning loosed upon it by the Judicators dissipated into sparks of harmless light. A snap of its mighty pinions sent a gale that staggered the hulking Retributors. A ghastly squawk that was part scream and part incantation bubbled from the daemon's beak and from the smouldering depths of its diamond throne shapes oozed into being, gaining in size and solidity until they stood within the hall – a mismatched horde of barbaric warriors and snarling beastmen. The Lord of Change extended its claw and the mongrel army leapt to the attack.

Sweeping the Cometstrike Sceptre overhead, the Celestant-Prime once more drew on the relic's divine power. The ribbon of holy energy swept outward, wrenching a fiery ball from the heavens, flinging the conjured flame full into the swarming foe. Scores of Chaos warriors and beastmen were immolated by the cosmic fury of the comet, their mangled bodies flung across the hall, crashing into the stunned ranks of the Prismatic King's vassals. Before the slaves of darkness could recover from their shock, the Stormcasts were charging towards them.

The Celestant-Prime led the advance. Faith and conviction were anathema to all things of Chaos, but it would need more than the valour of men to overcome a fiend as ancient and steeped in evil as the Prismatic King. Only a weapon as mighty and sacred as Ghal Maraz could vanquish the daemon.

The Judicators unleashed their skybolts across the hall. The Prismatic King didn't squander any of its sorcery to protect its slaves, however. Dozens of mortal warriors fell, their blackened mail pierced by the crackling missiles. The Retributors took position before the Judicators, defending the archers against the rush of snarling gors eager for their blood. With precision honed over numberless battles, they swung their massive mauls in a brutal arc, breaking bones and crushing horned skulls. Soon the ground before them was littered with the battered bodies of dead and dying beastkin.

As the Prismatic King's warriors struck the ring of Retributors, the Liberators pushed their way to the vanguard. With swords and hammers, the Thriceblessed wrought vengeful havoc against the minions of Chaos.

The Celestant-Prime cast down rank after rank of barbarous foes. Each strike from Ghal Maraz sent a thunderous clamour echoing through the hall. With one swing he obliterated a clutch of barbaric reavers. Another blow reduced a pack of horned gors into a heap of bloodied flesh and shattered bone. A hulking, bull-headed minotaur lunged for him, trampling the Thriceblessed who strayed into its path. A glancing blow of the godhammer tore the head from the beast's powerful body and sent it crashing among the monstrous throng still emerging from the diamond throne.

Any mortal would have known despair as he contemplated the innumerable foes the Prismatic King had already conjured from the depths of its throne. To see still more swarming forth would have broken them. But the Stormcasts had transcended such limits. They had been recast by the God-King, transformed into instruments of Sigmar's holy retribution. For them, there was no fear in battle, no such thing as unopposable odds. While they lived, they fought and while they fought they did so knowing that the glory of Sigmar shone within each of them.

None embodied this stalwart conviction more than the Celestant-Prime. Here was the fire in which he would be tested, the flame in which he would be proved. Yet as he would have pressed forwards, as he would have battered his way through the hordes of Chaos, a tiny warning made him hesitate. Had the Prismatic King, master of deceit and illusion, limited itself to such crude and obvious measures to protect its domain?

The Celestant-Prime looked beyond the crush of battle and the fires of his own righteous thirst for justice. Despite the ferocity of the fight, none of the Stormcasts had fallen. The chaotic horde was only trying to delay the warriors of Sigmar. After the Maze of Reflection, he could guess their hideous purpose.

Slain, the Stormcasts would dissipate, returning to the Anvil of the Apotheosis to be reforged. Trapped within the mirrors of the Prismatic King, however, they would be lost to the God-King. That was the peril which now threatened the Thriceblessed. The Prismatic King was going to work some feat of sorcery to achieve the same foul enchantment as the maze.

'Devyndus!' the Celestant-Prime's voice thundered above the carnage. 'The daemon's slaves are trying to delay us, to give their master time to trap us all.'

The Lord-Celestant bellowed commands to the Thriceblessed near him, who in turn passed the orders down the line. The Judicators loosed a concentrated barrage of lightning-arrows into the midst of the vicious horde, focussing their shafts along a narrow front. Into this momentary gap surged a phalanx of Liberators, their shields locked together to form a wall of sigmarite that would stem the tide of warriors sweeping around them. The Celestant-Prime rushed through the narrow path the Liberators had created for him, Lord-Celestant Devyndus dispatching Deucius to protect the champion's flank. In their wake, the wizard Throl scrambled towards the forefront of the battle.

Again and again, the Celestant-Prime swept the fury of Ghal Maraz across the ranks of savage reavers who stood before him. By the score the marauders perished, their broken bodies flung across the hall, yet still they came. Beyond them, the champion could see the huge daemon, its eyes glazed, its wings aglow as it summoned more magic into its loathsome conjurations. The transparent diamond of the Prismatic King's throne was becoming steadily darker, assuming a reflective sheen. The daemon was exploiting the essence of Chamon itself, using the vibrations of the Realm of Metal to help it transmute the diamond throne into a nest of mirrors – a new maze in which to recapture the Thriceblessed.

'Don't let it complete its conjuration!' Throl wailed, a stream of fire erupting from his splayed fingers to ignite a pack of gors, reducing the beastmen to heaps of ash. Deucius smashed down a dog-faced beastlord that had escaped the immolation of its followers, cracking the brute's skull with his hammer.

The Celestant-Prime surged forwards, howling a challenge to the daemon. The flesh around the Prismatic King's eyes twitched in fear but the Lord of Change was too committed to its mighty conjuration to break away from the spell. The creatures still emerging from the throne diverted towards the Celestant-Prime, seeking to answer the threat their master couldn't face. Already the transmutive energies had wrought a change upon the throne, however. The creatures that staggered and crawled towards the hero were obscene half-formed things, their bodies as opaque as glass, their armour as brittle. When Ghal Maraz struck them, they disintegrated in a spray of shards that were both glass and flesh.

Reaching the daemon, the Celestant-Prime raised the godhammer, ready to strike it down with the fury of Sigmar's wrath. As he started to swing, his eye strayed to the golden sheen of the hammer's head. In that mirror-like surface, he could see the Prismatic King, towering and terrible. He could also see the shadows of its diamond throne and the creatures emerging from it stretching towards the wall. These shadows were constant, yet that of the daemon flickered with a grisly inconstancy. Only in the reflection of the godhammer was this weird effect revealed. Looking directly at the shadow, it seemed no different.

When Ghal Maraz cracked against the Prismatic King's leg, the limb burst apart in a spray of light and thunder. The daemon shuddered, sagging back towards its throne. The shadow it cast flickered once more, then faded completely. The Celestant-Prime advanced on the reeling Lord of Change, but again there sounded within the deepest layers of his mind a cry of warning. Again he wondered at the trickery of a foe who could manipulate the senses as thoroughly as the Prismatic King.

He turned his eyes to the golden surface of Ghal Maraz. There, in the godhammer's sheen, he saw only an empty throne. There was no daemon, no Prismatic King. Not even a flicker of the fiend. The monster's sorcery could deceive mortal senses, but it couldn't obfuscate the holy relic with its trickery. The Celestant-Prime turned, staring at the reflection in the hammer, searching for the true shape of the Prismatic King.

What he found was Throl. In the godhammer, the wizard's shadow was a long ribbon of darkness, vast and hideous – the daemon had entered the man's body. The Celestant-Prime glared at his enemy. Around them, the sounds of battle faded away, diminishing into nothingness.

'Much better than the last time,' the Prismatic King grinned, laughing at the shock the words provoked.

'If we'd met before, you would already have found your doom,' the Celestant-Prime snarled, advancing upon the daemon.

'Only if you win,' the daemon hissed. 'You haven't. Not now, and not then.' Its gemlike eyes sparkled with malignance. 'Haven't you wondered, all those dim memories tugging at you, pulling you here and there?'

'They brought me here,' the Celestant-Prime said. 'They led me here to destroy you.'

The thing wearing Throl's body laughed again. 'That is because you've been here before. Some foolish test set by your god for you to prove your worth. Didn't you know? Didn't your little godling tell you? We've danced this dance before, you and I.'

The Celestant-Prime raised godhammer. 'I've no stomach for the lies of daemons,' he snarled.

'The best lies are hidden in the truth,' the daemon mocked. The flesh around its mouth began to shrivel, scraps of blistered skin sloughing away from the bones. 'There was a real Throl. He thought he could resist me. I even let his identity linger when I assumed his flesh. But there is only so long a mortal shell can contain the grand enormity of my spirit.'

A rending crash rumbled through the hall. Cries of bewilderment rose from the Stormcasts as their erstwhile foes disintegrated into broken glass. The vast shape that leaned against the throne broke apart like a reflection lost in a rippling pool.

'Kill it, my lord,' Deucius cried out as he turned away from the wreckage of his last enemy. Other Thriceblessed were converging upon the strange tableau now, surrounding the wizard who had deceived them for so long.

'Destroy the traitor and have done with it,' Othmar cursed.

The Prismatic King held its decaying hand towards the Celestant-Prime. 'Wouldn't you like to know where the Pillar of Whispers is? I will tell you. Such was ever my purpose, great Ghal Maraz. I will admit, Sigmar is clever in his way. The Maze of Reflection can thwart his cunning but is hardly capable of holding the hero chosen to bear the godhammer. No, I couldn't kill you and I couldn't trap you.' The gloating daemon's jaw fell off, crumbling to dust as it struck the floor. Still the fiend's voice slithered from its decaying mantle of flesh. 'All that was left to me was to destroy you.'

'Then you have failed, monster,' Deucius declared. 'The Celestant-Prime is triumphant. It is you and your slaves that are vanquished!'

'Do you know where the Pillar of Whispers is hidden?' the daemon mocked. 'It is locked away, buried inside a vessel of my own creation. I have held the Thriceblessed a very long time.

While they were my guests, I fashioned a simulacrum in their shape. I took one of the Stormcasts from my maze and replaced him with my copy. A perfect copy. A reflection so complete that even it believes itself to be real! That, Ghal Maraz, is where the Pillar of Whispers is hidden! To find the realmgate, you must destroy the simulacrum! Only the godhammer will free it from its mantle of flesh!'

'More lies!' Othmar raged. He swung his hammer at the disintegrating body, collapsing its ribs and smashing the carcass to the floor. The desiccated head continued to grin up at the Celestant-Prime.

'How many must die to unlock the realmgate?' the Prismatic King's mockery bubbled up from the bodiless head. 'Will it be the first or the second, or the two-hundred and second? How many can you strike down before your spirit is broken? How much innocent blood can stain your hands before you are unfit to carry the godhammer?'

The Celestant-Prime listened to no more. Throwing back his head in a roar of outrage and frustration, he brought Ghal Maraz smashing down, obliterating the last shred of what had been Throl's body and the Prismatic King's vessel. Denied its host, the daemon's spirit would be cast back into the Realm of Chaos.

But it was destruction, not defeat. The daemon was vanquished, yet its evil lingered on.

'It can't be true,' Lord-Celestant Devyndus declared. 'The daemon lies. We are all of us true Stormcasts. You have seen us fight. You have seen us cut down the slaves of Chaos!'

Deucius gestured to the dust that had been Throl. 'That thing did the same, killing its own servants, springing its own traps all so that it could lull us into trusting it.'

'But if the simulacrum doesn't even know it's false, how can we discover it?' Othmar asked.

The Celestant-Prime was silent, brooding upon the choice the Prismatic King had put before him. Striking down the Thriceblessed would send them back to Sigmaron, but each time a Stormcast was reforged, he left something of himself behind, becoming less and less human with each incarnation. More, it would blacken his own spirit to massacre his own comrades. He would be tainted, befouled. Unfit to bear Ghal Maraz.

The champion stared down at the sacred hammer. As he did so, he studied the golden sheen. The reflection within the god-hammer – the only true reflection within the deceit of the Eyrie. Inspired, the Celestant-Prime held the hammer aloft.

'Sigmar will show me the way,' he said. 'The glory of the God-King will reveal the simulacrum!' Spreading his wings, he rose into the air above the Thriceblessed, circling above them as he studied the image within the hammer's golden sheen.

It was when he looked to one stalwart warrior who had fought so valiantly throughout their long march to the fields of Uthyr, that the Celestant-Prime saw a disruption in the reflection. Like the Prismatic King's daemonic husk, the shadow of the warrior had no presence in the reflection Ghal Maraz revealed to him. The Stormcast wasn't real, he was naught but a conjuration endowed with shape and form.

The Celestant-Prime returned to the floor, wings folding against his back as he sombrely marched past the Thriceblessed. He could feel the relief issue from each warrior he passed and the trepidation of those he had yet to approach. There was only one, however, who had reason to fear.

Deucius fell to his knees in shock when he saw the Celestant-Prime walk towards him and shake his head.

'But I know who I am,' he said.

'You know who the Prismatic King made you to be,' the Celestant-Prime corrected him. 'Know this – by your sacrifice is the daemon undone. We will not forget you. We will mourn you. The realmgate will be secured and the darkness of Chaos will never again befoul it. By Sigmar, this I vow!'

One blow of Ghal Maraz was enough to shatter the simulacrum. The semblance of Deucius shattered in a blaze of light. From the midst of that destruction, a torrent of molten sapphire bubbled and oozed. Gyrating, spinning in a coruscating maelstrom, the Pillar of Whispers stood unleashed. The Celestant-Prime could feel the discordant vibrations spilling from the midst of the whirlpool, the opposing cadences of a different world.

'A path back to Azyr?' Lord-Celestant Devyndus wondered as he peered into the maelstrom.

'A path away from here, at least,' Othmar said. Staring down at the whirlpool, the warrior stepped out into the pulsating waves of force, diminishing as he was drawn through the gate. One after another, the rest of the Stormcasts followed.

The Celestant-Prime was the last to pass through the realmgate. In his mind, he wondered at the fiendish snare the Prismatic King had laid for him and at the daemon's claims that theirs was an old struggle. The premonitions that had affected him so strongly – had they been premonitions, or memories of some failed effort from the past?

Whatever the truth, the Celestant-Prime had proven himself now. He would ascend with the Thriceblessed and take his place in the God-King's war.

ABOUT THE AUTHORS

Darius Hinks' first novel, *Warrior Priest*, won the David Gemmell Morningstar award for best newcomer. Since then he has carved a bloody swathe through the Warhammer World in works such as *Island of Blood*, *Sigvald*, *Razumov's Tomb* and the Orion trilogy. He has also ventured into the Warhammer 40,000 universe with the Space Marine Battles novella *Sanctus*.

C L Werner's Black Library credits include the Space Marine Battles novel *The Siege of Castellax*, the End Times novel *Deathblade*, the War of Vengeance novel *The Curse of the Phoenix Crown*, *Mathias Thulmann: Witch Hunter*, *Runefang*, the Brunner the Bounty Hunter trilogy, the Thanquol and Boneripper series and the Time of Legends: The Black Plague series. Currently living in the American south-west, he continues to write stories of mayhem and madness set in the worlds of Warhammer and Warhammer 40,000.